Brina,)

God Bless You!
Remember Psalm!

No Wasted
Tears

SYLVIA D. CARTER

NO WASTED TEARS

TATE PUBLISHING
AND ENTERPRISES, LLC

No Wasted Tears
Copyright © 2012 by Sylvia Carter. All rights reserved.

No part of this publication may be reproduced, stored in a retrieval system or transmitted in any way by any means, electronic, mechanical, photocopy, recording or otherwise without the prior permission of the author except as provided by USA copyright law.

The opinions expressed by the author are not necessarily those of Tate Publishing, LLC.

Published by Tate Publishing & Enterprises, LLC
127 E. Trade Center Terrace | Mustang, Oklahoma 73064 USA
1.888.361.9473 | www.tatepublishing.com

Tate Publishing is committed to excellence in the publishing industry. The company reflects the philosophy established by the founders, based on Psalm 68:11,
"The Lord gave the word and great was the company of those who published it."

Book design copyright © 2013 by Tate Publishing, LLC. All rights reserved.
Cover design by Lauro Talibong
Interior design by Joana Quilantang

Published in the United States of America

ISBN: 978-1-62024-741-9
1. Fiction / Christian / Romance
2. Fiction / Christian / General
12.12.14

DEDICATION

This book is dedicated to Josephine Bullard
who spoke it before I conceived it.

ACKNOWLEDGEMENTS

I would like to thank my gracious heavenly Father, who anointed me to begin and complete this work. It would not have been completed without you using my hand as a pen. All praise, honor, and glory to Your name. In the beginning this book was to be a self-help book for women dealing with past hurts and rejection. But God had other plans because as I began to write, the anointing of God took control and today it is *No Wasted Tears* a novel.

A special thank you goes to Jonathon Carter, my husband and friend, who believed from the very beginning and never doubted I could accomplish this God-given assignment. I love you for being a man after God's own heart. The best is yet to come for both of us.

Thaydra and Jonathon, my children who have always given me unceasing love and constant support, know that you inspire me to do so much more. Truly you both are my inspirations, Mommy loves you both.

What can I say about my sister Sandra? You were a constant source of strength when I became discouraged and wanted to quit during my most difficult struggles. Your prayers pushed me to never give up. Thank you for being my bouncing board and for reading every chapter I sent you without complaining but always encouraging. Thank you Calvin for understanding and never complaining when this project took time away from you.

Craig and Chad you have supported, prayed, and encouraged me, all I can say is, that your big sister loves you. Devlyn and Brenda thank you for your prayers. I would also like to acknowledge the love and support of my parents Jenese and Warren thank you for instilling Christian morals and values in my life. I thank God for both of you on a daily basis. Mother you have always been a source of strength for me your tenacity has taught me to press on in spite any trial or tribulation.

There are others of you not listed, but who have supported me through prayers and positive thoughts for the success of *No Wasted Tears*, please know I am grateful.

Finally, to the best church family in the whole world, Siloam Church International, I love each of you forever and a day!

To all of the readers who have weathered the torrential downpours that have occurred in your lives, you survived. I know personally what it's like to believe God in the dark. But believe me God is still with you even in the darkest times of your life. Never let the devil see you sweat because all he has is a roar. You my dear readers have the victory because you are on the winning team. All of you made the decision to be victorious rather than being victims. I celebrate you, and this book was written as a testimony for all of our many tests in life.

PROLOGUE

Adam Wheeler knew he was in trouble the minute he saw her. He didn't know why she of all people snagged his attention, considering he was just in a conference full of the most beautiful females in the church world. He'd seen all shapes, colors, and ages, but none who seem to possess the innate ability to discern that he was looking for more than just a skirt to be his wife. This woman had his attention even while he approached his seat in the aisle. She wasn't totally composed; as a matter of fact, she was crying. But she had a face that was strikingly beautiful.

Adam examined her with greater care. Everything about her appeared quiet and understated. She'd let her hair hang loose around her face. She looked impossibly young, and yet one glimpse of those eyes warned of someone who'd been through the pits of hell and back again. They overflowed with vulnerability that he discerned could only have been gained through some type of pain.

He didn't know what it was in particular about her appearance that aroused such intense interest. It was something subtle. Something that stirred instincts he'd honed during his years surviving as a single pastor in the shark-infested waters of the church world. Those instincts warned that this woman, while appearing so calm and controlled on the outside, had a deeply rooted secret. Adam thought she was the most beautiful woman he had ever seen; she looked like a lost child. Only last evening, he'd been standing outside in a light rain, looking upward to ask God for another chance at love. He had recovered from the scandal he faced a few years earlier. There was once a time he thought he'd never get past the embarrassment or the hurt he suffered because of befriending the wrong woman. But it was a lesson learned. He praised the Lord for bringing him out.

The one thing he had learned as a ministry leader was that you had to be honest with yourself before you could effectively minister to your congregation. Never would he have thought that he would struggle with lust, pornography, or any other sexual sin. But he knew he had to repent and deal with the issues in his life. Realizing what triggered his downward spiral into sexual sin was a major part of his healing process. He knew what a broken heart was after experiencing a bad breakup with his fiancée. Pondering that thought, he now knew the breakup was part of the reason he found himself on the Internet.

But God had cleansed his heart and prepared him to help heal others. Now he could smile about it because he understood how David felt after he had committed adultery with Bathsheba. He lifted his eyes slightly while saying, "Thank you for creating a right spirit in me and giving me a ministry that teaches the lost your ways so that they can find their way home."

Adam would always be grateful that he had a loving family. It had been a year and a half since the whole incident took place. He'd heard just recently that the same woman was causing havoc in the life of another pastor in the city. He didn't want her life ruined; he just wanted her to be delivered.

He had cried many a night because of the lust of his flesh. After his deliverance, Adam began speaking truthfully about pornography and sexual sin. He stopped shying away from teaching the full biblical revelation regarding human sexuality. He had learned to be proactive and real. By being honest and as open as he could be on the subject, many Christians who felt as if they were the only ones struggling with this sin were encouraged by his openness. If he had continued to beat around the bush, it would have only added to the secrecy and shame that he and those who were struggling felt.

Now it was his goal to inform all pastors to preach about it from the pulpit. Adam learned that sexual sins were not just a guy's issue. Men, women, and many young adults were struggling with sexual sin at an ever-increasing rate. The more openly he discussed sexual sins as well as God's intent for biblical sexuality, the more his congregation was beginning to feel free enough to share their struggles and to seek help and guidance. He'd told many a pastor not to give in to the temptation of softening the message in their attempt to not offend anyone.

Now he was on a mission to help other ministers who had gotten caught in this sinful web. Since Adam had begun this new journey, God had pivoted his ministry to the next level. He was traveling all over the country telling others about the dangers of this addiction.

After spending time with the other ministers during the conference, he finally realized what was missing in his life. It was the companionship of a godly woman. While walking back from one of his sessions during the conference in the rain, he had poured his heart out to God in prayer asking him to send him true love. And now here he was looking into the most beautiful pair of eyes he'd ever seen. True enough he was tired. It had been a long week of meetings and lectures. He thanked God for all of the souls that had been won for Jesus. He also thanked God for being faithful, and that's when he heard God in a still small voice say, *Adam, tonight you're going to meet your destiny.*

He thought about the fact that it was a little scary knowing that God had spoken to him. So as a man full of faith, he refused to let the devil make him nervous. He knew that as a pastor he had run a good race, and surely if he was to leave this earth, then he must have finished his life's mission. So all he could say was, "Thank God."

It was at that moment he felt a squeeze on his hand.

CHAPTER 1

Slowly her eyes opened. Destiny took one, then another, deep, calming breath. What had she been thinking? Although she ached all over, at first glance, she seemed to be in one piece; there was still so much to do, and time was running out. She knew there was no time for daydreaming. Bishop's message "Moving Day" would forever stay with her, and this time she had heard him in her spirit man, letting her know it was time to move forward and get closer to the Lord.

Her eyes remained on the bedroom door from the bathroom where she was trying to clean the blood from her face. Her eyes were a little swollen, but some makeup would do the job. Every once in a while the noise from the settling of the house made her jump. She knew she had to hurry in order to make her flight.

Seattle, Washington was just a thought two months ago, but now it was her destination. It was far away from Charleston, South Carolina and him. Rushing to the closet where she had hidden her bank account information, she grabbed it out of a shoebox. Listening and watching, Destiny pulled the documents out and looked again at the balance. Learning not to buy new things or spend unnecessary money, she'd saved enough money to transfer the balance from her bank account to one under her auntie's name. No one knew this but her aunt Sara and her uncle Willie, and she trusted both of them. After putting her checkbook in the purse, she took a quick glance at the clock. There were less than two hours to make it to the airport.

The next few moments passed by as a blur. Destiny was lost, staring intently at the floor while her mind drifted elsewhere. Fear seemed to course through her veins. No matter how hard

Destiny willed herself to be strong, she just couldn't. Tears continued to form; she couldn't stop the migraine that was on the verge of causing an explosion in her head. She knew how lucky she had been tonight, no the correct word was how blessed she had been. Destiny swallowed. What if? She had read a story a couple of years ago about a young woman who had lost her life after a horrific attack by her husband. Her whole life had changed as a result. Her only mistake today had been not cooking. Stanley told her last night he would be going out. How stupid was it not to cook the steaks that were left in the refrigerator? She needed everything to go smoothly. One stupid mistake could have ruined everything, landing her in the hospital.

Stanley was gone now, and in thirty minutes, she would be out of this house forever and closer to her promised promises. After double-checking the room for anything that she could have missed and leaving behind everything that she did not need, Destiny started down the stairs. The suitcase was in the car. She'd purchased one last week while she was at Walmart and kept it in the trunk along with everything she anticipated needing for this move to Seattle. She even had living arrangements. All she had to do now was make it to her car.

Destiny was beat; she usually put in fewer hours at the office, but she knew her last check would come in handy. Bishop Carter preached a sermon last week about a man by the name of Zacchaues who had been trying to see Jesus, but his view was blocked. However, he did not give up. He climbed a tree in order to get a view of the Master. Destiny was feeling like that little man, and just like him, if it took booking a flight on Delta and changing her name, no one was going to stop her, not this time. Her dreams had been buried and left for dead her senior year in college. But the desire to be more than what she saw in the mirror had never died; somewhere deep inside there had always been a nudging for her to do more. She heard her dreams calling her name although she'd laid them to rest years ago. Today would be the first day of their resurrection.

It was odd, really. Destiny couldn't remember feeling so weak before she'd gotten involved with Stanley. How often had her aunt commented on her strong-will and determination? Since Stanley had come into her life, she felt like she was slowly crumbling on the inside. It was time to reinvent herself, she still had some fight left.

After turning on the porch light, she crept outside, listening carefully just in case Stanley hadn't driven off. Who would have imagined that she would have to creep around the house in fear? She found herself laughing at the farcicality of her life, leaving the front porch she went into the front yard taking a moment to look around for any signs of trouble. Their neighborhood had always been quiet, filled with elegant homes and respectable families. Stanley had a closed mind when it came to their gated community because he always felt it kept out the rift raft.

Still with all of its luxury, Destiny felt they lived in an elegant mausoleum instead of a home. Moving over to the window, she placed the house key where she told her uncle Willie it would be hidden. Turning her eyes away from the house she looked up to heaven, Destiny stood there for only a moment before she heard the voice of Holy Spirit speak to her, "home can only be found in the peace of God." The familiar voice caused chills to run down her spine. The same soft, gentle voice had often called to her when she was alone and feeling down trodden. It comforted her, even if it was just a trick of her imagination, because she wasn't as strong in faith as she needed to be, people saw her smile, never recognizing the pain it was hiding. The voice was her only respite, and she needed it. She went back inside the living room to wait for her uncle. Sitting only for a few minutes, she found herself stretching out on the sofa to relax but instead groaned with unbearable pain because it still hurt to move.

Willie controlled his irritation as he watched Destiny through the window. How many times had he told her to call him if she ever found herself in trouble? And yet, she constantly insisted that she could handle her problems with Stanley by herself. With Destiny, he found that he was on edge most of the time, because she constantly took risks. His irritation with those risks was the cause of the few arguments they had. She called him Uncle Willie but refused to allow him to interfere with her relationship with Stanley. Needless to say he was surprised when she called and asked for his help. He silently praised God for her deciding to leave him. Maybe it was his fatherly instincts but he had always suspected Stanley had physically abused her.

Chagrined by the look of fear he saw on her face, he reached for the key that she had hidden for him on the window seal. Unlocking the door he pushed it open, silently thanking God for his little spy. Sara, Destiny's aunt, kept him abreast of everything that occurred in her niece's life. When he stepped inside, she sat up on the sofa, recognition and relief chased each other across her facial expression and a hint of some other emotion. Sadness? Tension? Or relief?

"Uncle Willie, we need to move quickly, we don't have much time," she rushed on to say, wrenching as she grabbed her purse and keys from the coffee table.

Yep, tension. Maybe even irritation. He had to suppress an expletive. He just prayed that Stanley hadn't hit her. He watched with concern as she moved around slowly making sure she had everything she needed.

"I saw the lights come on and knew that was my code for the coast being clear. But just as precautionary measure, I double check to make sure there was no signs of him as the taxi pulled into the drive." He shook his head at how different she'd become because she was once an aggravatingly independent young woman who visited him often with his niece from college. She'd never admit it but he knew in his heart of hearts that this new aspect of her character, vulnerability, was an annoyance to her.

"Need some help?" he asked, wanting to do something other than just standing by idly watching her. She hesitated, glancing toward the door. He could read her thoughts. The sooner they got out of here the better, so he began moving toward the front door. Instead after having a second thought he asked, "Why don't I make sure your bags are situated in the trunk of the car?"

"Okay, but let me help you with that," she said, moving to follow him in the opposite direction toward the garage. Willie didn't know what was going on but upon opening the door to the garage they found her car was missing. Maybe she had changed her plans; he'd prayed she hadn't. So he asked, "Where's your car? What's going on?"

Destiny glanced into the garage and that's when Willie saw a slight frown, which caused her brows to arch. Something about this situation seemed to have disturbed her. "He took my car. I can't believe he took it." He knew from the tension in her voice that she was perturbed. He understood because he'd felt that way on several occasions it was as if every devil in hell was waging a war against you.

"What do you need me to do?" He asked with anxiousness and concern, willing to do anything she needed.

"I've already taken care of all the necessities, and if he hasn't taken his extra set of keys, I'll take his car and make the switch," she answered him as she rummaged through a drawer in the kitchen. Pulling them out she turned to him with relief written on her facial expression.

"So do you think he suspects anything?"

"I doubt it. I know he'll be drinking with his friends for a couple of hours, but if he is inebriated enough, maybe he won't check the trunk alerting him that something fishy may be going on."

"Then we need to hurry." He picked up her purse, watching her closely.

She was hesitating, nibbling on her lower lip. Something he knew she did often when she was nervous. *Please, God, let us be able to get her out of here safely.*

"Destiny, let's get out of here; there is not much time left." It was then that he saw she'd processed every detail of what he was saying because her face suddenly changed from one of defeat to determination; it seemed to pull her back to reality. Looking over at the SUV that he never allowed her to drive, she moved toward it. Getting in, she put her keys in the ignition. He followed and got in on the passenger's side. After he closed the door, she started the engine, and they were on their way.

Twenty minutes later, falling rain pelted the SUV with big drops, and it was impossible to see more than a few inches ahead. The traffic had slowed to a crawl in order for everyone to navigate the streets safely in the rain. As she drove, he noticed other vehicles had completely stopped. That was not an option for them. Destiny stated earlier that she knew where he was, and that she was going to stop at the restaurant and make the switch with the car, he would then drive her car to the South Carolina port as they had planned so that it could be shipped to Seattle.

Turning into Charlie's Bar and Grill, he saw the full parking lot. He heard her take a deep calming breath; he assumed it was because there were no visible people outside. After pulling up to her car she got out and he followed suit. They both were careful not to make any unnecessary noise. Checking the trunk to make sure he had not seen the suitcase was their first objective. After a quick inspection, he closed the trunk as easily as he could without being seen or heard. From the corner of his eye, he noticed a lone figure approaching. Bending down, they pretended to be looking for something on the ground. Glory to God, they walked past. She put her key in the lock and got in. It was so easy. Pulling her car out of its parking space, he pulled Stanley's in its place, leaving the key in the seat. Then, joining her, they began to drive out of the parking lot.

It was then that they saw Stanley walking out of the restaurant surrounded by a group of his friends. Staying to watch the fireworks was not their priority. She had to make her flight, and there was only an hour and forty-five minutes left. The traffic had gotten better and was moving faster. Finally he saw a smile grace her face. Reaching over he grabbed her hand giving it a gentle squeeze. They had done it. After checking her in curbside and saying their goodbyes, he watched her go through the sliding glass doors. Driving off he said, "*Thank you, Lord. You make hard things easy.*"

Destiny found a seat in the waiting area. Holding her hands tightly in her lap, she tried to remain calm. The events of the day were catching up with her with lightning speed. She took a few slow, deep, breaths and let them out, hoping they would begin the boarding process soon. The fear of being caught lingered on her mind. If she let it, Destiny knew, it would take over completely. All she desired was to be on that plane, but because they had another fifteen minutes before the boarding process she kept herself occupied by people watching. There were mothers pointing things out to their children, chatting mindlessly about the plane and all its features. Even with all of the activity around her, she could sense someone's presence near her, that awareness caused prickles along her skin. Turning, she saw a young lady with her head wrapped in a beautiful scarf that looked away just as she turned to see who was watching. She had what looked like a computer of some kind in her lap and her hands were moving quickly across its keys. Maybe she hadn't been staring at her after all. It was just as well because she didn't want to be recognized by anyone who could possibly know Stanley. Destiny stiffened, upset by the nature of her own thoughts…Stanley. No, she refused to think of Stanley, after all of her months of planning, this uncontrollable fear of him was causing her to doubt. Surely she was tougher than that? God had not given her the spirit of fear. Although all of this was a new experience for her, things had gone pretty much as planned expect for the mishap with the car, and still she and Willie manage to get to the airport on time. Her gaze wandered back to the young lady seated across from her, who now appeared to be busy on her computer tapping the keys with the speed of a gazelle.

Destiny couldn't look away, even when she looked up. Her gaze settled on the face of the woman, and there was such sadness in her eyes that it caused her to wonder at her purpose for traveling to Seattle. Destiny could not look away…and neither could the other woman. They stared at each other, and Destiny felt a connection. She seemed oddly familiar but she couldn't place her. Then her expression softened. Her lips formed a slight smile before she looked back at her computer. Destiny sagged against her seat. She was tired, but also amazed and unnerved by how affected she'd been by a simple look.

The flight would be leaving in just a few minutes, and she was becoming antsy waiting to board. There was something about that woman. She knew her and she was absolutely certain of that, but for now all her concentration had to be on getting to Seattle. It made her nervous not knowing where she knew her from but she'd remember if not now, maybe later after she was on the plane. Thinking about this now was ridiculous because, while South Carolina certainly held many painful memories, Destiny didn't have that many friends she wouldn't recognize when she saw them, nor did Stanley. Just thinking of Stanley, of everything that had happened, made her feel dizzy, and she forced herself to push it away. She couldn't wait to say one day that it was a lifetime ago. A lifetime she'd never forget. And a mistake she'd never make again…and certainly not with anyone like Stanley.

Straightening, Destiny turned to face the boarding attendant. It was time to start her new life.

After what felt like hours, Destiny was on the plane, seated, and prepared for take off. One of her biggest regrets was the woman she'd become after her decision to move in with Stanley. It was one of the main reasons why she'd decided to pack up and move to Seattle. She needed a fresh start, a chance to start over in a place where the memory of Stanley's abuse and infidelities wouldn't be constant reminders of her own failures. She had heard her Bishop say, "that although we may have aborted our dream, destiny, or purpose, God had the power to speak life to it because he impregnated us with it in our mother's womb." That was reason enough to rejoice about her future. Seattle was exactly what she needed, a place where no one knew her and, furthermore, no one cared about her past.

Her pulse thudded in her ears as the gravity of the situation finally hit her. Her skin broke out in a sweat, the palms of her hands were hot and moist caused by fear. Was she dreaming? She was actually going to start over in a city where the only people she considered important in her life knew her. Since she'd made the decision to move months ago, she'd tried not to think about what would come next. Sure she had a good sum of money in the bank and a house, but then what? Her possibilities were endless.

Destiny stared out the window because she was nervous—not about being on a plane, but about the thought of him coming on board to drag her off. Crazy thoughts were coming from all over the place, and it felt like she had more than one hundred demons fighting against her. Auntie always said that the Lord had angels who defended her on a daily basis. She had to admit her angels must have won the first part of the battle because she was on the plane safe and sound. She had learned from Bible study that fear was just false evidence that appears to be real. The only way to conquer a fear was to tackle it head on with faith. Today she had begun to do just that because everything had gone according to plan. All she had to do was relax. All the drama from earlier was now over.

Despite the pain and her frantically thumping heart, she could still hear his accusatory voice yelling because she didn't have his dinner prepared on time. Just thinking about the way he hit her made her angry. The physical pain had almost been unbearable but there was nothing to be done about it now. All she wanted was to get away. The depression that she had fallen into during her senior year in college had consumed her. Her thoughts had become bitter and angry. Then, Stanley had offered her a job and a home, some sense of security. At the time Destiny had desperately wanted something normal and steady in her life, someone who could be strong for her when her world was suddenly so off balance. So she had accepted his offer and then literally overnight, he had changed. He began finding fault with everything she did, even raising his hand to hit her.

Earlier he had stood there looking at her with his eyes rolling around like a deranged man. "You know you made me do this, right?"

Too weak to do anything, she scrunched her eyes closed and forced herself to concentrate, but her head pounded sickeningly as she tried to recall the last few days. It was all a blur, a foggy indistinct blur that made little, if any sense. What had she done now to trigger this? She had just lain there, balled in a tight knot. Trying to nod her head, Destiny had wanted to tell him anything so he would leave her alone. As if by looking at her made him sick, he straddled her already aching body once again. With the full force of at least ten men, he began to throw blows to her head.

Covering her face the best she could with her hands, she finally let the tears fall. She moistened her lips again, trying to find a way out of the confusing labyrinthine of her mind. "I'm sorry...Please stop...I'm sorry..."

Speechless with rage, he just looked at her, his wide nostrils flared and his breathing blasted out in ragged spurts. His top lip lifted in a movement that should have been a wry smile but somehow Destiny suspected it wasn't. "Where's the God that's supposed to be your shield and buckler? All I do for you, and you can't even get dinner on the table when I get home." Chuckling, he began again. "I told you before nobody wanted your sorry behind but me. Why did you come back? I never wanted you! I was supposed to marry Denise. Now she's marrying the man that was my best friend before I met you. You ruined my life. It's funny now." He laughed like a deranged person. "I befriended you in hopes of making Denise jealous, and now three years later she's marrying Curtis Watson. Now get up and fix me something to eat, and act like you're glad to do it!"

Reaching out with both hands, he grabbed her bloodied face and kissed her swollen lips and then whispered in her ear, "Don't make me have to do this again."

Nodding, Destiny just wanted him to leave. Her head hit the floor with so much force, and then he walked out of the kitchen. When he got to the door, he turned around.

Panicking, thinking he was coming back, Destiny covered her face.

"Oh, yeah, I forgot to tell you I'm hanging with the boys tonight. I'll get something to eat while I'm out! But let this be a lesson to you that when a man gets home, he wants his food. Now get up and clean your nasty-looking self up before you make me sicker than I already am."

Knowing that laying there would only make him angrier, she got up, resting on her knees. Too frightened to submit to the exhaustion she felt, Destiny tried once more to slowly get up. Lifting her hand slightly, she wiped the stray tear that cascaded down her face.

Silently, thoughts were running through her head. Why did she stay with this fool? She had a degree and a good job. A recent promotion had just put her in the six-figure range.

She put her hand against the window and looked down, reflecting on the last six months. Destiny shivered. Her eyes burned with tears and her whole body ached. She'd been so busy being an obedient boxing bag that she hadn't had a chance to figure out who she was or what she wanted from life. But now she had all the time in the world...and it scared her to death.

Her chest tightened uncomfortably, and her breaths came quick and shallow. Who was she kidding? She wasn't the type of person who could start over. She should get off this plane right now. At least then she wouldn't have to face the uncertainty of the future and the possibility of failing.

Her eyes watered, and she curled closer to the window, staring at the woman she'd become, asking what happened to the Destiny who once was so full of life. She pulled her ponytail holder out of her hair and ran her fingers through it. It had been too long since she had a life she could call her own. Shaking her head, with the realization that she'd given up everything for him, it never got better like he'd promised. It just got worse. In the beginning, before they'd moved in together, he had been so charming and so very attentive. He was protective, not possessive, forceful, not dominating. He was constantly telling her how much he loved her. It was all so flattering.

Destiny, however, had had no illusions about her feelings. She didn't love Stanley. She'd liked him well enough and thought that, perhaps, she would grow to love him. He always said, "Baby, you know I love you. It hurts me when I have to do this. I'm a good man, and any woman would be glad to have a man that drives a Bentley and lives in this neighborhood with a salary like mine."

Suddenly a claustrophobic wave overcame her, causing her to heave deep breaths. She tried to calm her racing heart, which seemed to match the roar of the plane's engine. It felt as if the plane was beginning to back up. It was at that moment she heard a voice in her head similar to Stanley's saying, *Where do you think you are going?* Then the speed on the plane picked up. *It's not too late to say stop, you made a mistake, and get off.* Rubbing her head, Destiny was starting to wonder if she did the right thing. Her head was pounding. What she needed to do was pray. *Lord, am I doing the right thing? I want a life. I deserve a life of happiness and joy. Please, Lord, give me a sign. In Jesus's name, amen."* She struggled to contain her composure by clutching at the armrest of the seat as if to anchor herself.

A hard thigh brushed against her hand, causing her to jump.

"Sorry." The voice was deep and filled with apology.

She gasped, hand clutched over her heart. Wiping the tears from her face with the back of her other hand, she said, "It's all right." Turning, she looked at the face of the voice she'd just heard.

"I can hold your hand if this take-off is making you nervous. I could even join you in prayer. It must be your first flight?"

Looking up, Destiny saw the man who was sitting next to her for the first time. Instantly, she noticed his warm brown eyes she felt tiny beads of sweat on her forehead while he appeared completely calm. His relaxed state eased some of the uncertainty she felt.

"Perhaps I should introduce myself," the man said, breaking through her tortured reverie. "We may as well get acquainted because for the next four-and-a-half hours we'll be seated next to each other. My name is Adam Wheeler, and what, may I ask, is yours?"

She never experienced the sensations floating around in her stomach. It felt like a flutter of joy, something that was reaching way down deep in her soul. It took her so long to answer him, he finally said, "At least let me hold your hand until we get in the air." She held out her right hand. After noticing it trembling, she hid it in her lap. She didn't want him to think she was a frightened little girl; her emotions were all over the place especially after everything she'd endured to make this flight. She was a big ball of confusion. Closing her eyes briefly, she inhaled, allowing the stored air in her lungs to slowly escape through her pursed lips before reopening her eyes to look at him.

Adam saw the trembling of her hand before she quickly hid it under her jacket. "It's Destiny…" she said after a moment, her spirits instantly lifting as she turned to looked out the window. Silence filled the air as the plane finally leveled off rapidly moving them toward their destination—the place where all of Destiny's hopes and dreams would come to fruition or dissipate into nothingness.

He could not believe his ears. "Excuse me…what did you say?" he asked. Destiny smiled lightly, in response to the astonishment that had crept into his expression despite his best efforts to conceal it. "Destiny. My name is Destiny Harper, and it's nice to meet you, Adam." She responded, sitting back and reflecting for a moment on what about her name seemed to excite him.

CHAPTER 2

There was something about the look on Adam's face that Destiny couldn't get out of her mind. Something about the sound of his voice—a contagious warmth that radiated from him, and she envied the peacefulness of it that she felt almost immediately. The cabin of the plane was dark now and the light above her seat cast a small circle around her. There were a few other lights on throughout the cabin. She was feeling some kind of way—almost a nagging sense of discontent. Adam must have had the same problem because he had been squirming in his seat, trying, it seemed, to find a comfortable position; he must have because his eyes were now closed. Shutting her own eyes she let herself sink into a mental fog, neither awake nor asleep.

It seemed she had been carried back in time. Time had healed some of the wounds, but nothing was ever going to be the same again. She was twenty-five and on the verge of turning twenty-six and two months ago her whole life changed. It was a regular Saturday in January. The weather was unusually warm for Charleston, South Carolina. Destiny should have known that a storm was brewing. The house was quiet when she returned home late following her trip with her aunt. Stanley must have left the hall light on for her after he'd gone out; she wasn't surprised by his absence, he never greeted her at the door so she wasn't expecting that but it would have been a nice change.

Picking up her suitcase, she headed up the stairs to their bedroom only to find all of her things scattered throughout the room in disarray. Immediately her survival skills kicked in as she tried to remember her last conversation with Stanley. It had been on the Thursday before she was scheduled to leave. She had been in her office taking care of some last-minute details before leaving for the annual pig pickin' held by her relatives every year on the third of January. A coworker came into her office to ask if she had heard the news.

"Hey, girl. Are you almost ready to take that trip?"

Destiny smiled. Shelia was the one person in her department whom she had come to really like. "I'm just about to get out of here. I have to take care of a few things before we hit the road."

Entering her office, Shelia leaned against her desk. "Well, I wanted to give you the latest news. You remember Curtis Watson, don't you?"

Destiny's eyes narrowed into thin slits. "I remember him." She snapped the folder in her hand, not looking up. "I really don't care to know or hear anything about him."

"He's getting married, Destiny."

Destiny looked into Shelia's eyes, her pulse rate picking up frantically. "To whom?"

"It's Stanley's ex-fiancée, Denise Jackson. The date is set for February fourteenth in Hilton Head. It's supposed to be a big to-do."

Pushing her chair away from the desk, Destiny's breathing became normal. He was getting married. Now all she had to deal with was the effect it was going to have on Stanley.

Standing to gaze out of her office window, Destiny turned slightly, looking directly at Shelia; she tried to be as casual as possible. "Well, I wish them the best. Listen, Shelia, I've got to get out of here. Let's do lunch when I get back from my trip."

"All right, girl. I'll see you on Monday." Shelia smiled and walked out of the office.

Destiny had no idea how Stanley was going to take the news, but knew she would find out sooner than later.

As if he'd read her thoughts, a voice broke into her space taking over the atmosphere. Shocked, and slightly disturbed by the fact that she had been staring off into space for so long, she quickly looked up to see Stanley, who stared at her in what looked to be a major annoyance. "I guess you heard what my ex-friend did?"

Destiny looked at Stanley. "I heard he's marrying Denise." She answered as calmly as she could.

Clearing his throat, Stanley came around the side of the desk looking directly at Destiny. "He knew I loved her! I can't believe he went behind my back."

It wasn't what she wanted to hear nor did she care to get into a long, drawn out discussion about it now obviously the only reason for his extended visit. She humored the notion of starting an argument for a moment, but what would be the point. Looking at the man who had stolen so many years from her only caused her more irritation, she wished his male charm had never had been used on her.

Shaking her head, a faint smile came to her lips. "I thought you loved me. If not, then why are we still together, Stanley?"

Pushing away from her desk, Stanley took a deep breath before rolling his eyes. "Please, Destiny, not today."

Destiny jumped up and began to walk out of her office. But Stanley blocked her way. "If you're not happy, when you pack your things for your little trip to Hicksville, don't come back. You were always my second choice anyway." With that being said, he turned and walked out of her office without a backward glance.

Stanley had shown up like a surprise storm and disappeared just as quickly carrying his gale force winds of anger back to his office, which didn't bother her in the least, he often locked himself in there to sulk. The silence that followed didn't dim Destiny's enthusiasm one bit. She was still excited about her trip. The enthusiasm leapt right across the desk where it hung in the air for what seemed like forever. Destiny couldn't recall much more about the conversation as she finished her day. The details didn't really matter. They were at an impasse. He had expressed his feelings about her and now she had to begin planning her future without him. There was time for that; tomorrow she was going on her annual trip with her aunt.

Kingstree, South Carolina, had a population of about three thousand. It was where her aunt, who ran the local club in their small rural community for several years, had raised her. She was royalty in their hometown. At sixty, she was still a thrill a minute.

Destiny smiled to herself as she thought about her. There was no other person like her. She put her bag in the trunk and got in the car. Her aunt never liked to be late. Destiny knew that the first thing she would notice when she hugged her would be the smell of roses. She always smelled the same no matter what time of day, always saying, "The sweetest thing about me is the roses I keep around my yard, and there isn't a better lotion for a woman than one with the smell of roses." She would laugh from deep down in her belly, making her eyes light up.

Most folk could not help noticing how attractive she was even now. Her heart-shaped face was still classically cut, even with signs of aging. Her eyes were the blackest and most beautiful pieces of coal you ever wanted to see. Men loved how her five-foot-eight frame handled her curves and her ample hips. Not too much but not too little.

She always said, "Most of them, men I mean, can't handle any more than this on a good day." Then she would run her hand gracefully down her sides, bat those eyes, add an extra shake to her hips, and strut out of the room.

Auntie always wanted to go visit her family for the annual pig pickin', and this year was no different. The pig pickin' in Kingstree was a big event, a party that involved the barbecuing of a whole hog. They always had a good time, and this year would not be an exception.

Focusing on the issue at hand, Destiny knew the time for daydreaming was not now. Her aunt was sitting on the front porch of her house when she drove up. Sara began to get up as she saw the car. Like many women her age, Auntie was always in a hurry. Opening her door and walking around to open the trunk, Destiny struggled putting the bag inside because she always packed like she'd be gone a year.

"I hope I'm not too late because I know you like to get an early start."

Auntie felt like she had to be the first one to arrive and the last one to leave. The food would not be the same unless she was there to help prepare it.

"Child, they don't know how to season food. I've got all of my secret spices, and nothing will taste right without them." This was what she said every year.

Destiny shook her head, watching as her aunt walked toward the car. Her arms opened, beckoning for them to give each other a hug.

"Put my bag in the car. We can beat the morning rush-hour traffic if we leave right now."

"I'm moving as fast as I can. Don't worry. We'll get there before the first piece of cabbage is cut for the coleslaw."

"Where is Stanley on this Friday morning?" Sara asked as she closed the door. "I know he gave you a specific time to get back on Saturday. Never seen a man so hell-bent on keeping up with one woman." She put her seat belt on, snapped it in place, and then turned to look at Destiny.

"He was dressed to play golf. What else? He bought a new set of clubs last week. You know he wants to try them out on the course today." Destiny shook her head and began to pull out of the drive.

"When's the last time he bought something new for you? Always spending money and showing off for those rich friends of his. I wonder what his friends would think if they knew the real Stanley Womack. Never did like that man." Sara crossed her arms, sucked her teeth, and stared out the window. "You think I don't know, baby girl? But I've seen those bruises on your arms and on your face. You try to cover them up. Always wearing those long blouses and using that makeup, but I've seen them." The anger in her voice was evident. "If I told you once, I've told you a hundred times to leave him. What is it that he has on you to make you stay? Your mama would be really disappointed if she were alive knowing you were being treated this way." Sara shook her head. "I just don't understand it."

"Auntie, I appreciate everything you've done for me, and I know you love me, but you just don't understand. Stanley is not all bad, and he was there for me when I needed him. I want to do the same for him. Look at all of the things he's done for me over the years." Knowing it was a cop-out, Destiny kept her eyes on the road and continued to drive. "So don't worry about me. I'll be all right."

"But I can't help it, honey." Sara stated. "I couldn't be there for you while you were in college."

"You were busy trying to keep a roof over our heads. I want you to know that all the things you did to keep me in college and give us a place to live will never be forgotten."

"Child, you are all the family I have. I wouldn't change all the memories we've created for anything in the world."

"If it weren't for me, you would have gotten married and had some kids of your own."

"If I really wanted to get married, it would have happened. Now, I don't want to hear anything else on the subject, you hear? Stop worrying about me. I'm too ornery and set in my ways now for any man to deal with me."

"Now, would I do that?" Smirking, Destiny kept her eyes on the road.

"Yes, if it was what you thought was best for me. You remind me so much of your mother. Margret was the real nurturer in the family even though I was older. She was always worrying about other people and never herself." The last few words caught in her aunt's throat.

Destiny glanced at her aunt and stated the obvious. "You two were closer than most sisters, weren't you?"

"Yes, we were. It's been a lot of years, and I still miss her. Always will."

"I wish I could have known her and my father. But you've been both mother and father to me. I love you, Auntie." She glanced over again to smile at the woman she trusted more than anyone else in the world.

They both settled into the drive to Kingstree with their own thoughts. The drive would take a couple of hours. Destiny put in her Anthony Hamilton CD and listened to him sing about corn bread, fish, and collard greens. It was easy to relax while listening to his rich, soulful voice.

Without warning, as she always did, Sara would start talking about the past as they headed to the old homestead in Kingstree.

"You know the good Lord knows who to give them to, children I mean, and who not too. I guess my name was on the not list." Smiling, she continued.

"But your mama, she was the sweetest thing in this world. She was always too trusting. She fell for your daddy the first night they met. Oh, she was smart, pretty, and had the cutest dimples. All the single men and some of the married ones in Kingstree were sweet on her. I told her when she met him he had too much going on in his life. But I knew it was over when he sang and danced with her that first night. They lit the whole place up. You could actually see the love. He told me that he was a pediatrician in Atlanta. He sent her flowers every day as well as bought her all kinds of gifts. She fell hard for him. Two weeks after they met, he was gone.

"Men like him came into the club all the time, you know." Laughing out loud to no one in particular, she continued. "They always walked around like they were the king of the world, flashing their money and buying drinks for all the ladies. I have to give him credit though. He was different from the other men who came around. He always treated your momma like a lady, always pulling her chair out, opening doors, and stuff like that."

Chuckling and running her hand down her thigh, she said, "Baby girl, let me tell you, your daddy has the prettiest caramel-colored eyes just like you and the same brown, wavy hair. It broke your momma's heart when he left. They were always together, but he didn't even let her know he was leaving. One day they were supposed to meet at the house for a special dinner, and he never showed up. She cried for many nights. There was nothing I could do. I tried everything, but nothing helped. She was devastated by his leaving." Auntie shifted in her seat. She started smoothing out invisible wrinkles in her shirt before continuing.

"She was twenty-nine years old when she got pregnant with you. It was the best present she could have gotten. She changed when she found out she was pregnant. She started talking about the future and all the things she aspired to do for you. I never could understand it. One day she was ready to give up on life, and then, all of a sudden, she was the Margret I knew before your daddy left. It was the strangest thing.

"When she went into labor, she started hemorrhaging badly. They couldn't stop the bleeding. I made a promise to my sister that night, and I kept it."

Auntie never got tired of telling Destiny the story, almost as if she didn't want her to forget.

"Your mama said, 'Sara, take care of her. She's your little girl now. You've always said that the good Lord knew who to give them to. I guess he found you worthy. You've been real good to me, Sara. You were the best sister anybody could have ever had. I know it wasn't easy raising me after Mama and Daddy died, but you did. Now she's part of your destiny and she's going to help give your life purpose. Both of you will be just fine. My little Destiny has a special angel. God sent her an angel, and he's going to take care of both of you.'"

She stopped again, the tears flowing steadily down her face.

"I knew then she was slipping away because she thought your daddy was standing in the door of that hospital room. It was only because I knew he was a pediatrician in Atlanta, and not Charleston that I didn't correct her, I just let her talk. 'Sara, tell the story of how we fell in love one night while we danced to Smokey Robinson. Tell her how he sang "The Track of my Tears." Tell her I chose her and God chose me.'

"She grabbed my hands, and at that point I could tell she was leaving me. She looked toward the door as if she saw Jesus himself. But it was that same doctor with his surgical mask covering his face, their gazes locked as if they knew each other. Her face began to light up with a happiness that I had not seen since she looked down at you. "I heard her whisper, 'I knew you were coming. Isn't she the prettiest thing you've ever seen? She has your caramel eyes and brown hair.' I turned around expecting to see him at the door, but the only person standing there was that doctor with his surgical mask and his assistant."

After pondering those thoughts in her mind, Auntie looked out the window of the car, turning slowly to look at Destiny.

"Destiny, sometimes you're able to see in hindsight what was right before your eyes. But while you were looking, you missed the important details. I believe it's true that our view about many things can be blocked by people, jealously, hate, and envy. Really, in my opinion people see what they want to see, baby."

She patted my leg before continuing. "But in reality there's always more if we would only allow the way we feel to be eliminated from what we see. Our own insecurities can block us from seeing what could actually bless our lives or become a blessing in our lives. After all the years that Margret has been gone, it's only now that I realize it was my anger and bitterness over the way my life had turned out that caused me to be jealous of the love Margret found."

Sara got quiet, caught up in her own thoughts.

A tear ran down the side of Sara's face. With a hand that had seen better days, she wiped it quickly away.

"Auntie, are you all right?"

And as if she had been in a trance, she looked at Destiny, wiped the tears, smiled that smile of hers, and said, "I did my best for you. Margret didn't want her baby girl working at no club and having babies by some 'ole no count man. And I kept all those boys that saw you filling out and looking like a china doll away. You were so smart just like your mama, and you loved all that science stuff. Every time I turned around you were either cutting up a frog or working on a concoction to make them better. Even back then your life was already poised for greatness, baby girl." She patted Destiny's thigh, after that statement, and closed her eyes. Destiny smiled looking at the road ahead of them moving closer to Kingstree.

CHAPTER 3

Coming out of her sleep, caused her head to jerk. Destiny ran her hand through her hair as the fog cleared in her head. She saw his lips moving before hearing his question. Then she noticed the flight attendant standing by her cart. "Would you like something to drink?"

She put her hand to her aching eyes, she was exhausted. "A Coke, please."

"Would you like some peanuts to go with that?"

"No, thank you. Just a Coke."

"We'll be back around in about forty-five minutes. If you need anything before then, just push the over head button to your right."

"Adam, can I offer you anything else to make your flight more comfortable?" She noticed the woman serving them was also serving up a view of her ample bosom. The sharp stab of jealously that ran through Destiny was as unexpected as it was unwanted. She turned her head and pretended that she was interested in the blackness outside of the window. Her slender, amber-colored, manicured fingers touched his shirt collar. Destiny could not believe the display that was unfolding before her eyes.

In a low, rusty voice, Adam responded, "No, thank you. The lady and I will inform you if we need anything else."

With that, she pushed the cart to the next set of seats.

"I didn't want to disturb you. They say you should never wake a person suddenly from their sleep." He said, taking a sip of his coffee. "First time for you?" He glanced at her for a brief moment.

"Huh?" She answered, being jolted out of her thoughts before turning from her window.

"Is this your first time on a plane?" he clarified as he raised his eyebrows.

"No, I've flown several times," she answered. "But this is my first trip to Seattle." She smiled at him "What about you?"

"Seattle is home for me." Laughing, he suddenly stopped as if he was pondering his next words. "Will you be traveling far when we land?"

She felt a little apprehensive about answering him. After all she knew very little about him. But she also knew there was something oddly different about him, something she couldn't put her finger on. It was the warmth that she felt from his eyes that made her comfortable enough to answer his question.

"I'm not familiar with the area. But my aunt and I have bought a home in the SeaTac area."

"I have a friend that lives in that area. Warren Revis. He pastors one of the local churches in Seattle. It's not far from the airport. It's a beautiful community, very peaceful, and the homes in the area are so reasonably priced. If you need a ride or help with your luggage, I'd be glad to give you one. No pressure, of course." Adam took another sip of the coffee he ordered.

Destiny thought that Adam's offer was kind. "I'm not really sure when I'll be leaving the airport. I am supposed to be meeting a young woman who will be living with us for a while. She's flying into Seattle tonight as well."

Adam took the napkin from his tray and wiped away the sandwich crumbs from his mouth that he had been eating.

"It's no problem. I can give you both a ride. I really don't mind. It will give me a chance to visit with Warren and his family."

She thought about what Adam had said, and it sure would beat paying unnecessary money for a taxi. "Maybe we will accept your offer."

"I truly don't mind at all. Lord knows there have been times when I needed a helping hand and someone was there for me."

Adam returned to the coffee he was drinking then turned his head and asked, "So are you nervous about your move to a new state? Maybe your houseguest can help you adjust."

Destiny took a drink of her Coke before answering. "Yes, I am a little nervous. I don't really know our guest; my aunt adopted a young lady that lived next door to her. From what I've been told, she's a wonderful person. She has two twin boys who are five years old. She's originally from the Seattle area, and is returning for the first time in several years."

Destiny was telling Adam about Cynthia's life. But it was better than telling him about hers. She had never met Cynthia, but her sons were adorable. They had the cutest dimples, curly hair, and brown eyes. Whenever she went to visit her aunt, she would have the boys. Auntie helped Cynthia out while she was going to school. It wasn't a problem. She had plenty of room.

"I'm a twin." Adam made that statement while still studying Destiny. "I have a brother, Marvin, who lives in Seattle as well. He's a real-estate investor. He made his first fortune when he got out of college and has been successful ever since. As a matter of fact, he just opened his own office. I guess you can tell I'm proud of him. My parents think he's who shot the bear." Chuckling, he took another sip of his coffee.

Destiny looked at Adam and wondered if his parents were proud of him as well. After a long moment she forced herself to meet his gaze once more. "Um…I know this might be a strange question but"—she quickly licked her lips for courage before she continued—"What about you? Are they proud of you as well?"

Adam looked at Destiny for a moment before his answer. "I guess that came out wrong. They're proud of both of us. I just traveled a different path than my brother. I graduated from Morehouse School of Religion, and I'm working on my doctorate at the University of Washington's School of Theology and I'm the pastor of the Greater Community Church of Faith. And now I'm returning home for some much needed rest since I've been in Charleston for a convention this past week.

Destiny turned her head to look out of the window. She saw her reflection, but she also saw something else.

Suddenly, Adam turned in her direction. Her stomach gave a funny tingle. *Is he watching me? And why on earth would he do that?* When she looked his way, he wasn't studying her but finishing the coffee, and his attention was squarely focused on that task.

She asked, "I thought you were in a conference. Didn't you get any rest while you were there?"

There it was again, she thought. A slight pause before he chose his words. "I did get a little rest, but I've been attending conferences for a while now. The one thing I've learned is that you must manage your time effectively between classes and reuniting with acquaintances." He seemed caught up in his thoughts once again, but this time it was delight that spread over her face. "I have very little time to relax with all of the workshops. I intend to relax on Friday, and I have all day Saturday to rest and get ready for Sunday morning. Such is the life of a pastor. I'm lucky. I don't have a wife, so I can really relax when I get home. What about you? Are you married?" He looked at her ring finger as he asked.

She blinked when she saw Adam watching her as she looked over at his wedding finger. Was it her imagination or was he smiling? Then again, she really didn't know him, which was the way she liked it and wanted to keep it. Getting too close to men—especially single, handsome, and apparently nice men—always led to trouble. At least that was her experience.

"Uh, I'm not married. I thank God for that because if I were, you would be sitting here alone."

Nodding his head with understanding, he replied, "Just thought I'd ask. You never know. These days a lot of couples don't wear their rings."

She blinked again. There he went again, and this time he was definitely smiling and laughing. The gentle curve of his mouth was uplifted. As he laughed, a hint of his dimples came to life in his brown cheeks. She felt a flutter of wonderment and dismissed it. She wasn't interested in Adam or any man, especially after this last disastrous relationship.

But she responded, "I believe that if I were married, I would definitely wear my ring because I know that my man would be worthy of wearing it for." Maybe she had said too much, but it was out now.

Adam watched Destiny's facial expressions. A man might think she was made of ice because she didn't smile much. But all evening he had been watching her. Although this was the picture she wanted to present, he believed there was another person wrapped up in all that hurt. He could see a woman who was vulnerable and damaged by the hurt that had occurred. He'd seen the look on her beautiful face when he asked to hold her hand.

She wasn't as tough as she pretended to be. You couldn't look at her physical appearance to judge this because she was beautiful. She had the most gorgeous hair, which fell on her shoulders, and her eyes were an extraordinary color with specks of gray when the light hit them, but it was the way her shoulders slumped when she spoke that made him curious. Now, as he watched her, he realized just how beautiful, lonely, and maybe even hurt she really was.

Why he was noticing, he couldn't really say. He'd given up on women for a while, and trusting them was the part he had to learn all over again. Regina had taught him that lesson well. Regina was the only woman he'd ever proposed to, believing he loved her. And he thought she loved him. That was until she discovered he was returning home to pastor in Seattle and wouldn't be staying in Atlanta, her hometown.

They had planned a beautiful fall wedding at her father's church in the city. New Haven Baptist Church was well known, as was her father. He was one of Adam's professors in seminary. Adam had developed great respect for not only Dr. Michael Webber but his wife, Mildred, also. He spent a lot of time at their home. Had eaten many Sunday dinners with them and some meals on occasion through the week. Dr. Webber even allowed him to minister from his pulpit. When he met their daughter, Regina, who was attending Spelman College, their relationship developed over the last two years of college. With all the time they spent together, it seemed only natural for them to fall in love. Adam always told Regina that he was going back home to pastor in the Seattle area. It was a burden he had since he received his calling at nineteen.

Regina seemed to be fine with that until he told her about the offer from the Greater Community Church of Faith in Seattle. She had refused to listen to reason.

She shook her head. "I can't leave Mom and Dad. I am their only child, and they might need me."

Adam stiffened; the warmth that was in his eyes faded. "Then, by all means, stay here with them." That was all he said as he began to walk away from her. This was not the way he had planned on ending his day. He thought she would be excited about his announcement.

"Don't do this to me, Adam, please," she said, her hand touching the curve of his jaw. "Don't make me feel as if I'm betraying you because I care about my parents."

The word *betraying* stayed with Adam as he said calmly, "Regina I'm going to accept this pastoral position, and either we agree on this or I guess the wedding's off." With that said, he walked toward his car from her parents' front porch.

"You're going to walk away from our wedding because of a church in Seattle?" she shouted so loud that her parents came to the front door. "Then go on, Adam, and be the pastor of some poverty-stricken community church in Seattle. You could have worked with Daddy becoming the pastor, but no. That was too easy. You have to be the inner-city warrior for your old community."

Regina began to cry. Watching from inside the screen door, her mother walked outside, wrapping her arms around her daughter.

Dr. Webber looked at Regina then at Adam. "Son, I wish things had turned out differently, but baby girl just isn't ready to leave home. Don't worry about the wedding. We will handle all the cancellations and let everyone know." He began walking toward Adam with his hand held out.

All he said was, "Son, you do what the Lord told you, and if God sees fit for Regina to be in your life, she will. But for now go and take your final exams, go home, and be the pastor that God called you to be." He had tears in his eyes when he spoke those words.

Adam took one final look at Regina, but she turned her head to her mother's chest and wept.

After hugging her father, he whispered, "I do love her, you know."

Dr. Webber responded, "I know you do, son, but Regina has some growing up to do. I'll tell her mother you said good-bye. God bless you, Adam."

And with that, Adam got in his car, drove off, and never looked back. His last thought was that when he did get a wife, she would have to support him in ministry.

CHAPTER 4

They landed slightly ahead of schedule. As the plane taxied to the gate, Destiny couldn't help but to feel a few nervous butterflies. She had enjoyed her conversation with Adam; it was easy to flow from one subject to another. He made her feel comfortable, which is probably why they both had enjoyed the in-flight movie. Now her focus was on meeting Cynthia at the baggage claim. Sara said that she'd be easy to recognize with her blonde braids.

After departing the plane, Destiny followed Adam, moving toward baggage claim, focused on finding Cynthia. Then they both could journey to their new home together. As they approached baggage claim, Destiny noticed the woman she had seen earlier with the beautiful scarf walking around the carousal. She was the same woman who avoided her gaze at the airport before this flight.

When she neared baggage claim, Destiny searched for anyone fitting the description that her aunt had given her. Unaware that someone had approached her from behind, she turned around, almost colliding with the woman she'd seen earlier. "Are you Destiny Harper?" she asked.

Destiny was slightly taken aback, shocked that she knew her name. Then it dawned on her, so she in turn asked, "Are you Cynthia Mason?"

"Yes, I am," she replied with a smile.

She was very pretty. Her eyes were dark, and her skin was the color of caramel. Destiny held out her hand, smiled, and said, "It's a pleasure to meet you, Cynthia. I was looking for blonde braids. How was your flight?"

Shaking her hand in return, she replied, "Good and it's a pleasure meeting you as well. I can't believe I saw you at the airport earlier. I didn't want to stare you down, but I knew you looked familiar. Your aunt told me about your eyes and I wouldn't be able to miss you, and she was right. They are unbelievable eyes."

"Wow, you're good for my ego. I think we are going to get along fine." Destiny answered.

Cynthia continued saying, "I wrapped my hair in this scarf because I knew the flight was going to be long, and I wanted to sleep worry free." She pointed to a couple of her braids that were peaking out.

"I was looking for braids." Destiny watched as Cynthia took her hand and touched her hair. "Girl, when you have twin boys, you do the simplest things possible to make life easy." They both laughed.

Nodding her head in agreement, Destiny stated the obvious. "I don't know about that yet, but your boys are adorable. They were the highlight of my visits every evening after work at my aunt's house."

"They are precious, but of course I'm biased. I can't wait to see them. I've missed them so much."

Destiny responded, "I'm sure they missed you as well."

She nodded her head. "Miss Sara wanted them to come with her so that I could make sure everything was done before leaving Charleston. Nothing would have been done with two rambunctious twins getting in the way. The Lord himself sent Miss Sara to me."

Noticing Adam pointing to the carousal, she indicated which bag belonged to her. As he reached for it, he must have seen his as well because his attention went right back to the carousal before she could tell him she'd found Cynthia.

The air was a little cool in the terminal, wrapping itself around her as the sliding glass doors continued to open and close. Her eyes darted back to Cynthia as she was putting her arms in her sweater; it was then that she noticed her fidgeting with the purse straps almost as if she was trying to avoid looking at Adam.

"I sat next to him on the plane. He's a pastor here in Seattle." Smiling, Destiny glanced at Adam. He was moving toward them.

"Cynthia? What are you doing here?"

Destiny watched as Cynthia's eyes froze on Adam. She tried but had no hope of disguising the look of shock on her face. She opened and closed her mouth, seemingly trying to get her voice to work. By the movement of her eyes her brain was flying off in all directions, confused, frightened, and lost. As if she were asking the question. "How could this be?"

Destiny noticed her hands shaking. Shifting to look at Adam's dark and intense gaze, she was a little surprised to see the gaze he was emitting was a little chilling but curious as well.

"I could ask you the same thing, Adam," she finally responded. Her tone was just as sharp as his had been. For a heart-stopping moment, no other sound left anyone's lips.

Adam looked over at Destiny, "I assume you two have met?"

"Yes, we have. Adam, this is Cynthia. She's the houseguest I've been telling you about."

Not quite letting the smile reach his face, Adam looked back at Cynthia. "I know Cynthia well. It's been a while, and I'm sure we'll have a lot of catching up to do." With that said, he began to move toward the airport exit.

Destiny, sensing something was going on, looked at her watch. "If you're ready, we can get going, Cynthia. Are you okay?" Destiny asked, concerned by the stricken look on Cynthia's face.

"Yes, I'm fine. Just surprised to see Adam."

"It's going to be all right. Let's get you to your boys," Destiny said as they walked toward the car. "Because honestly, Cynthia, you don't look all right to me."

Cynthia didn't argue. She just waited with Destiny as Adam brought the Range Rover around to pick them up. While Adam put the bags in the back, Destiny opened the door for Cynthia.

Adam eased the car into traffic. "Destiny, we are going to SeaTac right? I know the general area. Just give me the street address." He looked over at her for a reply.

Destiny began to look into her purse for the paper she had written the address on. Once she found it, she told Adam and placed the sheet back in her purse.

Destiny glanced at the backseat when she heard Cynthia mutter something crossly, just before she pulled her cell phone out of her purse. The strain on her face evaporated once she began her conversation with whoever was on the other end. Turning around, she whispered curiously to Adam, "So how do you know Cynthia?"

It was a moment before he answered. Destiny couldn't help feeling he was holding something back from her, something important. Inhaling, Adam's brain flew through what he knew about Cynthia Mason, wondering what brought her back to Seattle, "We all graduated from high school the same year. She went to school on Mercer Island. Marvin and I attended Bellevue High." He focused on the road ahead of him.

Finally his lips stretched into a brief on-off smile that didn't involve his eyes. "That doesn't seem to merit the reaction she had when she saw you walk through the door." Destiny tried to read his expression, to see if any slight movement of his lips, eyes or forehead would provide some clue to the state of the relationship they apparently shared once. He gave a slight frown but did not elaborate on his response. She wondered if they'd been a couple.

Adam couldn't help but notice the look on Destiny's face and the strange arch of her brows. "Cynthia and my twin, Marvin, dated from the eighth grade until they were seniors in high school. They were really in love. I thought if I ever were in love,

I'd want it to be like theirs. But I guess it wasn't meant to be. Cynthia's parents, Edward and Gwendolyn Mason…"

"You mean the Dynamic Duo? At least that's what they're called on CNN. They own the Mason Law Offices, right? And they handle all the high-profile cases." Destiny gulped.

Adam chuckled. "That's them. Cynthia's parents didn't approve of her relationship with Marvin. Didn't think he was good enough. So on the night of our graduation, Mr. Mason paid a visit to Marvin, and in not so many words he was ordered to stay away from his daughter or there would be consequences he did not want to pay. That's the long and the short of it."

Adam reached out and touched Destiny's hand before quickly pulling it back. "So you see why I was shocked, but it seemed to take a whole lot more out of her. I can only imagine Marvin's reaction after he finds out she's back in the city."

Destiny sensed that it was much more. Just seeing Adam could not have garnered that kind of reaction from Cynthia. Destiny also noticed that Adam never mentioned anything about Cynthia having children, which meant maybe he didn't know. It wouldn't be hard to put two and two together. Adam and Marvin were twins, and Cynthia had two beautiful twin boys. Come to think of it, they looked a lot like Adam. If Cynthia didn't mention it, then she would keep her thoughts on the matter to herself. Besides, she would be dealing with her own skeletons in a few days. They would deal with Cynthia and the twins when they arrived at the house.

Turning her head toward the window Destiny's eyes filled with amazement realizing why Tina, her best friend from college, and her husband Richard were so in love with Seattle. They had been living in Seattle since the Seahawks drafted Richard in his senior year. Tina told Destiny that she would love it here when she begged her to relocate. She looked out the window, and in the distance she could see the rolling hills that looked as if they had been sprayed with a soft mist. Tina told her about the trees and the misty, grassy fields. She described the summers as being soft and relaxing caused by the rushing of the river that ran behind their home on Mercer Island. That's where Adam said Cynthia's parents lived, which also meant that Cynthia's parents had money. So why had Cynthia been living like a pauper? It made no sense to her. But maybe when Cynthia was comfortable they would really talk. It was easy to sense she needed a friend. Maybe they could become good friends especially since they'd be living in the same house. That thought brought a genuine smile to her face.

"I never get tired of the scenery here," Adam commented. "It's like looking at the face of God and being in awe of his majesty."

"I agree. I didn't know it would look like this. My college roommate, Tina, lives here with her husband and their daughter. You may have heard of him. Richard Wilson?"

"The Richard Wilson? The all-pro running back for the Seahawks?" He looked at her in awe.

Laughing, Destiny said, "They're one and the same."

"Wow, he's an awesome running back and a great person. He's done a lot of charity work throughout the city."

"I'm not surprised. Tina and Richard were very active in the Fellowship for Christian Athletes during college. They started dating during their junior year, and later the same year they both became born-again Christians. They're my closest friends, besides my aunt."

"I hope that one day you will consider me a friend, Destiny." Adam glanced over at her. Destiny tried to picture it but her mind continued to be a blank. *Could he?* she asked herself as soon as the thought settled into her head.

One of the last messages she heard from her bishop in South Carolina was about God knowing the plans for her life, and if he knew the plans, then surely it was all going to work together for her good.

When her mother could not be there for her during child-hood, Aunt Sara showed up to raise her. When she needed a friend in college, Tina was there. Looking back on the events of today, she knew that God sat her in that seat beside Adam. So yes, she was certain he'd become a friend.

As far as anything else, that would have to be seen. As she looked over at Adam, she responded, "Yes, I believe I will one day consider you a friend." That lightning-quick movement came and went in his gaze again, it was like the hand of an illusionist making something disappear before the audience could see how it was done.

They both heard Cynthia saying goodbye, indicating she'd gotten off the phone. Destiny saw her hit the off button on the little white cell phone and then she sat back in the deep, black leather seat. Whoever she'd been talking to seemed to calm her because her face seemed to relax as she closed her eyes. That thought pulled her eyes away from the back seat. They all had a multitude of issues to sort out.

A melancholy mood settled in her spirit. Although her aunt and her friend Tina were here, it felt like they were as far away as the moon. She felt a sadness she couldn't explain. She hated leav-ing South Carolina for more reasons than she could name. But to let a relationship destroy her life was humiliating. Of course she'd had some rough patches, but it was home—the only home she had ever known, and there was still some uncertainty about whether or not Stanley would be looking for her.

Her gaze drifted out to the hills of the green covering across the landscape in the distance. Tears of unwanted frustration threatened, but she beat them back. She hadn't been here two hours, and already she was worrying about what life would be like here. She could still hear Stanley's voice reminding her she didn't belong anywhere.

The thought that she didn't belong anywhere cut through her spirit like a sharp dagger. After all of these years she still had difficulties dealing with the abandonment of her father. If he had loved her, wouldn't he have stayed or at least have tried to find her? But in all of these years there had been no contact whatsoever. That's why she appreciated Uncle Willie; although he wasn't a blood relative, he'd been there to support her, for that she was thankful.

The phone in her bag beeped to life, dragging her away from her thoughts. She glanced down at it. With a sigh, she touched the on button and lifted it to her ear. "Hi, auntie."

"Oh, Destiny. Good. So you've landed?"

There was no pause to let her answer, and she didn't bother to try. She knew there wouldn't be one.

"Yes, and we're in route to the house."

"Are you excited about being here; isn't it beautiful?" The sigh said more than she'd been able to say so far. Her mind had ways of betraying her at the most inopportune moments. But she said nothing. Her gaze slid to the vast expanses of the land beyond. "I don't know. Everything is just hills of green but it is beautiful."

"Good, at least you noticed. You can't be more than twenty minutes out. When you get here, I'll have dinner waiting for you and Cynthia. I know you both connected right away."

"We did and we can't wait to see you."

"I'll see you in a few."

"Okay." Ten more words, and Destiny hung up. Glancing over at Adam, she too relaxed now. All she wanted was to get a great meal and find a nice, soft bed where she could finally sleep.

As Adam pulled into the driveway, she saw a welcoming pot of bright pink geraniums beside the doormat and a garden filled with sunshine. Destiny could already picture her life here. In the mornings, she could bring a book, cup of tea, or her laptop and sit to watch the sun come up across the horizon. Yes, maybe this was going to be a wonderful place to call home after all.

CHAPTER 5

Humming happily, Sara reached for the drying cloth that lay on the kitchen counter. She had been getting things together at the house all day. She knew that with Cynthia and Destiny arriving, they would at least want their beds ready. She had put David and Jonathan down for a nap. That had given her a little time to finish up with the girls' rooms and fix them a light dinner. She was sure they would be hungry after such a long flight. She smiled while walking out of the kitchen into the living area. The four-bedroom craftsman was the cutest little home, and it would be perfect for her, the girls, and the twins.

Looking in on the twins, she couldn't help but think to herself. This was perfect for two high-spirited boys. They would be happy in this room together. Especially since both of them were so much alike. There was a cushioned window seat that could be used for storage. It was the perfect place to store all of their cars, trains, and games. The window looked out over the front yard. It was small but just large enough for them. The backyard was fenced in, and the children had enough room to run and play.

Leaving the twins' room, she went to the kitchen where she heard the car door slam. With excitement and anticipation, she took off her apron and then hung it on the hook behind the kitchen door.

She barely had time to straighten her hair and smooth her yellow blouse over her dark-green corduroy skirt when she heard small footsteps running down the hall. The boys wasted no time opening the door. They thudded across the planking of the front porch. Already smiling and stifling the urge to hurry, she moved through the dining and the living room, crossing to the entry. Looking out the door, she said, "Welcome, everyone."

"Mommy!" the children shouted in unison, throwing the gate open and running to their mother's waiting arms.

"You glad to see us, Mommy?" Jonathan asked.

"I sure am," Cynthia answered, closing her eyes and hugging both of her children tightly.

"We had a good trip, Auntie," Destiny said as she got out of the car.

"Cynthia, are you all right?" She noticed her watching the gentleman coming around to help Destiny out of the car.

"I'm fine, Miss Sara. Just a little tired and hungry. I'm glad to be here. This is such a beautiful house." She looked around at the house while watching Adam get their bags out of the car.

Destiny made her way over to give her auntie a warm embrace. "I second that, Auntie. It looks lovely, and I know from the pictures you sent that the inside looks just as gorgeous. I love it already."

She took the opportunity to look around the front yard. It was well manicured with a lot of flowers. Smiling, she knew what her aunt liked about the beautiful brick craftsman with its rustic wood shutters. Her favorite was the porch that had a cute swing that would be perfect for relaxing; the entire home was fenced in, which would be good for the twins.

Adam walked over to where Destiny was standing. "Where should I put these bags, ladies?"

One of the twins he saw hanging on to Cynthia ran over to him, reaching for one of the bags. "Hi, mister. I'm David. I'm real strong. Can I carry one of those bags?"

"So you want to help, huh?" Adam hunkered down eye level with David. "I'll be glad to let you help if we can get your brother to help as well." He saw the other boy standing off to the side, watching their interchange. "What's your brother's name, David?"

"His name is Jonathan. Jonathan Wheeler." He glanced over to look at his brother while yelling, "Come on, Jonathan. He said we could help carry the bags!"

Adam, after straightening, shifted his gaze to the approaching figure. "David and Jonathan, I'm Pastor Adam Wheeler."

Sara, overhearing the conversation, walked over to officially introduce herself. She extended her hand. "Pastor Wheeler, it's nice to finally meet you. We've attended your church a couple of times since we have been here. You have a wonderful church, with a powerful word and a wonderful congregation."

Sara looked over to Destiny. "Destiny is my niece, but she's really a daughter, as well as Cynthia."

"Well, come on, guys," Cynthia interrupted. "Let's get in the house so Mommy can see your room."

"Oh boy, Mommy! Me-ma let us have our own room. She said we were big boys now," David said while grabbing her hand and forgetting about Adam.

"Yeah, Mommy, and guess what else?" Jonathan said, grabbing her other hand.

Laughing, Cynthia said, "I give up. What else?"

Jonathan looked at her and responded, "We have our own bed. Me-ma said that they were twin beds just like us. So I call mine Jonathan."

David interrupted, saying, "And I call mine David."

Destiny grabbed two bags and started walking ahead of Adam. Turning, she said, "You can come on inside. My aunt always cooks more than enough. I know you're hungry." Destiny spoke over her shoulder.

Sara laughed. "The boys are always hungry. I made a salad along with some spaghetti. You are more than welcome, Pastor."

Adam spoke as he entered the small foyer. "Thank you, Miss Sara, but I'll be leaving. I have to stop by another pastor's house before I turn in tonight."

"Well anytime you're in the area you're welcomed to stop by. We don't know too many people. So it's always nice having company. Now if you don't mind, I'm going to show Cynthia the boys' room, and then hers." With that said, she turned and walked down the hall to the boys' room.

Destiny returned from her room. At least she assumed it was her room. There were some of her personal things inside.

"Well, Pastor Wheeler, will you be staying for dinner?"

"Not tonight. Remember I told you about my friend Warren, the pastor who lives in the area? He's expecting me, so I'd better get going." He started moving to the front door. Before he opened it, he turned to Destiny. Extending his hand to shake hers, he gave an infectious smile before saying, "It was a pleasure keeping you company today. I really enjoyed our time together."

"I enjoyed meeting you as well. I think I'm really going to like it here," she said with exhaustion clearly in my voice. "I've already met one kind person here, but now the real work begins. I'll be up to my eyeballs in unpacking and helping to make this our home." She responded.

Adam nodded his head in obvious understanding. "I've been here for years, and I wouldn't live anywhere else." He then added, "Why don't you come to church on Sunday?"

"Thank you, I'd love to come, as a matter of fact, we'll all come." She paused for a moment. Shifting her weight, she felt fatigue sinking into her bones, although the conversation was interesting, it was time to bring it to an end.

With that, Adam opened the door stepping out, he turned and then waved.

Destiny closed the door and leaned back on it while smiling to herself. She didn't hear Cynthia and her aunt walk in the room.

"It looks to me like someone is excited about more than just this new house," Sara stated as she turned to head toward the kitchen.

"So do you think Adam realized he was talking to his nephews?" Cynthia asked in a cautious voice.

Destiny was a little shocked to hear this information so soon. But she gave Cynthia a reassuring embrace. "We're here for each other. Don't worry about something that hasn't happened yet. God will work it out for you if you put it in his hands. Don't ask me why I'm saying this because usually I'm the one seeking answers for my life. But just like for me, God has all of your answers, Cynthia."

Pulling back to look her in the eyes, she continued, "And if he did recognize the resemblance, he didn't say anything. Let's just take one day at time. It's all going to work out in the end. Now let's have dinner in our new home." They both headed to the kitchen to help Sara.

After settling in for the night, Destiny finally let rip a whoop of joy. She sang and danced on the spot as she took in the room again. She quieted as she rounded the room, touching everything—bedspreads, curtains, wardrobe, dresser, mirror, and chairs. The wonderful house was made even better because she owned it along with her aunt. And then there was that attractive Pastor Wheeler that had driven her and Cynthia home. She knelt down and said a quick prayer of thanks.

As Adam got in the car, he was in deep thought. He wondered what he was going to say to his brother. When he saw Jonathan and David, he knew right away. They looked identical to the pictures of him and his brother that their mother had on the mantle above the fireplace. *My God, how did Cynthia do it all by herself?* He knew that she hadn't been home in years. Cynthia's parents disowned her shortly after she left for college. Now he understood why. But why didn't she tell Marvin?

After a short visit with his friend in SeaTac, Adam drove home. He loved attending conferences, but there was no place like home. Adam shut the door to his condominium. It was his retreat. The inside of it surrounded him with all the things that soothed his soul. Laying his briefcase on the marble kitchen counter, Adam removed his shoes. He sunk his sock-covered feet into the richness of the rug that lay over his dark hardwood floor. Running a slender hand over his coarse, cropped hair, he closed his eyes and inhaled deeply before slowly letting out his breath. This was an exercise he'd learned to do to release the tension and anxiety he was feeling. He walked over to the sink, turned on a steady flow of cool water, and softly splashed his face. He then headed to his bedroom to get cleaned up from his long day of travel.

He sat on the chaise lounge at the foot of his king-size bed. A clock on the mantel of the massive fireplace chimed the hour. It was ten o'clock. He had miles to go before he slept. As he began to unpack his luggage, he couldn't help but to reflect on his evening spent with Destiny.

He smiled when he remembered how nervous she was when she'd gotten on the plane in Charleston. She was really something—a little afraid to open up at first and she seemed to be a good listener. She also had a sensitive side that was really refreshing. He knew she was not a strong believer, but she had a desire to know the Lord, and he wanted to be the one to introduce her to the blessings of knowing Jesus as Lord and Savior. He had sworn off trying to develop any kind of relationship until he established himself as a pastor. That had been years ago. Now he had a strong desire to find someone to love and someone to share his life with. Greater Community had always been his second love. But now he realized not having someone to share it with was lonely.

On the plane he had talked to Destiny and one thing was certain he knew that she had been hurt somewhere in her life. He sensed that she was running from something, but only God could work that out for her. It was just last week that he had taught the singles that God hates it when they have vain imaginations, according to Romans 1:21 and 2 Corinthians 10:5. Many single women suffered from vain imaginations more than any other group of women. One imagination that single women have was the "prince on a white horse" belief.

When a woman started to imagine that God had magically chosen a husband for her, she engages in what the Bible calls a "vain imagination." It's an empty imagination, not supported by scriptures. The only "prince on a white horse" whom they would encounter was one named Jesus Christ. Because of the man shortage that they say is in the land, an alarmingly large number of single women are stricken with desperation, panic, anxiety, fear, and anger. He believed these negative emotions had to be dealt with, or they would destroy a woman.

Adam wanted a woman who stood out in the crowd. He'd been patient waiting for what God wanted for him in a wife. He had foolishly put a time limit on God saying that he was going to give him three years to find him the right woman. But maybe God had other plans. One thing was for sure: Adam knew his wife had to be special to understand his calling. She had to love the Lord and love people.

For now he hoped his reaction to seeing Cynthia again had not raised too many red flags. There was something about Destiny that had his heart palpitating. For now, he wanted to be her friend. He wanted them to learn as much about each other as possible. If she came to church on Sunday, he would make it his priority to talk to her about them spending time with each other.

CHAPTER 6

On Sunday morning Adam rose slowly from his knees and sat on the edge of his bed. He raised his hands, praising God for blessing him to see another day. Looking around the room, he admired all that God had blessed him with since he began his patronage at Greater Community. Serving the Lord was worth all of the sacrifices he had made, and with every passing day God proved it more and more.

Looking around for his briefcase, he picked up his Bible from the nightstand, grabbed his suit jacket, and walked out of his bedroom toward the front of the house. He could not help but hear the words to Psalms 118:24: *"This is the day the Lord has made; let us rejoice and be glad in it."* Truly this was the day he had made, and he could not wait to see what else God would do with it. Smiling, he opened the door to head for Greater Community.

Adam already knew that the Spirit of the Lord was in the sanctuary as he listened to cries of "Sing choir!" "Hallelujah!" and "Praise the Lord!" coming from every corner of the church. From his seat, Adam agreed. He could see the spirit of the Lord on the faces of the worshipers as they clapped their hands, stomped their feet, and lifted their hands in praise to the Almighty. He knew that there would be a great outpouring of the spirit throughout the service.

It took everything in him to contain himself as young Anthony Hodges took the mic and began to sing, "Awesome." He closed his eyes as the spirit of the Lord took him where no one in the world could, into the presence of God. It was an exuberating experience. His prayer was that one day this would be an experience he would share with his helpmate. Upon opening his eyes, he saw Destiny had just taken her seat along with Miss

Sara, Cynthia, and the twins. Adam allowed himself to enjoy the warmth that flooded his soul as he watched her.

She looked beautiful in her canary yellow suit. She had such poise and gracefulness, classy, but not overdone, and she stood out amongst the other worshipers, whether she wanted to or not. He took the time to look at her as she glanced at the worshipers around her. She was young in the Lord, and he had no problem with that because he saw the sincerity in her.

The thing that amazed him was the behavior of the boys. They were dressed in khaki pants and polo-style shirts. Each of them were standing and clapping their hands as if this was the norm for them. Miss Sara would fit right in with the mothers at Greater Community. She had on a beautiful pink dress with a hat to match, and not once did she sit down upon entering the sanctuary. Destiny was clapping as well as smiling, but from the movement of her head, he knew she was checking everything out. Cynthia must have been accustomed to this type of worship as well because she was standing right along with Sara. Her eyes were closed, but he could see her tears from where he was sitting. She seemed to be in that place he was in before he looked up to see Destiny entering the sanctuary.

Cynthia was dressed beautifully as well. She chose to wear no hat, but she did have on a beautiful silver suit.

The church was hit by a wave of the Holy Spirit, and the service took on a new level of worship. The ministerial staff had finished with all of their duties. Minister Susan Falson was about to do the offertory appeal, and Adam knew his time to minister would come after she finished. Rachel, one of the soloists in the choir, moved to take the mic after the offering was completed, and as she opened her mouth to sing the beginning bars of "Just One Touch," Adam began to silently pray before he stood behind the book board to speak the words of the Lord for the day.

Father, truly you are awesome in all of your ways. Your majesty leaves us, as mere humans, speechless at times. Truly, it is just as the words in this song say; it only takes one touch as you pass by that causes us to know that you will listen to the faintest cry. It is with that knowledge that I ask you to use me as a vessel to change the lives of the souls who are looking to hear from you today.

Adam knew the voice of Rachel because she often sang the lead to many of the selections in the choir. But the voice he was hearing now was one that sounded like the voice of a thousand angels. As he lifted his head and opened his eyes, it was in amazement as he heard a voice, just as strong as Rachel's, singing the words to "Just One Touch." With her eyes closed, oblivious to all that was happening around her, Cynthia was crying and singing those words. It moved him more than he could ever say when he heard her sing the words, "Just one touch and he makes me whole, speaks sweet peace to my sin-sick soul; at his feet all my burdens roll, cured by the Healer divine just one touch!"

It was at this point that Rachel stopped singing, so moved by the voice of one who seemed to have been anointed by God at that moment to usher in his presence. Everyone in the church was looking in Cynthia's direction, but she never once opened her eyes. From where she was standing in the pews, she continued to sing, "And the work is done, I am saved by the blessed Son. I will sing while the ages run, cured by the Healer divine." The only sounds that were heard by anyone were a chorus of, "Praise the Lord," "Hallelujah," "I love you, God," and, "Thank you, Jesus."

Everyone was affected by the beautiful voice of Cynthia, and as she finished the last verse, the sanctuary was filled with his glory. When she opened her eyes, Destiny hugged her. Miss Sara was crying in between saying, "Bless you, Lord."

The twins were both holding on to the legs of their mom, and Adam saw his congregation nudging each other, pointing in Cynthia's direction.

It was then that he rose and walked toward the podium to do what he knew he'd been called to do. Opening his mouth, he began to preach. "Let the church say amen, for the Lord is surely in this place today. Can I get another amen?" He heard a return chorus of "amens."

"I don't know about you all, but I know the presence of the Lord is here. Today, would you open your Bibles to John, the fourth chapter?" Adam smiled when he heard all of the Bible pages turning.

"I want you to take a trip with me to the town of Samaria. Adam looked out over his congregation before continuing. "I want to invite you all to come see a man."

Adam began by saying, "I want you to listen in on a conversation between Jesus and the woman at the well. Having met her at Jacob's well and being very thirsty, Jesus asked her for a drink. The woman refused because he was a Jew and therefore could not expect favors from a Samaritan."

As always, Adam made the story personal to everyone in the audience by going on to say, "Now, if you don't know, let me inform you all that Jesus had a rep that not many can duplicate. So when he flipped the script and started to talk about living water, he then turned around and informed her that if she only knew the gift of God that was in her presence, she would ask him for water. Can I give it to you in today's language?"

Looking at the faces of his audience, he heard some of them shout back, "Say it, Pastor!" or, "Go on with your bad self!" Adam smiled and continued.

"The trouble with this woman was that she put Jesus in the same category of every other man she had met. She didn't know of whom she was standing in the presence of at that time. She was blinded by the negative views of all the men who had approached her before Jesus!"

Adam asked before he could think, "Can I get somebody to look at their neighbor and say, 'Excuse me, but you're blocking my view'?"

Continuing in his extraordinary fashion, he said, "This woman was a notorious sinner, even by Samaritan standards. She had been married five times and was presently living with her sixth lover. Although she was a sinner, there was hope for her because she just met a man that would change her life."

He stepped back and looked over the church and said, "Can I get somebody to say, 'I met a man'?"

The church was on fire, and people were standing and shouting their replies loud and proud. The presence of the Lord was strongly on him.

He continued, "She had just met Jesus. He had to pass through Samaria that day to save this woman. He had asked her for a drink because he was thirsty. How many of you know it wasn't a physical thirst?" he asked. "Just as Jesus is thirsting for the salvation of this woman, he longs to save someone today. Because just like she needed living water, you need the healing waters of grace and salvation."

Adam paused to asked, "Now, brothers, if you don't mind, can I ask the sisters something that only they can answer?"

He heard the brothers respond, "Ask them, Pastor."

He laughed while saying, "Sisters, how many of you all out there have misunderstood his question, just like this sister, but you had enough intelligence to realize that this man was talking about a special kind of water? You knew enough to see that this brother wasn't like any of the ones you met before." Adam asked the ladies, "Can I get some sisters to say, 'Talk to me, Jesus?'"

The church was really rocking now. Adam told them, "Guess what she asked him? According to John 4:15, she said, 'Give me this water, that I thirst not, neither come hither to draw.'

"Then my Jesus and your Jesus bluntly said to her, 'Go call your husband.' And, church, do you know why he said this, to make her realize what her problem was? She had to know how much she needed him. Her problem was a spiritual one. She was a sinner. That's why he says, 'Go call your husband!' This changed the whole conversation because when Jesus told her to get her husband, she came face-to-face with her problem.

"'I have no husband,' she replied evasively. She was startled by this strange request. She was even more startled by Jesus's next remark: 'You are right about that. You've had five husbands already, and the man you now have is not your husband.'

"She deliberately gives an ambiguous answer. Why? Church, don't you, like me, want to know why she answered this way? Is she single then? Or maybe she is a widow? But no, church, can I tell you she was neither? She deliberately gives an ambiguous answer."

Adam said with much conviction. "Church, let me tell you why. It's because she wants to hide her shame. She is on her guard. She doesn't want full exposure. Not yet, anyway.

"Now, Greater Community," Adam asked, "do you see yourself here? We too are good at using evasive tactics. We will admit that we are sinners, of course, but we prefer not to go into any details. 'I have no husband' is her curt reply. It is the truth, Church, but not the whole truth. Yet that is what Jesus is after, you all. He wants the whole truth and nothing but the truth."

Adam continued by saying, "Now some men may not mind being number two or your back-up man. But that's not how my Jesus rolls. He doesn't play second to anyone, so he says, 'Thou hast well said, I have no husband, for thou hast had five husbands; and he whom thou now hast is not thy husband: in that saidst thou truly.'

"'Go get your husband,' Jesus said to this woman." Adam looked out at the audience and asked them, "What would you say if Jesus came at you with this question?" He went on to say, "You do understand, Church, what he means by saying, 'Bring me your husband,' don't you?"

"Tell us, Pastor, tell us," was the chorus throughout the sanctuary by men and women alike.

Adam continued, "What Jesus was asking, Church, is this."

Being so caught up, he was jumping up and clapping his hands, and he even twirled around before saying, "Make Pastor feel like preaching, Church! Jesus was asking her to bring him her sin. *Husband* here means your sin, or whatever it is that you are thirsting for instead of God. What are you longing for or craving after? What do you live for every day?

"Now, Greater Community, Jesus knows us better than we know ourselves. But he'll still ask you personal questions. He wants us to face the fact that we are sinners. If we confess all our sins to him and seek him, then he will cleanse us from all unrighteousness. Therefore, Greater Community, go call your husband. Tell Jesus what your sin is, confess it to him, and don't try to cover it up." He drew in a breath and released it slowly as he watched his congregation.

"Greater Community, what I want you to realize this morning is that when Jesus tells this woman to get her husband, he puts his finger on the wound in her life that has not been healed, and it still causes her to hurt. It was maybe physical trauma, wherein you were torn or a cut to your soul or your heart was punctured and required emergency medical attention. His eyes came back to theirs, studying them for a pulsing moment before he continued.

"That's why he said what he said, Greater Community. It wasn't to discourage her so that she would go away and never come back. No, Church, he meant for her to come back with her husband. Bring him here. Bring him to me!"

"Greater Community," he said, "go and I know that word touched many of our consciences, but he wants your hearts to say come."

Adam looked around. He was so moved by the response to the Word of the Lord. He saw men and women getting up from their seats moving to the front of the church. Many of them were crying and bowing before the Lord around the altar.

He felt that the Lord wanted him to make one more appeal. So he opened his mouth to say, "Maybe some of you feel that you are too sinful to come to Jesus. You feel that you've been out of his will for too long. You've even been asking yourselves, how can the Lord do anything with me? Let me tell you on this glorious day that you are no worse than this woman of Samaria. Even if you were, wouldn't Jesus be able to help you? And doesn't this story show that he is very willing, too?

"Today, if you hear his voice, then do not harden your heart. Come. Nothing you have done is so bad that it will keep Jesus from loving you. Some of you may surprise others or even shock them, but you can't shock Jesus."

Adam went on to say, "Perhaps you're a regular churchgoer who is new to the area and seeking a church community. Maybe you left the church some time ago and are feeling an impulse to come back. Possibly the Christian faith is something you've never explored. Whatever your situations, we at Greater Community invite you to 'come and see.'"

The outpouring of the spirit of the Lord was so great it was overwhelming. The ministers were at the altar laying hands and praying. The altar workers were busy assisting in any way they could. It took a few minutes for Adam to come down from the high he was on with the Lord. His head was bowed in worship to the Lord. The tears of joy were still flowing from his eyes, but he lifted his head, and when he saw her, he began to weep all the more.

Destiny did not really know when she began to walk, but she was moving toward the altar. She wanted that water that Jesus offered the woman at well. So when she heard the voice of one holier than Adam quietly whisper to her, "Come," she slowly rose from her seat. As she was moving, she thought about the fact that she had restrained herself from crying during the entire message. But that was before the Lord spoke and told her to come.

With slow, cautious steps, she moved around the twins and Cynthia. She made brief eye contact with her aunt, who smiled and nudged her on into the aisle. She continued to move forward until she arrived at the altar. When she realized where she was and what was happening, she became filled with so much joy that she began to weep.

Pastor Wheeler stepped down from the pulpit. He had a handkerchief in his hand because sweat was still pouring from his face. As he moved between the crowd of new believers and those wanting prayer, he kept his eyes on Destiny. He was stopped by one of the altar workers to pray for a brother, which he did while still making his way toward Destiny.

When Adam finally made it to her, he reached down, took her hand, and smiled at her. He extended his hands toward her, waiting for her to accept his. When she looked up, Adam's breath caught in his throat. He pulled her closer and asked her to bow her head so that he could pray.

"Destiny, God is ready to receive you right now. I know personally that when we come to him with our sins of the past or present, we are to turn away from those sins and not commit them anymore." Then he began to pray, "Father, we want you to forgive us of our sins. God, do an amazing thing in Destiny's life. Take away all of her sins and place them on Jesus. And God, take Jesus's goodness and his righteousness and transfer it to her. We believe that Jesus died for our sins. We believe that now he sits on the right hand of the Father, interceding for us. And today Destiny is saved and qualified for heaven, and she will be a member of the family of God forever. In Jesus's name, amen."

As he stood at the altar, he knew that God was not only changing Destiny's life, but he knew his was changed on this day as well.

Watching shrewdly as a group of women walked by, a woman, sitting on the back row, put down the Bible she had been pretending to read. She leaned over and asked her companion, "Whose that?"

The man next to her smiled and said, "Who? The one in the canary yellow suit?"

"I want you to find out who she is. I've never seen her here before."

"I'll get on it right away. I've never seen him respond to anyone like that either, not even you."

The woman nodded, acknowledging the man who had just spoken. Putting the Bible in the seat beside her, she stood and left the sanctuary.

CHAPTER 7

Reflecting on her day so far, Destiny wondered if she had imagined it on today or had she been the center of attention? Maybe she shouldn't even worry about it, the service had been wonderful and everything else didn't matter. After standing in line after the morning service to shake the pastor's hand, he'd invited Destiny and her family to be his guest at a local seafood restaurant for Sunday lunch.

He would be a hard one to say no to, she imagined. So, she took a couple of deep breaths, then walked the final few feet to the restaurant with her family. Pushing on the glass door, they stepped into the beautiful interior. After a quick glance around, she requested a table for their party, then they were escorted to a table. Not long after, she saw Adam waving to few people he recognized, making his way over to where she and the others were sitting. He pulled out a chair while acknowledging everyone at the table.

She was anxious to find out what happened after they left the church. "I hope we didn't raise too many eyebrows this morning," Destiny whispered to Adam while the others were placing their orders.

"Nothing that I couldn't handle. I'm so glad that all of you came. I was really anxious to see you again."

Picking up a menu, Destiny scanned it quickly. Everything looked good. She was thinking about ordering the fried lobster.

"You sure can preach real good, Pastor Wheeler," Jonathan said while coloring the picture of a boat on his menu.

David looked up from his coloring and said, "Yeah, and we didn't even go to sleep like we used to at our old church. We used to go to sleep right after Mommy finished singing. Right, Jonathan?"

Laughing, David said, "Jonathan, Mommy said not to tell anyone that we sleep in church. They may think she's not a good mom and that we don't sleep at home. But she's the best mommy in the world, Pastor Wheeler. Honest." They both looked at Adam with puppy-dog eyes.

Adam nodded in agreement. "I know you both have a great mother. I knew your mom when she was in middle school and high school. She was a friend of my family. We spent a lot of time together." Adam looked over at Cynthia and smiled. "Guess what, guys? She used to sing all the time."

"Shattering glasses and windows." She chuckled. "But thank you for the compliment," she said, looking back at the menu.

Their waitress arrived. She rattled off the list of specials before pulling out her pad and pen.

Everyone gave their order, but the twins took a few minutes because they didn't want to eat Nemo. So they decided on grilled cheese sandwiches, chicken nuggets, and applesauce.

"Adam," Cynthia asked, "did your parents ask about me after the service was over?"

"No," Adam admitted. He draped an arm around the chair that Destiny was sitting in. "I'm not sure if they knew for sure that it was you. But if they listened closely to your voice, they had to know. I could recognize your voice anywhere. I'm really not sure if I should be the one to tell them about you being back."

Sara, who had been sitting silently listening to the conversation, said, "I know that God had a plan when he sent you back home. I'm not sure how he's going to work it out, but he does have a plan for your life. Keep Jeremiah 29:11 in your spirit and be confident in God's Word. He backs up what he said: 'For I know the thoughts that I think toward you, saith the LORD, thoughts of peace, and not of evil, to give you an expected end.' Everything is going to work out for you. I feel it in my spirit." She patted the hand on Cynthia's lap.

"Cynthia," Destiny said her name. Cynthia met her concerned gaze as she continued by saying, "the one thing I do know is that news travels fast. If anyone did recognize you this morning, then your parents will know you are back in town."

Destiny reached for her glass to take a sip of water.

"I knew it was going to happen at some point, so I may as well get it over with as soon as possible. They probably won't want to see me now any more than they did after I left," Cynthia murmured.

"I hate that things turned out this way for you and your parents," Adam said, reaching for his glass of tea. "If you and your parents could talk face-to-face, it probably would be better for everyone involved. Give it time. Now that you are back in the city, everyone involved in your life and the life of the twins will have to talk at some point."

Cynthia agreed. "Besides, this is not about me, it's about the boys. I know the Lord loves us, and he'll surely take care of this situation. He has a plan or he wouldn't have told me to come home."

While eating his food, Adam looked at Cynthia. "Do you have any regrets?" It was a simple enough question. "What did you end up doing after you left here? One time you were talking about becoming a lawyer, but you could have made it in the music industry."

She shook her head and felt her body going rigid with remembered pain. "I can't believe you still remember that. I love singing but it was not my career choice. I finished college and got my master's through online and evening courses. I'm now a certified commercial real-estate specialist with a degree in real-estate management. It was a choice I'd make again without a second thought," she said with a wistful look in her eyes.

"I know what you mean. I feel the same way about my calling to be a pastor," Adam agreed.

She took a sip of tea before saying, "Marvin and I always knew there was something special you would do with your life. You becoming a pastor is such a wonderful thing, Adam. Your church is beautiful, and your message was powerful. I'm proud to know you." Cynthia looked over to see the twins were struggling with their grilled cheese sandwiches. Reaching over to grab a knife, she began to cut their sandwiches in fours.

"Mommy, I can do it," Jonathon whined picking up his sandwich before she could cut it.

Cynthia pulled her hands away and held them up. "Okay, you go for it then," she said.

"Thanks, Mom," Jonathan said before biting into his sandwich. Both of them went back to eating their sandwiches.

By the time everyone had finished a fantastic seafood meal and was waiting for their key lime pie to arrive, Adam and Sara were becoming instant friends. Their conversation started with his sermon and led to just about everything else. Cynthia and Destiny could barely get in on the conversation as the two new acquaintances talked nonstop. Of course, Adam was quite intrigued with Sara's interest in Seattle and his work at Greater Community. Likewise, Sara was interested in the young man who had captured the attention of her niece.

Since she couldn't talk to Adam with her aunt pressing him with questions, Destiny turned to Cynthia. "You've got to tell me what it was like raising two twin boys," she urged, knowing Cynthia had to have some fascinating stories about her sons.

"Let's see." Cynthia sighed, leaning back and looking at the two pair of eyes that were suddenly upon her. She leaned back in her leather chair. "If you'd like me to give you the short version, they were a handful. It was hard at first learning how to balance taking care of two at once. When I finally got the hang of it, I was a force to be reckoned with. But it was all-good or should I say all God, because he alone brought me through that season. The long nights and long days were sometimes challenging, and a few times I thought I would lose my mind." She laughed, joining Jonathan and David laughing, as if they knew everything that she had to endure.

Destiny looked at the boys. They were adorable and had the best manners, but she could tell they were getting a little restless. It would soon be time to take them home so that they could run around outside and play.

Destiny turned back to look at Cynthia. "I can only imagine them being a handful, and it's amazing we were at the same college but never met."

Cynthia nodded her head. "Yeah, that was amazing, but I'm glad we know each other now. Growing up, I was an only child. So having the boys brought me so much joy. I didn't have any help. When I found out I was pregnant, I knew I had to drop out of college." Cynthia looked out the window as if she was seeing a movie of her life. She squeezed her eyes shut as if looking in instead of out.

"I met a young lady at Clemson whose parents had a rental property that they gave to her. She allowed me to live there for as long as I needed it. When I think about it now, it was really just the size of my parents' guesthouse, but it was enough for us. Then I met Miss Sara, and my whole life changed. I was able to work and finish my classes at night. Miss Sara was a godsend to me and the twins." Cynthia reached for Sara's hand squeezing it gently as a reminder of the love she felt for her.

Marvin was at the hostess's podium scanning the restaurant for his brother. Earlier he'd talked to his mother. She had been ecstatic about this morning's worship service. Her conversation had been non-stop, all centering around a young woman who had the voice of an angel. Before ending their call she'd told him that they were going to meet for dinner, so he decided in haste that he'd join them. Now two hours later he found himself at the restaurant with a female companion.

It was the sound of a familiar voice that sent Marvin's heart into an uncontrolled spin. He shifted his gaze from his date, colliding with the woman who'd haunted his memory for several years. She was still breathtaking. For a fraction of a second, time stopped, and he and Cynthia were back in high school.

If possible, she was more beautiful than he'd remembered. The years had lent her an appealing air of maturity and confidence. Her hair was braided now, but it was still beautiful, and his hands trembled with the memory of sliding his fingers through the silky strands. Her incredible, dark eyes, wiser with age, pulled him in as they had when they were teenagers.

Even from where she was sitting he could tell that at six three he still towered over Cynthia's five-foot-six-inch frame, making him feel the urge to protect and shelter her. It was a ridiculous notion, considering he had not seen her in years.

Laughter erupted from their table. Destiny, Cynthia, and Sara were sharing stories with each other but quickly silenced when they noticed Cynthia's eyes travel across the room.

"What is he…?" Adam breathed, catching sight of his brother moving their way from across the dining room.

Cynthia shook her head as if she was in a daze. She knew it had to be Marvin. Obviously he had decided on the Lighthouse as his restaurant of choice for dinner as well. Unfortunately, he didn't come alone. Cynthia returned her gaze to Marvin and then wished she hadn't. But seeing him reminded her of all of the reasons she'd fallen head over heels for him back in high school. He'd been the guy all the girls had wanted.

She also noticed Marvin's date, who looked a lot like Kristen Milton, a girl she knew from his old high school. At that time, she was very promiscuous. If memory served her right, she had a baby before she got out of high school. Even then she was always in Marvin's face. She had a thing for athletes then, maybe because she played basketball. Cynthia didn't know what kind of men she was chasing now. She prayed she'd pull off a convincing job of looking cool and unfazed seeing him for the first time in years. Though they were quite a distance from one another, Cynthia knew that he was looking directly at her.

"God, this would be a good time for you to intervene," Adam muttered, standing as Marvin and his companion headed toward the table.

"I'll take the boys out for some fresh air." Sara spoke to no one in particular because everyone's eyes were glued on Marvin.

"What's she doing here?" Marvin's first words were snarled in his brother's ear once the distance closed between them.

"I invited Destiny and her guest to dinner after service today," Adam shared, a little put out by Marvin's tone.

Silence settled around them, and it was quite uncomfortable. To break the ever-thickening ice, Destiny stood and extended her hand in a gesture of welcome to Marvin and the woman at his side.

"I'm Destiny Harper, a friend of Adam's," she said with a smile.

"Hi, I'm Kristen Milton." She started giggling. It didn't surprise Cynthia; she was always the dumb-blond type a hustler of the female persuasion.

"Kristen, it's so nice to meet you. This is Cynthia Mason," Destiny said.

"Oh, my God. Cynthia, is that you? I still remember you coming to the school to watch Marvin play ball. Girl, where have you been? You look so good. I love the braids, and you put on some much-needed weight in all the right places. What happened you dropped off the face of the earth? It's good seeing you again, and girl, we're looking good for twenty-five, aren't we?" She gestured with her hand at their bodies. The two women hugged each other lightly without the smile reaching either of their eyes.

Cynthia arched one slim eyebrow as she caught Marvin's eyes roaming over her body.

"Have a seat, Kristen," Adam urged, already pulling out the seats vacated by Sara and the twins. He began to walk away with Marvin. "We need to talk," he grated to Marvin once Kristen was comfortable.

"What's she doin' here, Adam?" Marvin demanded as the two of them headed for the lounge of the beautifully lit dining room.

Laughter lilted somewhere in the distance, and both men turned to find that it was the ladies whom they had left at the table. Destiny, Cynthia, and Kristen were all giggles and smiles. "Well, praise the Lord. They all are getting along fine," Adam remarked in a stressed voice.

Marvin rolled his eyes. "Whoopi doo."

Adam stopped in the area just off the lobby and folded his hand across the sleeve of his brother's shirt. "What are you doing here, Marvin? I thought you were going to be at church today. Then you show up for dinner with a woman. Why is she here?"

"First of all, I didn't come to church because I overslept. Secondly, I definitely didn't know that Cynthia was back in town. Thirdly, Kristen is just a friend. She called me today and asked what I was doing. Since I hadn't eaten, I thought she would be good company," Marvin snapped his answer and pulled his arm away from his brother.

"Mom told me that you had your nose opened by someone at church today. I wasn't coming here without someone when I knew you were going to have a date," he stated flatly.

Adam chuckled. "Right, like I have dates all the time. What about all the times I had to be the third wheel with you and

Cynthia? Did I ever complain? No, I showed up. We had a good time. I went home, and you took Cynthia home. End of story."

"That really hurts a brother's feelings, Adam. You act like I was insensitive," Marvin said, holding a hand over his heart.

"The truth will make you free, brother."

They both laughed. Marvin stopped Adam from leaving by catching the cuff of the blue sports coat he wore. "Adam, what is she really doing here after all these years?" he said in a serious tone. "You know if I knew Cynthia was here, I never would have brought a date."

"Hey, guys," Cynthia, said as she strolled over. Their conversation silenced immediately. Marvin was speechless. He was enjoying the scent of Cynthia's perfume that settled beneath his nostrils.

"I wanted to say good-bye. I'm going to take Miss Sara back to the house," she told them.

"What about the key lime pie we ordered earlier?" Adam was having a good time and didn't want their day to end just yet. In actuality, he didn't want his time with Destiny to be cut short.

Cynthia knew Adam wanted to spend more time with Destiny. But she had to get out of there. How could she cope with this right now? What she wanted was breathing space. She needed time to get her head clear, away from Marvin, and time to think. Kristen told her she worked for Marvin's company, so they must have had a cozy set up with her being right at his fingertips.

"This is my dessert." She lifted the box in a gesture to show them both that she was prepared to leave. "Adam, I realize that you may want to spend more time with Destiny, so I took the liberty of telling her that you could bring her later."

"I would have enjoyed your company as well, Cynthia, but if you have to go, I understand," Adam replied.

Marvin watched the exchange between Cynthia and his brother. He smiled, smoothing a hand across the front of the blue branded collar shirt he wore. He thought about how incredible she still looked.

"I have to leave anyway," she whispered again. "I start my new job with the real estate company tomorrow, M and W Enterprises. I have some things I need to do tonight before I meet my boss. So I guess I'll see you both later." She leaned in close to hug Adam. She spoke a hushed good-bye to Marvin and was about to ease by.

"Cynthia, wait," Marvin softly urged, his hand folding across the overlong cuff of her silver suit. "I'm sorry for what happened a few minutes ago," he apologized once Adam walked off.

"Sorry?" Cynthia spoke, confused.

Marvin blinked. "Walking in here with a date," he clarified, looking at her as if he could not believe she misunderstood his apology.

Cynthia shrugged. "Kristen is all right if you like her type, and obviously you do."

"But if I had known you would be here, I would have come alone or not at all," he continued.

"You don't owe me any apologies, Marvin," she assured him. She looked at his hand still holding her wrist.

Marvin watched Cynthia's eyes and felt a sudden rush of sensations from a single touch of her flesh. Brushing his thumb across the pulse point below her wrist, he finally released her.

Cynthia turned and left. She ignored her desire to look back, knowing that if she did the boys would approach her in front of Marvin, and she wasn't ready for that.

Marvin watched Cynthia leave the restaurant. He then looked over to the table where his brother and the two ladies were sitting.

"I ordered us some dessert," Kristen was telling Marvin when he returned to the table.

"Thanks, Kristen, but I've decided not to stay," he said, fixing his date with a stare that showed regret. "I'm sorry, but would you mind if we left early?" he asked her.

Kristen reassured him that she was willing to leave early by giving him a wink. "Just promise me that we'll do it again." She smiled before saying good-bye to Adam and Destiny.

"Destiny, it was nice to meet you," Kristen said.

"Where is she staying?" Marvin asked Adam.

"She lives with Destiny and Sara in the SeaTac area. But it'll be easy for you to get the exact address from her resume since she will be working for you starting tomorrow." Adam smiled at his brother before saying, "God works in mysterious ways."

Marvin looked at his brother before turning to walk away. "He sure does," he replied, and with that, he joined Kristen before leaving the restaurant. *Yes*, he thought to himself. *Tomorrow won't be soon enough to talk with Cynthia.*

Adam had been looking forward to his private time with Destiny. Since no one else was at the table, he moved to one of the vacant chairs. This way their conversation could be a little more personal.

Scanning the restaurant Destiny didn't want to appear squeamish because he moved his chair closer to hers. Her gaze returned to his, two small frown lines sectioning her forehead. "This is a beautiful restaurant—you eat here often?" she asked. She pressed her lips together and looked away again like a shy schoolgirl.

"I do but most of the time it's on Saturdays when I'm not preparing for Sunday worship. It gets me out of the house and I can sit by the lake and listen letting the Lord speak to me at one of those picnic tables, weather permitting."

"Are you a workaholic?"

"I guess I could have tendencies in that direction, but to me it isn't really work because I love serving the Lord. I enjoy the challenge of putting together a dynamic sermon."

Marvin was watching her and it made her a little nervous she avoided his eyes by looking at their surroundings yet again.

Wistfully, Destiny replied, "I could just sit down in the grass out there and look at the lake and trees all day. It seems so peaceful here and I can see why you fell in love with it." He watched her reach for the pitcher of water on the table and refilled her glass before continuing their conversation.

"So tell me about yourself." Adam asked as he watched her squint her eyes as if she was trying to decide what she wanted to say to him. "What do you want to know?"

"I don't know. Tell me everything, anything. How does your family feel about you moving to Washington with your aunt?"

"Well, let's see...my aunt raised me from a newborn, so I had no family to consider in my move to Seattle but Auntie." Looking up, she found him watching her.

Adam gave her an encouraging smile. He wanted to hear more. "Your aunt sounds like a wonderful person. I could tell she loves you very much from our conversation earlier during dinner." Adam looked up from the after-dinner coffee he was drinking and focused on Destiny. "What happened to your parents, brothers, sisters?"

"I'm an only child. My mother died in childbirth, and I really don't know much about my father besides what my aunt has told me. From what I know, he left before my mother died. Sara worked hard owning a club, but back in her day, they called it a juke joint. After I finished college at Clemson, she moved us to Charleston. So here I am in Seattle, hoping that God will continue to guide me and all of my decisions from here on out." Destiny looked up from the key lime pie she was pushing around on her plate.

The finality of the statement kept Adam from asking anything else about her life or the relationship she was in.

"Well," Adam said, "I can say that God is already doing his part. If he weren't, you wouldn't have gotten saved and totally surrendered to him. I know God had something to do with us meeting. I'm happy about it."

Adam must have sensed that his statement made her a little uncomfortable, so he changed the subject. "So tell me, where are you going to be working here in Seattle?"

"For Kintama Chemicals, designing and managing a network of receivers that can pick up signals from tagged salmon known as the Pacific Ocean Shelf Tracking project." I'm really excited about it." He watched the spark of excitement in her eyes light up like fireworks as she talked about her career.

"My best friend, Tina, the one I told you about, recommended me for the job. We had the same majors in college. She knows the president, and they were really excited about me joining their team," Destiny said around a bite of pie.

His low soothing tone was her undoing, causing her stomach to flutter. He chuckled before responding. "Okay, I can tell you love your work by the way your face lights up while you talk about it."

She tilted her head slightly and asked, "Is that a bad thing?"

"No problem with me. I love what I do as well," he stated as he took the last bite of his pie.

He was constantly watching her expression even when she looked away there seemed to be a magnetic force that caused her head to turn back. Destiny couldn't take her eyes off his mouth; the enigmatic tilt of it fascinated her. The way he half-smiled, as if he was enjoying the edge he had over her in knowing something that he only had privy to.

It was a hard task to stay focused with her voice sounding so seductive. He knew it was not intentional, but it was still hard to stay focused on their conversation. Praise the Lord they were in a place that helped keep his flesh in check Adam thought to himself.

They left the restaurant after he took care of the bill.

As Adam drove toward SeaTac, he watched Destiny out of the corner of his eye. Calling her a beautiful woman was an understatement. Her flawless face was the color of rich caramel, and when she smiled or laughed, her eyes danced with excitement and passion at the same time. He had been struggling all day to keep his eyes off her. He wanted to show everyone some attention, but there was something about this woman that moved him.

As he pulled into the driveway of the house, he noticed that she still looked a little nervous as he turned off the ignition. The only thing he could fathom was that she probably was a little nervous about how they would end this evening. Adam got out the car and came around to help her out. He reached for her hand and felt an electrical charge run up his arm. She must have felt it as well because she dropped his hand immediately. They walked side by side to the door.

Adam reached around her to open the screen door, and Destiny jumped, causing the door to slam shut. She looked at him with those caramel eyes sparkling.

"Why are you so jumpy? Relax. I won't do anything you don't want me to," he whispered softly. "I should probably go," he managed to mutter as he tried to calm himself down. Not doing anything he would regret later.

A red strain formed on her cheeks, and her eyes fluttered. *Destiny*, she chastised herself, *this is a pastor, for Christ's sake! What must he think?* Her face became the picture of embarrassment as she put distance between them by reopening the screen door. She moved inside the house while letting the screen door be a barrier between them, leaning her face against it.

"Adam, I mean Pastor Wheeler, I really enjoyed dinner. There is something happening between us. I'm not sure what that means with you being a pastor. I just want us to take our time being friends." She looked at him with such sincerity that he wanted to kiss her but knew this was not the time.

"No, I would love for us to be friends. I really enjoyed our afternoon. Can you promise me something?" he asked.

She felt her breath stall in her throat not certain of what he wanted to ask. "Yes, if I can."

Getting serious again and making her nervous, he said, "When we are alone together, will you please call me Adam? I love knowing that I'm your pastor, but when it's just you and me, I want to be your Adam and you can to be my Destiny."

She sighed and looked away. Boy, was she relieved. She answered him, "Yes, I think I can handle that."

Reaching around the screen door, he ran his fingers over her long brown curls. "Before I go…would it be all right if I called you?" he asked.

She agreed, giving him the number he requested.

Adam turned and started down the steps. "Aren't you going to write it down?" she called after him.

Looking back, he repeated the number. Then he opened the door and got in the car. He waited for her to go inside. When the door closed, he began to back out of the driveway. He didn't even realize he was singing. "This is the day, this is the day that the Lord has made, that the Lord has made. We shall rejoice. We shall rejoice and be glad in it."

Marvin's heart was racing as he lay in bed. Picking up the phone, he called his brother.

"Hello?"

"Hey, man, what's up? I didn't want to bombard you with questions at the restaurant—"

"I know how you must feel. It was a shock when I saw her as well. But she's back now."

Marvin's heart started racing all over again, his mind filling with questions. *Back? Back from where? Had she been alone, or had there been a man with her? Someone who would be exactly what her parents wanted for her? Did she complete her education?* He didn't voice even one of these questions. He had no business wondering what she'd done over the years. He swore silently. He couldn't stop himself from asking, "How is she?"

"She seems to be doing well. She completed her degree."

Marvin nodded his head in satisfaction. "I'm happy for her. She deserves to be happy even if we didn't make it."

"From the looks of things today, there's still something there. You two were very much in love and hurt because of the breakup."

"All of that is history. If I see her again, I'm sure she'll tell me all about her new man," he offered.

"We'll see how it goes in the morning, okay, brother? It's easy to say that because you're not in her presence."

Deciding to change the subject, Marvin said, "I didn't mention that tomorrow I should close on that real-estate deal I was working on in Oakland. I'm excited about this opportunity. It's really going to put the company on the map."

Adam laughed. "I never doubted you for one second. You wanted it, and you all worked hard on closing that deal."

Marvin ended the call with his brother after a few more minutes of small talk. He found himself still struggling to wrap his mind around the fact that Cynthia was in Seattle. He wasn't surprised that Adam was excited about her being back. He really expected no less from his brother the pastor. Just because he and she had been high school sweethearts didn't mean anything. People grew up and moved on with their lives. Adam hadn't thought so, but he wouldn't be surprised if Cynthia was engaged by now. There hadn't been a ring, but nowadays that meant nothing. She was an incredibly beautiful woman. Time had been good to her. What difference did it even make at this late date? A lot of time had passed, and what they'd shared in high school was gone. It no longer mattered why they'd broken up or who was responsible. He wanted her to be happy. Seeing her in the morning might prove to be awkward because of what they'd once shared, but that was okay. They had both moved on with their lives.

CHAPTER 8

Opening her eyes, she couldn't believe that she had ended up here again. It wasn't until he threw his leg across her that she realized he had stayed the night. This was getting old real quick. She had been in Seattle for four months without much success of accomplishing her goal. Yes, it had been easy finding the church because he was very popular in the area, but getting closer to him was proving to be more difficult than she realized.

Her plan was to come here and become the wife she should have been years ago. All of the clubbing and partying was getting old. Plus, the drinking had become a habit that she couldn't seem to shake. Her parents saw her once when she was a little intoxicated, and suddenly, she had become an alcoholic in their eyes. If she had been honest, she would have told them that she only drank when she went out. But being who they were in their self-righteous ways, they found fault in everything she did. Even her mother, who was once her biggest ally, had turned on her.

She still remembered her words: "Now, dear, you should avoid the very appearance of evil." That was after she saw her out with a few friends drinking at one of their favorite restaurants. As far as she was concerned, who she spent time with was no one's business. She had been in the church convention circuit since she was a little girl. Men loved her and she loved them. She had a thing for older men. It was her life. So what if she enjoyed the company of tall, not so dark, and very handsome men? There were women all over the world just like her. Since she was attractive and by many standards a real beauty, she had been linked to several men over the years. Most of them were just friends, but a few had been friends with benefits. She'd even been introduced to some of the men by her father. That in itself was reason enough to laugh. They were all supposed to be godly men. And they were when he was around. But just like the old school song says, "The freaks come out at night."

What was a girl supposed to do? She was a freak. Her name was well known among most of the preachers in Atlanta married and single. Her parents had put her out of the house. Therefore, she had to find a means of support, and most of the guys fit the bill: good looking, large bank accounts, and partiers.

She felt his movement, pulling her into a kiss. It wasn't the kiss that bothered her so much. He had become far too familiar with her and apparently assumed they had a relationship that didn't exist, showing up when he got ready. It was really getting old. On the other hand, hadn't she put that idea into his head a few nights ago? He had agreed to help her at a price. There could not be a romantic involvement. But for now she would give him what he wanted because in a few days she'd have what she wanted. Finally relaxing, she began to return his kiss as he pulled her deeper into the sheets. She smiled because soon all her dreams would be coming true.

CHAPTER 9

Everyone in the house was up early. The sun found Cynthia on her knees praying for God's guidance as the day started.

She heard her boys running up and down the hall. Glancing over at the clock, it was time to get up and get moving. Looking around the room, she was proud of what she saw, loving everything about her new home. She had chosen a soft pink paint that Sara had sent her swatches of, which the painters applied perfectly. They even sprinkled the white spots on top of the paint, and the effect was dazzling. Sara made the curtains; they gave the room a feminine appeal. She had a window seat in which she put several pillows. It would be a great spot to read and reflect after work.

She thought about her confrontation yesterday at the Lighthouse with Marvin, wondereding how long he and Kristen had been dating. A sharp stab of jealousy ran through her. She knew that she had no rights where Marvin was concerned, but it still hurt seeing him with another woman. She had promised herself that if she saw him, she would remain calm and act like an adult. Cynthia was proud of the way she handled everything. Miss Sara had been a lifesaver, taking the boys out of the restaurant before Marvin saw them.

Adam had not shared the information about the twins with him. She knew for sure that his parents saw her at church on Sunday. Mary Wheeler was very observant, and she knew that if she got close enough she could tell that the boys were her grandsons. God had shown her some grace, but she knew that she would have to tell him and soon.

Cynthia knew she couldn't worry too long about Marvin. She had to meet with her boss today at M and W. That was going to require some much-needed strength. She made up her bed headed to the bathroom for a shower.

Across the hall Destiny was gasping for breath, caused by the sobs rising in her throat from a terrible dream that interrupted her sleep. Sitting upright, she was relieved to know she was in her own bed. The sound of the rain against her windowpane was refreshing. It took a few seconds before the panic subsided and the sight of her new room steadied her a little. As if on cue, the alarm clock announced with a song that it was time to get up.

"It was a dream," Destiny said aloud as she brushed a hand over her tangled hair and scrambled out of bed. She was in Seattle. That fact alone gave her peace of mind.

As Destiny and Miss Sara sat at the kitchen counter, Cynthia entered, inhaling the smell of the freshly brewed coffee. She glanced in on the boys and told them to put away their toys before coming to breakfast.

"Good morning, Destiny, Miss Sara," she said while moving toward the cabinet to get a mug for her coffee.

Destiny looked at Cynthia. "If they base hiring on how good you look, then you have a new job."

She smiled before taking a sip of her coffee.

Sara looked up from her newspaper to comment. "I tried to get the boys to stay calm this morning, but they are excited about attending their new school. It's really a blessing that I got them on the list for Little Lambs Christian Academy when I moved here in February. It's not far from where you'll be working."

Cynthia looked over at Miss Sara as she took the makings for breakfast from the refrigerator. "The boys and I drove over to the school when I went to the mall to pick up some things for decorating my room. I also went by the M and W to make sure I knew how to get there today."

Sara gazed at her. "The boys asked who Marvin was yesterday when they saw you talking to him. Jonathan said that he looked like Adam, just like he looked like David." Laughing, she went on to say, "David told him that was because Marvin and Adam were twins just like them." Sara looked at Cynthia and in a serious tone said, "Don't wait too long to tell them the truth."

"I'm going to tell them just as soon as I tell Marvin. I also want them to know all of their grandparents," she replied.

Sara walked over and put her arms around Cynthia before saying, "Trust your feelings and trust what God is telling you to do." She looked up when she heard the boys entering the kitchen.

"What's God telling you, Mommy?"

Her sons were coming in the kitchen, talking at the same time.

"God is always telling me how wonderful my sons are and how much they love me. Now come give Mommy a hug. Did you all say good morning to Destiny and Miss Sara?" she asked them.

Both Jonathan and David left their mother and responded, "Good morning, Miss Destiny, and good morning, Me-ma." They gave hugs to each of them.

Jonathan smiled up at Cynthia. "Mommy, are you going to fix us some pancakes?"

"We want chocolate chips inside," David added.

"Um-hum," Jonathan responded.

Destiny grinned. "Why chocolate chips, guys?" she asked as she was putting her mug in the sink.

"That's what Mommy always does to start our week off right. Today we start Little Lambs Christian Academy. We promised we would be good." David looked sheepishly at Destiny.

"Can we sit in front of the television and eat them, Mommy?" Jonathan asked.

"Not today, guys. Mommy has to get you to the school, and I have an interview," she told both of them. "We'll watch cartoons on Saturday and eat pancakes. Deal, guys?"

They looked up at Cynthia, and said, "Deal."

"I believe that a prayer is in order for all of us today," Sara said. "Cynthia, you have an interview. Destiny, you are going to visit Tina and her family. David and Jonathan are starting a new school, and I'm going to be right here interceding for us all." She looked at everyone in the kitchen, and then she held out her hands.

Everyone walked over to join in the prayer. Sara began in a voice of authority to pray for her family as they began to walk in the purpose for which God called them.

"Gracious God, there are so many requests that we have for our lives this morning, but before we start asking, we just want to say thank you. For we know, God, that there are so many people who live alone in this world without family to encourage them, listen to them, and support them. We realize that we have you. For that, we just want to say thank you. You have blessed us to be family—not through a blood relationship of a mother or father but by the blood of your only Son, Jesus. For that, we want to say thank you. Now, God, we realize that we all came to Seattle for different reasons. One of us is a scorned child wanting to reconcile with a family that doesn't know you. One of us has come to this place looking for self-renewal and your divine will for her life. God, my Father, I realize that you know all about me. My only request is that my daughters and my godchildren be granted their requests. I know you will take care of me and all my needs will be taken care of. In your Son, Jesus's, name, we all say amen."

Each person agreed with her and said, "Amen." Cynthia and Destiny set about making breakfast while Sara checked the boys' ears and went through their book bags before they left for school. Today was going to be a great day for all of them.

Cynthia drove her car into the garage of M and W Enterprises Real Estate Investors, Inc. as Charles Mullins instructed her to do when he called Saturday to confirm their meeting time. Stopping at the gate, she let the automatic window down and looked at the attendant.

"Hi. I'm Cynthia Mason, and I have a meeting this morning with Charles Mullins." Cynthia watched as the gentleman checked for her name. Finding it, he leaned out the booth, pointed to the area where she could park her car, and showed her the entrance she would use to enter the building.

Cynthia drove her car to the K-level where she found a parking space close to the elevators. Gathering her briefcase she headed for the elevator doors. As she boarded, she took a deep calming breath. Others got on the elevator and got off on different floors. Checking herself in the mirror one last time to make sure her braids were still pinned up and her suit was wrinkle free gave her the confidence needed for her appointment. She was determined to get this job, not because of who her parents were but because she was qualified. When the elevator stopped on her floor, she got off and followed the signs M and W Enterprises Real Estate Investors, Inc. She opened the glass doors that led to her new career.

CHAPTER 10

Destiny thought about how she had tossed and turned that night, her dreams filled with images of Stanley. Later the dreams changed; she was no longer in Seattle but back in Charleston running through a swamp bare footed with Stanley in fast pursuit. The faster she tried to run, the slower she moved, her feet were growing heavier, weighed down by muddy swamp water. She wanted to escape the swamp, but she couldn't make her legs turn in the direction of the light she saw. Finally, she found herself on dry land, moving quickly, no mud holding her feet back. But when she looked up to see the source of the light, it was a flashlight being held by her archenemy Stanley. As he moved toward her she was unable to move; all she could do was stand there while he laughed hysterically, holding the flashlight baring down on her. Then she woke with a start.

"Calm down," she chided herself firmly, waiting until her breathing had returned to normal before she moved. Sitting up, she shook her head slowly, stealing a look around the room and knowing full well no one was there. The dream had been so real. She wiped the sweat from her brow and stretched; she knew it was time for her to get the day started. But these dreams were giving her pause. There had to be a way to eliminate her uneasiness concerning Stanley, but for now she had something else to do.

Two hours later, after their family prayer she was on her way to Tina's house. Her daughter, Taylor, probably had grown so much since the last time she'd seen her. Destiny thought about her god-daughter as she maneuvered through traffic. The directions were pretty straightforward and easy to follow. She was excited about seeing her. They really were more like sisters, having been roommates for the entire time they were in college. That's how she'd met Willie, who she lovingly called Uncle, in actuality he was Tina's uncle, but Destiny had spent so many weekends and holidays with the family she began calling him by the same term of endearment.

When she thought about Tina, it was easy to get emotional because Tina knew her history. Tina and her husband Richard were both there to support her. They had not judged her; they just loved her and supported her decision as difficult as it was at the time. Destiny parked in the driveway as per Tina's instructions. She checked the address again, took a deep breath, and then turned off the ignition. Exiting the car, her heart was beating a mile a minute. Focusing on her surroundings, she turned her attention to the gorgeous house. Destiny sucked in a breath of cool air as she climbed the front steps. She was only on the second step when the door opened to an excited Taylor yelling, "Auntie Destiny!" But that alone wasn't enough for little Miss Taylor. She jumped up in Destiny's arms; hugging her with all her might, the force alone caused Destiny to stumble back to the first porch step.

"Hi, Auntie Destiny. We've been waiting on you for a long time. And guess what? I made a picture just for you. Do you want to come see it?"

Just as quickly as Taylor had jumped in her arms, Destiny couldn't believe she was now jumping down and dragging her by the arm toward the front door.

Destiny couldn't believe how beautiful Tina looked pregnant. She was smiling as Taylor led her to the front door. Dropping Taylor's hands, Destiny studied her friend, searching for something, maybe she needed to see the happiness that she hadn't seen in her own eyes so many years ago. Tina held still until, seemingly satisfied, Destiny lowered her eyes gently rubbing her swelling stomach. Destiny threw her arms around her best friend.

It had been so long since they had seen one another. Releasing her, Destiny saw the shimmer of glistening tears in her eyes.

"Girl, it's so good to see you again. You look good. How's my auntie, and what do you think of Seattle?"

Destiny chuckled because Tina had not changed a bit. She was a little bigger around the middle, but other than that, she looked good. She was always the talkative one, so Destiny knew before she left she would be drilled on everything from Stanley to her trip to Seattle.

"To answer your first question, Auntie sends her love. And I can't believe how much you have grown," she said, rubbing Tina's stomach again, "and Taylor as well. She's beautiful."

"Come on, you guys. Let's go eat lunch before all of my hard work in the kitchen goes to waste." Tina was heading for the door. "Come on, Destiny. We have a lot of catching up to do. We may as well get started."

After a satisfying lunch, Tina sat with Destiny in the family room as they both looked out over the gorgeous view of her backyard. It was everything Tina had told her and more.

"So tell me about Pastor Adam Wheeler," Tina said, breaking the silence between them. "You sat next to this handsome brother all the way from Charleston to Seattle. For you to visit his church and join, he had to have made a great impression."

Hearing a noise, Destiny looked around to see if Richard had returned. Seeing no one, her attention went back to Tina. She'd told Tina about meeting Adam while they were cleaning up the kitchen earlier. "I'm a little nervous, Tina. I really like him a lot, but I don't know about dating a pastor so we agreed to be friends for now."

Tina scratched her head. "Girl, being a pastor is what he does, but a natural born man is what he is. His title does not change the fact that he is like any other man. He just has a calling on his life to do God's work."

They both looked at each other and laughed as they gave each other high fives. "I know that's right!"

"So you're nervous, huh?" Tina asked.

"I guess it's just that I want to do everything right, Tina. I don't want to mess this up. I believe that I deserve to be loved by a good man. But I've had so many mess-ups in my life that I'm a little scared. I did do one thing I'm proud of." She paused for a second. "On Sunday, I gave my life to the Lord." Destiny used her hand to wipe the tears that were falling.

"Oh, my God, I prayed that you would come to know Jesus and the true nature of his love. He won't fail you, Destiny. He'll be there every step of the way on your journey to discovering yourself." Tina took her time and looked Destiny right in the eyes while placing her hands on Destiny's heart.

"You have the Holy Spirit within you, Destiny, to help you become more and more like Jesus. When we have an experience with the power of God like you did on Sunday, our lives begin to change. You, Destiny, are now empowered to walk in authority like Jesus. That's why you were able to walk away from the place you were in because when you discover who you are, you can move from where you are to where you need to be."

She breathed out a sigh of relief because her sister understood what she was feeling without her having to explain. "I've never felt like this, Tina." She closed her eyes and laid her head back on the sofa where they were sitting, her body relaxing before she looked over at Tina. "This morning I woke to the phone ringing, and do you know who it was? It was Adam. He said he was calling to pray with me and to give me a scripture to meditate on for the day. It was just what I needed. Listen to this—" Destiny pulled a sticky note from her pocket—Psalm 66:17-19. Sitting upright again she read, "'I cried out to him with my mouth; his praise was on my tongue. If I had cherished sin in my heart, the Lord would not have listened; but God has surely listened and heard my voice in prayer.'"

"And then we prayed together. Can you believe it? I have never prayed with a man on the phone before. I feel free for the first time in my life. I know that my life is going to be different. I'm so ready for God to show me what to do next in my walk with him. I started going to church last year in Charleston, and my bishop was great. His preaching gave me the courage I needed to leave. I feel better than I have in years but I still have a ways to go. God, I'm so happy!"

Destiny jumped up from the sofa, danced around in a circle, and pulled Tina up to join her. They were both laughing and crying tears of joy. "I could shout it to the mountain tops!" Destiny lifted her hands, giving God silent praise for the wonderful things he had done and was still doing in her life.

Tina grabbed both of Destiny's hands, and, looking at her, she said, "Well, I might as well give you something else to celebrate. The baby's a boy!"

Destiny dropped Tina's hands, jumping up and down with joy. This time she ran around the sofa and began to dance.

"Oh, my God, oh, my God, you're going to have a boy! I'm so happy for you, Tina!" Destiny flopped back down on the sofa, touching Tina's stomach.

"I have only five more months to go. Destiny, I'm so happy because now Taylor will have a brother and Richard will have a boy to share his love of football with, although Taylor thinks she's the next Seahawks quarterback." Tina grabbed a tissue from the coffee table and wiped her eyes.

"Destiny, I want you to know that from the day Richard and I brought Taylor home from the hospital, we loved her just like she was our own. We had read every book, and besides, we went to all of the doctor's visits so we were ready for anything. She is such a precious child, and I don't know what our lives would be like if she weren't in it." Now the tears were falling from both of their eyes.

"Tina, you know I didn't know anything about the Lord when I got pregnant. I thought I would lose my mind, especially after finding out that I was pregnant after the rape. But you and Richard were truly angels sent to me by God. I knew I couldn't destroy a life. She deserved to be here even though I didn't deserve to be raped. God is a giver of life, not a taker. Remember that verse you quoted to me on the night I delivered her? Psalms 77:14: 'You are the God who performs miracles. You display your power among the people.' I never forgot that scripture because he used me to give you a miracle, and he showed both of us his power." They both leaned in to hug each other.

"I know that I'll have to share what happened to me with Adam, especially if we are going to have a relationship. But I want to see how it goes first, and then I will tell him everything. But in the meantime, I'm going to develop a relationship with the Lord and let him take care of the rest." Tina reached for Destiny's hand and squeezed it tightly.

"I've never been so proud of you, Destiny. You are going to be just fine." Tina raised her eyebrow. "But you know that, don't you?"

"I know you and Richard love me, and it means the world to me. When we were in college, you, Shawn, and Uncle Willie were always family. I felt this way because you all showed me love unconditionally, and I'll always love all of you for it. I cherish all of the time we spent together as a family during breaks, and those long weekends were great being able to share them with you all." Destiny reached for her glass of iced tea that was sitting on the coffee table and took a sip as she listened for Tina's response.

"You know we enjoyed you as much as you enjoyed us; now enough about me. Tell me, what do you think of Cynthia and the boys?" she quizzed and waited for an answer.

"Tina, I absolutely love Cynthia, and once you meet her, I think you will also. We connected the moment we met at the airport. The twins are the most adorable little boys. They are older than Taylor by three years. I have to give her credit because as a single mother she has done a wonderful job of raising them. They are very polite and well mannered." Destiny reached over and touched Tina's hand to emphasize her statement.

"You know Auntie kept the twins when we were in Charleston," she stated.

"I remember Sara telling me about two boys." Tina smiled at Destiny because she could imagine them both in her mind.

"I spent time with them, but I never had the opportunity to meet their mother until we arrived in Seattle. Can you believe that we were on the same flight?"

The shock of what Destiny shared showed on her friend's face. "Oh my God, you have got to be kidding me."

"I wouldn't lie about something like this, Tina. She was sitting in the seat in front of us. But, girl, this tops it all!" Destiny hit her legs with her hands. "Can you believe that the father of her twins is Adam's brother, Marvin? The sticky part about all of this is that he doesn't even know they exist." Destiny could tell by the expression in Tina's face that she was shocked by this revelation.

"You mean to tell me that her twins are Marvin Wheeler's?" She asked with alarm in her voice and questions in her eyes. "Richard and I met him last year at a fundraiser during the Christmas holidays. He's a generous man and gives large donations to charities around the city. His generosity made such a great impression on us, and we became rather fond of him, friends actually. It's not often that you find young, single, black males giving back to their communities, but I can truly say Marvin Wheeler is an outstanding individual. Is she going to keep the boys a secret?" Tina inquired with questioning eyes.

"Heavens no. You won't believe this, but there is another twist in this whole situation. When Cynthia left Charleston, she applied for a position with M and W Enterprises Real Estate Investors Inc." Destiny chuckled when she saw the raise of Tina's eyebrows in recognition of the company's name.

"Am I correct in assuming that she didn't know that Marvin owned M and W?" Tina began to laugh uncontrollably. "The Bible says that my God shall supply all your needs according to his riches in glory by Christ Jesus. God is so awesome. He orchestrated this whole thing. Look at this."

Tina slapped her thighs with her hands. Then she lifted up her fingers to illustrate her point. "Number one, you and Adam meet on the plane." She raised one finger. "Number two, Cynthia just so happens to sit in the seat in front of both of you." The second finger went up. "Number three, Adam is the pastor of one of the largest churches in the city, and his brother just so happens to be Cynthia's babies' daddy and her new boss. Now tell me that God didn't set this all up. It has his handy work all over it."

Tina threw both of her hands up. "Let me throw this in for good measure. Richard and I have been trying to decide on a ministry to join, and we had thought about Pastor Wheeler, but now I know why we waited. However, this Sunday, we will be the newest members of Greater Community.

Tina looked over at Destiny and added, "Plus, he likes you, and you seem to like him as well. Am I correct?" Tina suggested in her usual helpful voice.

"It's true. I do like him. Adam's sweet, and I believe we've gotten to know a little about each other." Destiny stated.

"I just feel God all over this thing. Don't worry about Adam. He's going to do only what God directs him to do and nothing else," Tina told Destiny. She didn't explain further.

Then Destiny focused on Tina. "The truth is, Tina, I don't know enough about the Word of God to be completely comfortable talking to Adam about the things of God or Stanley for that matter."

Looking at Destiny like she had grown a second head, Tina responded, "are you concerned about Stanley finding you here?"

She nodded. "I find myself double checking everything and I constantly have nightmares about him." Destiny abruptly stopped talking and smiled meekly. "I've been going on and on about everything but that. But in all honesty it scares me to death."

"I'm sorry." Tina's expression became thoughtful. "I should have asked you about him sooner. I know that it's been a difficult time for you." Her voice was unsteady. "Why didn't you tell me sooner about your feelings?"

She didn't really want to say that her fear of Stanley weighed heavily on her mind on a daily basis. Bleakly she wondered if she'd ever get over that fear. She flicked a glance at Tina, who had a pensive look on her face as she sat on the couch. She seemed to be sensing something was wrong. Destiny could only imagine how angry she would be if she knew all of the abuse she'd encountered at his hand. The injustice of it brought tears to her eyes because she had not anticipated this, had not wanted to bring him into what had been a wonderful day up to this point. Yet still she accepted the futile inevitability of the moment, of the truth.

Tina eyed her with sympathy. "It's okay, Destiny, it's all going to work out. I know it will."

Destiny nodded her head in agreement, knowing there was no point. She couldn't keep the truth from Tina. She would have to reveal her secrets after all. "No. It's fine." She hesitated, her expression pensive. "This isn't our first time down this road with Stanley, but, Tina…I can assure you it will be our last."

Tina smiled encouragingly, her gaze firmly focused on Destiny. "When you're ready, there are counselors that can help and this time the authorities should be involved."

"I know," Destiny mused. She felt numb now as she faced Tina directly. "I believe I'm ready to do that for the first time. I'm ready to move on with my life."

"And, Destiny, the Lord will let you live your life to it's fullest because you deserve it."

"That's what I want." She swallowed and took a breath. "It's all I've ever wanted." She stared down at her lap.

Tina put a gentle hand on Destiny's shoulder. "The God you gave your heart to will not fail you. Don't for a moment think Adam sitting beside you was a coincidence. I believe it was in God's providential will for your life. Sure, he doesn't know everything about you yet, but he will. The one thing that I have learned is that friendship doesn't know age, color, or national origin. Love is just love, plain and simple. We can't always explain it, but it is what it is, and if it's real love, then it will work every time.

"Richard told me once that he had an 'every time love.' Every time he looked at me, he saw another reason for loving me. Every time he called my name, he heard another reason for loving me. Every time he thought of me, he thought of reasons for loving me. Every time I smiled at him, he was reminded of why he loved me. He said every time he closed his eyes and prayed, God would say to him, 'My love works every time.' He always said, 'Every time I turn around, I find another reason to love you.' So as a believer, I have come to realize that love is what God created it to be from the beginning of time. Love is God, and without him in our lives, we will never understand or identify with how it feels, how it is expressed, and how it works. So love is God's ultimate expression of what he feels every time he looks at us."

Destiny wiped the tears that were falling from her eyes. "I have never heard of love explained quite that way. One thing I do know after you explained it is that I want a love that works every time."

Destiny leaned over to hug Tina. "Tina, my love for you is a love that works every time."

Smiling, Tina replied, "Ditto."

CHAPTER 11

Cynthia could not believe that she had been working for Marvin almost four months. Him not being in the lobby to greet her after she got off the elevator was strange. It had become a morning ritual for them. Susan her secretary, informed her that Marvin had to leave for Chicago. That was two weeks ago. The negotiations for a piece of prime property were about to fall through, and he had to go salvage the deal. The only time she talked to him was when he called on Monday for their weekly department meeting. But that was fine with her. It gave her the time she needed to decide how she would tell him about the twins. She also needed to build up her confidence before calling her parents to let them know she was back in town. It was something that had to be done before someone else did it.

She was proud of the way things were going with Destiny and Miss Sara. They were becoming family. They spent time together on weekends running from one mall to another. Jonathan and David enjoyed spending time with them, especially when they were able to play in the Kid's Land and get something to eat from the food court. When they weren't at the malls shopping for their new home, they could be found in the living room laughing at a Disney movie or just sitting around eating popcorn and watching old black-and-white movies. They had settled into a nice routine, and it felt like a home.

Today, Sara had surprised the boys with a cake. She had arranged everything while Cynthia was outside playing with the boys. Everything on the table was decorated in blue. The boys loved blue. She even had candles on the table, which she had lit before returning to the kitchen with the food. After they had finished eating a wonderful dinner, Sara went into the kitchen and walked back out with a beautiful cake. The icing was white with blue borders and Nemo decorations. Everything tasted wonderful. After dinner, they took their slices of cake and a gallon of vanilla ice cream into the den to eat as they watched television.

Leaving the boys in the living room watching television, the women moved to the front porch of the house. They spent a lot of time there. They had bought beautiful furniture that was comfortable enough to relax.

"Well, ladies, I'm going back inside to clean the kitchen and put my dinner on for tomorrow." Sara grabbed the emptied dishes on the table between Cynthia and Destiny before disappearing back in the house.

"So, Destiny, how's everything going with you and our pastor?" Cynthia inquired while wiping frosting from her mouth.

Destiny replied, "It's amazing. I really cannot believe how well everything has been going in my life lately. When I think about Adam, I feel my heart beating like a drum. It feels almost like I'm a teenager again. It's amazing, and he treats me like a lady. I'm not used to it. Sometimes I have to pinch myself to prove it's all real." She felt her insides give another fluttery movement as she thought about him. "But for now I'm glad we agreed to be just friends."

Cynthia's eyes widened as she swallowed hard. "I think that's a wise move."

There it was, a slight pause before Destiny spoke, choosing her words. Her eyes shifted away from Cynthia's, her throat doing that nervous up and down thing again, "I've been having these reoccurring dreams about Stanley."

Cynthia saw the shadow of grief pass through her eyes before she averted her gaze. "When did they start?" she asked, surprised by this new revelation. She fought back her anger toward Stanley, reminding herself that Destiny was safe here in Seattle.

Cynthia wanted to know how frightened Destiny really was but thought her eyes were like shuttered windows, not revealing much. "I've been having them since we moved to Seattle," she said. "I told Tina that I needed to talk with someone about them."

Cynthia bit her lip, her fingers plucking at the invisible lint on her blouse. "That's a great idea…I'd hate it if you were continuously tormented by these dreams. You can't allow Stanley to continue holding you hostage even through your dreams."

She didn't answer. She just sat there looking down at her with that expressionless face, making Cynthia feel a little uncomfortable. If she were deeply in love with him she would have stayed with him, surely? What sort of man could cause one woman so much pain? From all she'd heard about him, it certainly didn't sound like he was very devoted to her.

After pondering her own thoughts for a long moment, she forced herself to meet Destiny's gaze once more. "Um…I know this might seem a strange question but," she quickly licked her lips for courage before she continued, "would you consider letting Adam counsel you?"

The question seemed to hang suspended in the air for a very long time.

She tried to read her expression, to see if any slight movement of her lips, eyes, or forehead would provide some clue of how she felt about that suggestion.

Finally her lips stretched into a brief on-off smile that didn't involve her eyes.

"I think it would be better if I got counseling from one of the other ministers on staff at the church," she said. "Right now we are just getting to know each other. I don't want to share too much too soon."

Cynthia searched her features once more. "I'm sorry…so very sorry for not recognizing any of the signs that now as I'm sitting here were kind of obvious…" She bit her lip again, releasing it to add, "If it were me in your place, I know I would be terrifyingly frightened."

Destiny's eyes searched hers for a beat or two before they fell away as she said, "I would love to have the strength I've seen in you since we've been living here as a family. It's my faith that gives me strength, and Destiny," she added, "disappointments won't last forever. At some point they have to leave and your next appointment will be filled with joy."

Cynthia reached out to rub her hand gently and whispered, "You're going to be fine."

Destiny really hoped that was true. "Thanks," she said with a pathetic attempt at laughing. "That really makes me feel better."

Cynthia gave her a long look and sighed again, taking her hand, she squeezed it before saying, "Sounds like you need more sugar."

"Sugar? But we just ate cake!" she said.

Cynthia held up her hands in a sign of surrender. "You are so right—I'll be right back."

"Here we go." Cynthia breezed back onto the porch with two additional slices of cake in her hand. She held them out for her viewing pleasure. "This is just what Sara ordered." She let the screen door shut behind her.

"Are you serious?"

Cynthia smiled because Sara said cream cheese frosting was Destiny's favorite.

"It's the best thing to take your mind off of anything negative and cause you to think of nothing but sugary bliss." She sat the plates on the table and settled into a rocker beside her.

"You're a good friend." Destiny said picking up a plate.

"I hear that all the time," Cynthia said, "now relax and let the sugar do its job."

Destiny rolled her eyes. "Hopefully on the lips only and not my hips." Cynthia watched her take a bite, closing her eyes to savor the taste. She wasn't sure but she thought she saw a slight release in Destiny's demeanor as she relaxed, and with those parting words she watched the twins play in the yard.

CHAPTER 12

Just after getting the boys off to school, Cynthia decided to call Tina for a girls' outing. After talking to Destiny, she'd decided it was time to make new friends. Her career was on track now especially after getting the position at Marvin's company. She had to laugh at the awesomeness of God. Nobody but the Lord would have orchestrated the course of events for her life. He was truly a comedian on top of being a deliverer, healer, and savior. Thinking about what they could do, she decided a shopping outing would be fun if Tina felt up to it being almost six months pregnant.

Hours later Cynthia was still thinking how wonderful her afternoon had been with Tina. She and Richard seemed to be such a wonderful couple.

The thought was still rewinding in her mind when she crawled into bed later that night. She and Tina had stopped by the Seattle market for a tour after they had a delicious lunch. They'd run into a few people they'd both known from the church. Now she stared at the ceiling in her bedroom. She felt as though someone had pulled the rug out from beneath her feet. It was amazing to know that Tina and Richard had been college sweethearts. They'd moved to Seattle right after the Seahawks drafted Richard.

They loved each other. Their future was all mapped out. They had an adorable daughter and a son on the way. Life. Cynthia couldn't get her head around it. It made her chest tight to think of how her life could have turned out if she hadn't gotten pregnant. There was no way she'd have made a different decision about her sons; they meant the world to her. Yes, her relationship with her parents had been jeopardized but she'd done it without their help. God had blessed them. She thought back to the night before she left for college, to the things they'd said to her. They both had agreed that her relationship with Marvin would only lead to a dead end, and with her father's help it had. Then one month after going to college she found out she was pregnant.

She twisted in bed, rolling over to her side. It was a time when she thought things were going to turn out differently and not end up in such a disaster. Even worse, she hadn't been around family to receive comfort and support from them because they'd pushed her out of their life when she'd needed them the most. Marvin had no idea she'd been pregnant or had his sons. She could still remember the conversations they shared about their future, and the way Marvin had looked at her when they were in love. She was drifting toward sleep when an insidious little thought weaseled its way into her mind: now that she was back in Seattle and Marvin was still free, maybe, just maybe, things could change between them. Her eyes snapped open. Her heart kicked out an urgent, panicky beat. Don't even think about it. Not for a second. What would he say about the boys?

But she was wide-awake and the thought was lodged in her brain, glowing like her night-light.

She was free to love again. That's if Marvin was interested in a second time around?

"Don't be an idiot," she said out loud.

Chapter 13

Destiny was on her way out the door when the phone rang. She glanced at her watch. It was already ten minutes past the time she was supposed to leave for the office. She reached for the phone. "Hello?"

She heard someone on the other line, but no one responded, so she repeated her greeting. "Hello?"

When the person continued to breathe in her ear and refused to say anything, Destiny decided she had more important things to do. Already late, she hung up the phone. She continued toward the door, remembering to lock it on the way out. Some people evidently had nothing better to do than to play on the phone.

Sitting at her desk, Destiny decided to make the phone call she had been putting off all day. She and Adam had agreed to talk today about plans for this week. They had enjoyed a wonderful dinner after church on Sunday. Adam had taken her to SkyCity, the Space Needle's five-hundred-foot-high restaurant, for a wonderful brunch. After a wonderful meal and delightful conversation, they had walked through the Space Needle's Pavilion. It was the most unique shopping experience.

Then she had gone home only to have another haunting nightmare. They disturbed her sleep, like the surprise spring storms that ran rapid throughout the south. Since coming to Seattle, she had fought hard to push all thoughts of Stanley and the past from her mind. She had started to believe she was succeeding. Despite the gloomy rainy climate of Seattle, the lab she ran at Kintama Chemicals kept her so busy that somehow being immersed in work for days on end she wouldn't have time to think of him or see his evil face. Last week she had talked to the secretary at Greater Community about support groups for battered women. She was excited to find that they did in fact have a support group, which met once a week.

She had been debating about inviting Adam to dinner. She had all the right reasons for why she shouldn't but they fell short of a legitimate reason. All of her haggling about it was causing her day to drag. The one good thing about today was that her test results were just what they'd been looking for in their latest research. So things in the lab had actually gone fairly smoothly. Maybe because she'd slept like the dead last night after her nightmare. She couldn't remember when she'd been out cold like that.

Her cell phone rang. "Saved by the bell." She'd been about to go off on another long analysis of why she should call Adam. One glance at the screen and she smiled. Tina.

The conversation lasted nearly an hour. Tina updated her on things with Taylor and her pregnancy. Her descriptions of Taylor's antics were hilarious. Her stories about Richard obsessing with the baby showed how in tune with one another they were, even in pregnancy. The perfect couple. That was what Destiny wanted.

She heaved a big, loud sigh. She could go to lunch early. But eating wouldn't help. If talking to Tina for the better part of an hour didn't do the trick, nothing would.

There was only one thing to do.

Call him. And see if he'd accept. After all they were friends and hadn't they said they'd get together?

The only question left was what kind of friends? She chewed her lip, pondering that for a minute. The kind of friends who supported each other through thick and thin in life or the kind that would eventually become a couple and all that it entails?

A grin stretched across her lips.

She picked up the phone and dialed.

"Hello?" he answered softly, his thick voice barely audible.

"Hi," she responded, suddenly embarrassed that she called at all. He had told her that Monday was a rest day for him.

"I was just thinking about calling you. How's your day been going in the lab?"

"Everything's fine. It's been busy but I've had a breakthrough in some research, and since I had a few minutes, I thought I would take a break to call you."

"You could have called me early this morning. It would have been nice hearing your voice," he responded, a hint of a smile in his voice.

"You probably were sleeping, especially after delivering such a wonderful message on Sunday. I didn't want to disturb you."

Adam laughed softly before he said, "I enjoyed our day. You were such a joy to be with."

Destiny could feel herself blushing profusely. She tried hard but couldn't stifle her giggle. It was very difficult to stay focused with Adam when he was being so charming. "Thank you. I had a good time as well."

"Don't you want to see me again?" he asked, his voice taking on a serious but cautious tone.

Destiny sighed heavily and then took a deep breath before proceeding. "Yes, I do, if you would like to."

Adam laughed to himself. "Well, that's good to know. So, Miss Destiny, when can we plan on getting together?"

Smiling, she replied, "Well, my schedule is fairly full these days, Pastor Wheeler, but I guess I can squeeze you in sometime between now and forever."

"Well, that's really wonderful to know. How does this evening look, say around seven?"

"Let me check my schedule." She paused for a minute before responding with a laugh. "I guess if I have to see you again, then tonight at seven will be perfect, and we can eat at the house. Auntie would love it, and please don't be late. Auntie likes to eat on time."

Adam smiled into the phone. "Me late? Never. I'll see you tonight at seven."

"I'm looking forward to it."

"Not as much as I am."

Pulling into the driveway, Destiny gave a peaceful sigh. Tina's car was in the driveway, which caused her spirits to lift automatically. Getting out of the car, she performed her normal ritual of scanning the area around the house. Walking up the porch steps to unlock the front door. She stuck the key in the lock without a second thought to look behind her. That probably would not have been smart if it was dark outside. She had taken a self-defense class before moving to Seattle. The fact that she had to take all of these precautious perturbed her more than anything right now. If Stanley had had something in mind, wouldn't he have already made his move?

It had been quite a while and there were only a few phone calls that concerned her right now. The decision she made to move here was imperative in order to put as much distance between him and her as possible. She stuck her key in the lock, thankful for her new life in Seattle. She heard the latch disconnect then she push the door open.

As soon as she stepped inside she automatically reached for the light switch. Realizing it was still daylight, she chuckled nervously to herself. With each passing day her paranoia was getting worst.

After turning around she gasped with surprise when she saw everyone staring curiously at her, "Hi, guys," there was some nervous tension in her voice. She managed a smile. Her stomach was churning. They had seen her caution as she entered the house. So she decided to act as if nothing was wrong.

Dropping her bags to the floor, Destiny sank down in the first chair she found. Cynthia must have been walking from the kitchen, along with Sara, because each of them had a tray of refreshments. Sweet smells wafted from the kitchen, filling the room with their aroma. Destiny could already taste the ham with its pineapple glaze. The biscuits sent her nose into overdrive, and she swore one of the smells was collard greens.

"Hi, Miss Destiny," she heard David and Jonathan say as they headed her way. From behind them she heard the voice of Taylor.

"Hi, Auntie," she said as they all ran to grab her at once.

"Hey, guys, I didn't expect to see all of you today. What have you been doing?" she inquired after giving each of them a hug.

Taylor hugged her before saying, "We've been waiting on you, Auntie. I have a recital, and we came to pick up David and Jonathan. Do you want to go?"

"Not this time, guys, but next time for sure." She smiled before making her way around the room to give everyone a hug and kiss.

"Destiny, I feel as though I have known Cynthia forever instead of just a few months. We could not stop talking during lunch last week. We shared so many aspects of our lives—Taylor, her sons, and the new addition on the way." She looked down and laid a hand on her growing stomach and smiled brightly.

"Cynthia, you and Destiny have become family. I prayed that God would send Destiny to Seattle, but he cared enough to send both of you."

They all squeezed hands, smiling at one another. In the distance they could hear Sara singing in the kitchen as if she didn't have a care in the world. They all settled back down in the living room. Destiny pulled off her heels, stretching out her toes while giving them a break for the first time today. After closing her eyes, enjoying the moment, she opened her eyes only to find both women looking at her.

"Well?" they said in unison. Tina and Cynthia looked at each other and fell into a spell of laughter.

"Well, what?" Destiny asked as if she didn't have a clue as to what they were talking about.

"Are you having dinner with Pastor tonight or what?" They were both waiting for an answer.

"We decided to get together tonight. I wanted him to get a little better acquainted with Sara, so I invited him to dinner. Then I called Sara, and I guess from the smells raffling through the house, she started cooking right away."

Tina stood, gathering her purse. "Well, everyone who's going with me needs to get their things. We're about to leave the station." She watched as all three of the children began to clean up their areas.

"Cynthia, it would be a joy and a lot of help if you wanted to tag along."

"I thought you'd never ask. Let me get my purse." Cynthia turned, heading down the hall.

"Enjoy yourself, Destiny." Tina winked as she started toward the door. "I'm sure you and Pastor will have an interesting dinner with Auntie. We should be back around ten this evening. We'll see you then." With that, she grabbed her keys, made sure the kids were ready, and headed for the car.

Destiny returned to the living room. She had plenty of time to relax. After she checked the lock on the door, she sat down and immediately closed her eyes. There were still a couple of hours before Adam would arrive.

Flipping on the lights in the living room, Sara relaxed against the doorframe, watching Destiny sleep. Her eyes scanned Destiny's outfit all the way down to her shoeless feet. Destiny never liked wearing shoes. Lord, she was so much like her mother. Sara's heart was full as she admired the young lady who had been through so much in life. It seemed as if everything in her life was changing since they had come to Seattle. She was happier than Sara had ever seen her, but some things in her behavior gave her a slight concern. She never failed to ask if any calls had come from Stanley and she was always checking the locks on the doors almost obsessively when she was home. Sara heard her crying in her room on several evenings after everyone went to bed. Even the way she had entered the house today alarmed her. She had been nervous as she came in the house, turning on the lights to the living room and porch only to realize that it wasn't even dark out yet. Maybe she needed some counseling for battered women.

She prayed that Destiny would inquire about the programs and if not at Greater Community then maybe a private center. *Bless her, Lord*, Sara said to herself. *My sister would be so proud of her*. Clearing her throat, she watched as Destiny's eyes opened.

"Baby girl, when are you going to start getting yourself ready for dinner? Pastor Wheeler will be here shortly." She smiled, deciding that now was a perfect time to wake her up.

"Thank you, Auntie. I need to get up and get started now," she responded, sitting upright.

"Baby, you don't owe me any thanks," her auntie said, kissing her lightly on the cheek. "I should be thanking you for being the best child anyone could ever want. Now go get dressed. Pastor will be here in a few minutes."

After dressing, Destiny went into the kitchen. When she didn't see any signs of her aunt, she began to set the table. Sara came in shortly after and began to hand her the silverware she needed.

"We'll put the food in the oven until Pastor gets here so it won't get cold," she said, heading for the living room. Destiny did as she was instructed and then followed her into the living room. Sara sat in the living room in her favorite chair, rocking back and forth. Destiny sat across from her, relaxing on the sofa.

Looking around the room, Destiny was pleased with how the house was becoming a home for each of them. Their tastes were different, but they managed to compromise on a lot of the decorations, giving the home a country, chic elegance. The family photos of the twins, Cynthia, Sara, and herself graced the tops of the tables and the walls. Destiny admired all of the pictures. Picking up the picture of Sara, she admired the softness that epitomized her character.

"What are you thinking about, Destiny? You've been kind of quiet the whole evening," Sara asked, breaking the silence.

Destiny shrugged. "Just thinking about everything that's happened and how wonderful God is to bring us to this point."

"God always takes care of his children."

"I'm learning so much about the goodness of God. Pastor Wheeler is an excellent teacher," Destiny stated, not realizing she was smiling.

"You're smiling like you won first place in a contest." Sara was laughing now.

Destiny laughed. "Is it wrong to be this happy? Sometimes I don't think I deserve all the happiness I'm feeling right now."

Sara looked and rolled her eyes. "The Lord wants all of us to be happy, and you deserve some happiness. You're a wonderful young woman, and your mama would be proud."

Destiny sighed. "I like him, but I'm worried that our going out might not be good for him. I noticed on Sunday how some of the young ladies were watching me at church. I don't want to cause problems. We've only been there a short while. Today, before I left for work, I got a phone call, but the person didn't say anything. It was strange, just a lot of breathing on the other end."

Sara sucked her teeth. "Child, it's been almost five months. It couldn't be anybody you know; just a wrong number or some kids making a prank. At least you're not running up behind him every Sunday or Wednesday like a dog in heat, trying to get his attention. It's a shame, but that's what it is. The man's probably been looking for a lady like you all of his life."

Before Destiny could comment, the doorbell rang. She jumped to her feet. She let Pastor Wheeler in as Sara came to her feet.

Destiny held the door open for Pastor Wheeler, and as he walked into the room, he stopped to hug her gently. Destiny smiled warmly at him.

"Hi, Destiny," he said quietly as he looked over at Sara.

"Hi, please come in." Taking him by the elbow, Destiny led him into the center of the room.

"Good evening, Miss Sara. I hope it wasn't too much trouble fixing dinner for three."

"No, no, not at all," Sara said while giving him a hug.

"I hope you're hungry," Destiny said as she took his jacket. "We put everything in the oven, waiting for your arrival."

"I am," Adam responded, "and it smells wonderful."

Adam and Destiny followed as Sara led the way into the kitchen. Sara instructed Pastor Wheeler to sit at the head of the table while Destiny filled each glass with the richly colored tea she considered the best. After placing a lemon on each glass, she placed them in their respective place. Sara brought out the food in the beautiful servers that she only used on Sundays. After making sure she had everything, she settled herself in the chair next to Destiny.

Sara gestured toward Pastor Wheeler. "Pastor Wheeler, if you don't mind, I would be honored if you would bless the food."

Adam was pleased. They all bowed their heads as he blessed the food as well as every occupant of their home.

"Amen," they all chorused at the end of the prayer. Then, reaching for the collards, Sara began to fill each plate with the delicious contents of each bowl.

"So Pastor Wheeler, how was your day at the church?" Sara inquired as she began to cut her ham.

Adam cut into his ham, taking a bite before responding. "I generally take Mondays off because of my schedule on Sunday. So today I relaxed and began to pray about what God wanted spoken to his people in the coming week."

SYLVIA CARTER

Sara took her time in responding. "I believe that every pastor should take a day of rest. God wants his men and women to be open to receive and not tired out by all of the issues they have to deal with throughout the week. You have to attend to your own spiritual, physical, and emotional needs because it's crucial to your ability to serve God."

"Auntie, I never heard you talk about the role of the pastor before. I knew you loved the Lord, but now I can see your respect for the role of a pastor," Destiny said while sipping her tea.

Sara chuckled. "I've never been married, but I do know that the relationship between the pastor and the church is like a good marriage."

Sara wasn't surprised when she noticed the rise of his brows, probably realizing she had a revelation that very few understood. "Yes, Miss Sara, the relationship between the pastor and his church is much like a marriage. It's a partnership, each giving one hundred percent to make sure they are caring equally for each other."

"So," Sara said, "have you lived in Seattle all of your life, Pastor?"

"Yes, ma'am. I was born here. My parents are still living, and I have a twin brother, Marvin, who lives here as well. The only time I left was to attend college in Atlanta."

Sara nodded. "I had never been to Seattle or anywhere else 'til Destiny told me about Tina wanting us to come and live here. But I do think I'm going to enjoy it here."

They ate freely, biting into the ham and dabbing the juices of their collards up on their plates with the homemade biscuits. They talked about everything from the weather to sports, business, and local events taking place in Seattle. Adam talked about his family with so much love and respect. Sara studied him and understood what so many of the women at his church saw in him.

Sara gave Destiny an approving smile. Pastor Wheeler had made her laugh at his jokes and cry when it came to his love for the ministry. Destiny would be treated like a real lady with this

118

man. He'd pulled her into his heart and he had done it in less than two hours.

Her niece seemed to be caught off guard by all that she had seen transpire between herself and Adam. Sara watched as she swallowed the food in her mouth, rinsing the last bite down with a gulp of tea.

Then she jumped up saying, "We'll clean up the kitchen, Auntie. You go and relax for a while." She picked up the empty plates and took them to the kitchen sink.

Sara sighed heavily before responding, "You're right, baby girl. It's been a long day." Rising from the table, she extended a hand toward Adam. "Pastor, please come by again. It was really nice having you here for dinner. Our house is always open to you. Try to get baby girl not to worry about that phone call she got today. I told her it was probably some kids playing on the phone."

"Thank you," he responded, rising to his feet. "Everything was delicious, Miss Sara. Thank you for having me over."

As she eased out of the room, she called good night to Destiny over her shoulder.

Adam and Destiny stood together in the kitchen doing the dishes. The low hum of the refrigerator was the only noise to be heard for a while, along with the running water. Rinsing the soap from each dish, Destiny was almost in tears, laughing as Adam spun story after story of his and Marvin's exploits as kids. With all the dishes dried and put away, Adam tossed the damp dishcloth across the sink and guided her back into the living room. They heard Sara singing as she prepared herself for bed.

Adam guided Destiny down onto the sofa beside him. He picked up the Bible that lay on the coffee table and opened it up. The first book that he came to was Matthew 6:33, and he began to read. "'But seek ye first the kingdom of God, and his righteousness; and all these things shall be added unto you.' I think this is a perfect scripture to meditate on for the evening. I really enjoyed this evening, but more than that, I appreciate your relationship with the Lord."

Smiling, Destiny answered, "God will have to come first in my life, plain and simple. Putting God first, as his Word says, is so important. Seek ye first the kingdom of God. It's a big sacrifice, but when you start the process, you realize and learn that God is just like a protective father watching out for his children."

Adam was amazed at the response Destiny gave him. "You know, Destiny, God is supervising his flock and won't let any harm come to you."

"My aunt told you?" she looked up from the Bible.

He looked at her, making sure she was comfortable with this conversation. "If you're not comfortable talking about this, we can change the subject." He closed the Bible he'd been holding in his hand.

He felt her tension; the way she gave a tiny, almost imperceptible flinch as she held the Bible in her hand. "When I think about those calls, it brings back the fear, anxiety, and insecurity that I felt in South Carolina."

Adam wanted her to trust him enough to confide in him. But she also had to be comfortable opening up to him. So he waited, not wanting to rush her.

She gave him a fleeting smile. "I believe that one day I'll be able to share more about my past with you." She shifted her attention to his face. There was something about the way he was watching her that must have caused the single tear he saw roll down her face. With a trembling hand she wiped it away quickly. He understood her reluctance to reveal her feelings, with him since she was just beginning to really know him.

"Destiny, I'm not trying to force you to…" He stopped speaking when he saw her get up and pace in front of him with her arms crossed over her chest.

"It's okay, Adam, I'm kind of tried." He sat quietly, absorbing that information, hoping he hadn't made her upset.

She twisted her mouth wryly. "To tell you the truth, I think I'll go to bed early." She was deliberately pushing him away, as if distance in this moment would protect her from whatever it was she was battling with in her past.

Destiny gave him an apologetic grimace as she sat back down. "I'm sorry."

He gave her a tight smile. "No problem, but if the phone calls persist, please let the authorities know."

His words seemed to shock her because she responded nervously. "Do you think that's necessary?"

"Yeah, I do, and because I don't know everything about your past. Those phone calls could be connected to it. But I want you to remember that you've got a friend who will listen if you need it." He rose from the sofa and gently helped her out of her seat. Reaching for her hand, he gave it a slight squeeze to reassure her.

"I'll remember," she said quickly. "I just don't want to bother you with all of my baggage."

Adam didn't want to sound impatient. "Just remember what I said if they persist: call the police." He looked down at her now, wondering if she had any idea of the war going on inside him. She was cautious around him, which was understandable given she seemed to have given so much of herself to someone who gave her a limited amount of themselves, which only leads to frustration.

He hesitated a moment longer. But she was right. Maybe he was taking on too much too soon. She'd even admitted that she had baggage. Heck, he didn't even know everything about her yet, and he certainly didn't want to turn her away. Not wanting to wear out his welcome, he reached for his jacket and slipped it on before turning around to face Destiny.

"I want to thank you and Miss Sara for a wonderful evening. I had a nice time tonight," he said politely, squeezing her hand beneath his.

"I'm glad you were able to come, and I hope we'll be able to do this again," Destiny confessed.

Adam took her into his arms. Taking a deep breath, he looked into her eyes before lowering his head but he didn't kiss her he pulled her to him in a light hug.

"I'll call you tomorrow. Maybe we can make plans for later this week. I want to take you to a special place that means a lot to me, okay?"

Adam was pleased to see her nod in response; he was looking forward to their day together.

Pausing, his hand on the knob, he turned to face her one last time, studying every detail of her face as if he wouldn't see her again.

"How long have we known each other?" he asked her.

"It's been over five months at least."

"It's been incredible, and I've enjoyed getting to know you, Destiny, but I want you to trust me as well." Adam stated.

"I want that as well," she said. "I'm getting there, and I know things are going to get better." Destiny returned the smile she was receiving from him. She walked over to where he was standing at the door.

"Don't forget, in all of this you've got to learn to trust yourself." He kissed her on the cheek and walked out the door.

After Adam climbed inside his car and started his engine, he noticed how Destiny clung to the door with her hand clutched tightly around the doorknob. There was still a lot he needed to know about her.

Adam pulled his car onto the expressway, rubbing his head, pondering the conversation he'd just had with Destiny. Before tonight he felt like they had made a connection but now it seemed as though they had a set back.

Adam was glad that he didn't accept the invitation he had received on Sunday from Sister Deloris Green to have dinner with her family tonight. Deloris had been trying to set him up with her daughter, Barbara, since he had come to Greater Community. He knew that her invitation came with strings attached that he had no intention of untying.

He had dated since coming to Greater Community, but never anyone from his ministry. None of the relationships were what he was looking for. They were too overbearing, too loud, too argumentative, too needy, too materialistic, or carrying too much excess baggage.

He knew that he didn't want to deal with any additional baggage. He had enough of his own and was still unpacking a lot of it. Destiny wasn't perfect, but he also knew that with God's help, they would be able to work through any issues she was dealing with from her past.

Adam didn't dare relax. He couldn't help but think about what he knew he shouldn't, "Lust, lust and more lust," he said out loud in the car. "Lord keep me delivered."

He recalled one of the conversations they had about the progression of their relationship. Destiny had pursed her lips, she seemed to hate the fact that she was blushing, or it may have been the fact that she hated him in that moment for watching her with such amusement. Then she told him in the most serious tone, "I can assure you I would never fall in lust with someone," she said. "I would only love someone I admired as a man, for his qualities as a person, not his possessions or social standing. And I most certainly wouldn't marry a man on physical attraction alone. If I didn't learn anything else in my past, I know this with everything in me."

Yes, he and Destiny still had a long way to go although it had only been five months, he knew God wasn't finished working on either of them. He had time, and he knew how to pray.

Tapping his fingers lightly on the steering wheel to the beat as he pulled his car into the driveway of his condominium. After pulling his key out of the ignition, he continued to sing the words to Jason Nelson's song "Shifting the Atmosphere" that he had been listening to in the car and couldn't help but smile. The song helped to push the negative thoughts to the back of his mind. Tomorrow was going to be a good day.

At home on Tuesday, Adam headed straight for his bedroom. He was tired, and it had been a long day of counseling. It was amazing that the week was going by so fast. There were no dinners with Destiny or her aunt to relax him. As a matter of fact, Destiny was the reason he was so agitated. He had known there was something she hadn't been telling him from the lags in their conversation today.

He could hear Destiny sigh on the phone, obviously not sure how to tackle her conversation with him. Adam wasn't surprised. After all, he didn't know what was bothering her. He could hear her hesitation right through the telephone.

"You don't have to tell me what's bothering you if you don't want to. I'm not going to force you, but I thought..." His voice trailed off, trying to find the words as he held the phone to his ear.

Apparently he wasn't the only person struggling to get their conversation started. Adam was surprised when he heard Destiny's breath catch through the phone. "You thought that we'd be further along in our relationship?" she asked softly. "I don't know what's going on," she said. "I don't know what's what any more..."

He had been curious about her unfinished sentence in spite of himself. Hadn't they just had this conversation a couple of days ago? Surely they had made some headway? "You don't know about what, Destiny?" he asked, his tone a little stronger than he'd meant.

Destiny sounded like she may have been hurt by something. "Us, Adam I don't know if I want us right now," she confessed.

"Hmm, I see," he responded. He decided to remind her of that fact. Adam had been confused by her concern. Odd, he'd have expected her to be ready for something new since moving here. But that wasn't the case. His efforts to get her to talk to him hadn't worked. He'd tried everything. Whatever it was, it had him concerned about her. Adam sat on the edge of his king-sized bed, bowed his head, and prayed.

CHAPTER 14

Shaking almost uncontrollably, Destiny awoke to the sounds of shattering glass. Her nightgown was soaking wet and fear immediately gripped her when she saw pieces of glass scatter on the floor from her bedroom window. It was in that instant she saw what appeared to be the shadow of someone move quickly across her bedroom. Her whole body froze as she slowly turned her head in the direction that she saw the shadow move.

Not realizing that glass covered her bed until she felt a sharp, piercing pain on her cheek, her hand rose to touch the side of her face where it came in contact with a wet substance she assumed was blood. Refusing to yell, she slowly rose out of the bed to move to the door. Putting one foot down she felt a hand wrap around her ankle causing her to trip and fall on the floor. She yelled with all of the strength she could muster, but the hand on her ankle was so strong she couldn't move any further. She felt more pain as her knees came in contact with the glass on the floor. Terrified, her legs went into automatic kick mode. Using all of her power, she freed herself and she pulled her herself across the floor.

Then she heard it, the sound of Stanley's laughter, as he stood over her body. Reaching for her, he pulled her badly aching body toward him. His hand began to run through her hair as he snatched her head back to look her in the eyes. His nose was flaring like it did every time he'd ever gotten angry with her. Leaning down, he smelled her neck, then without warning, he bit her. Again she yelped out in pain, bringing no response from anyone in the house. Struggling, she tried to free herself from his grasp only to feel a slap across her face. His eyes were filled with the evilness she had become accustomed with while living with him. How did he find her? She could taste the blood from the cut on her face as it was pooling at the corner of her mouth.

Finally, she heard someone banging on the door. With a renewed sense of strength she twisted around to fight back. He must have heard the noise coming from the door as well because she felt his death grip on her arm release, and she collapsed to the floor. Looking up for a brief moment she saw her rescuer as he burst through the door.

Shaking the cobwebs from her head she looked again making sure her eyes weren't deceiving her. It was Adam! Praising God silently she didn't have time to figure out what he was doing in the house because Stanley rushed him, slamming his body against the doorframe. Frantically she began to scan the room looking for anything she could use as a weapon.

Catching Adam's eye she saw him shaking his head mouthing "no!" Then she heard his voice say, "This kind of demon can only be driven out through prayer and fasting." Something resituated in her spirit when she heard those words that gave her spirit a peace. She felt her body release the fear she was feeling.

In an instant her eyes stung from the light that flooded her room. Her eyes were blurred from the tears that had been falling but her nostrils were filled with the scent of roses, letting her know it was her aunt's arms that were gently rocking her back and forth. Her arms felt like dead weights as she stretched them out to wrap them around her aunt. A sigh of relief caused her body to relax even the more.

"Thank you, auntie." Time seem to stand still as she lay on her aunt's chest. She pushed back all of the negative vibes she'd been feeling during her nightmare. It felt so real but she couldn't help but to praise God that it wasn't. Something had to be done because her life was at a stand still and she couldn't move forward without getting some counseling soon.

CHAPTER 15

"Auntie Destiny?"

Destiny had to listen again because her name had been spoken so softly.

Taylor usually went to bed on time when Destiny baby-sat but not tonight. She seemed unusually restless earlier. It took a while but she had finally gotten her comfortable with watching a Disney movie, but now her eyes were drooping as her head was bobbing a little bit more, trying to stay awake. The pajamas she had on were adorable—purple with pictures of little dinosaurs all over them.

Destiny pulled her closer as she called her name, "what is it, precious?"

"I'm sleepy." A huge yawn escaped her as she tried to cover her mouth. "But I want my daddy to put me to sleep."

"He's still out with your mommy, baby." Destiny stood, scooping her up in her arms. "Let's get you to bed and when they get home, I'll tell them to come and say goodnight." Destiny started for the bedroom. "How does that sound?"

"You, promise?"

"Have I ever broken a promise to you?"

Taylor shook her head and then laid it back down on Destiny's shoulder. Destiny opened the door with one hand as she held on to Taylor with the other. Gently she pulled back the covers, lowering her into the bed.

"Now doesn't that feel better than sitting up on that sofa?"

"Yes." Taylor sighed before her eyes starting to close. Destiny had to wonder what her life would have been like if Tina and Richard had not been apart of it.

Her life had been nightmare living with Stanley—never knowing what she would do or say that would set him off. But she made up her mind that she was leaving after one of his brutal assaults left her in the hospital. It had been so terrifying and alarming that it almost left her deaf because he punched her so hard across the side of her face. Sara had broken down into tears when she saw her in the hospital bed.

But now, a year later, she was in a different state, changing her life for the better.

"Goodnight, Taylor." She gently rubbed her hand across her brow as she closed her eyes.

Small hands touch hers, grabbing her pillow as she pulled the covers up around her. Destiny patted the comforter as a last reassuring gesture and Taylor smiled.

As she walked back toward the living room, Destiny felt a sense of peace. She had made some tough decisions as a young woman but this one was a blessing. Taylor was a special child and one day she would have a family just as Tina did and she would love them with all of her heart. In her soul she knew that God had a plan for her life. Her faith was growing everyday. It was becoming as solid as a rock. So she knew that one day she would have this dream of children and marriage.

She checked the locks on all of the doors then settled down to finish watching the movie. Her cell phone began to ring and not wanting it to wake up Taylor she reached for it saying, "hello?" No one responded so she hung up and laid it on the arm of the sofa. Picking up the television remote, she turned off the television, and laying her head back she closed her eyes.

The chiming security system alerted her to the arrival of Tina and Richard. Sure enough she heard them giggling before she saw them. They must have had a great time because the happiness on their faces filled the room with joy.

Tina tossed her purse on the sofa and sat down next to Destiny.

"How did everything go?" she asked while struggling to pull off her shoes. Destiny watched Richard kneel down to assist her. He massaged each foot as he removed a shoe.

"Taylor and I had a great time together. She fell asleep in the middle of *The Princess and the Frog*."

Destiny couldn't help but laugh as she watched as Tina lay her head back on the sofa while Richard massaged her feet. "A girl could get use to this." She signed.

"How was your dinner?" Destiny inquired as she watched the interaction between the both of them.

"It was wonderful when no one was asking for his autograph." There was a hint of aggravation in her voice. "I don't think I'll ever get use to it but some people do respect our time."

God had blessed Tina and Richard tremendously. Richard's professional football career had provided them with a lifestyle that many people would never experience. They were not caught up in the lifestyle of the rich and famous. They both had a humbleness seen by all who came in contact with them. God had been gracious to both of them.

Destiny wondered where she would be today if she'd never gotten involved with Stanley.

"You seem to have a lot on your mind." Tina adjusted her body on the sofa.

"Is there something troubling you? You always get that troubled look when Stanley had done something stupid. Have you heard from him?" Destiny heard the concern in her voice.

"I'm not sure but I have been getting some harassing calls. You know calling and then hanging up." She watched the expression on Tina's face register some shock at that revelation.

"Well, I remember when I visited you two summers ago, and he was relentless in keeping tabs on you. Calling the phone every five minutes or so."

"If it is him I don't know how he found me." She ran her hands through her hair showing her frustration.

"Have you asked who was calling?"

"Yes, but I never get an answer. One time there was laughter but I couldn't tell if it was a woman or a man."

"Well, it could be some kids playing with the phone. Stanley has to know that it is officially over."

Destiny laughed when she saw Tina roll her eyes.

"And you're celebrating right?"

"And you know it!" She almost yelled but stopped herself before she woke Taylor.

"Don't worry, I'm not the same silly woman I was a year ago, full of fear. It's so over, I'm taking back everything the devil has stolen!" Glancing around the room, Destiny searched for signs of Richard.

"Where did Richard go?"

"He's pretty tired as well especially with spring training coming soon. He's been working out with some of his teammates. Probably just giving us some girl time."

"He's always been good to you." Destiny pulled her feet up on the sofa as she got more comfortable.

"I know. Everyday I thank God for him." Destiny loved to hear Tina talk of her love for her husband.

"Are you ready for your counseling to begin?"

The one thing Destiny didn't want to talk about was her past. Having to talk about the phone calls was enough.

"Oh, let's not talk about that now," she answered. "I should be asking you if you're okay." She noticed Tina rubbing her stomach, which had grown even larger with the baby.

Taking both hands she laid them across her swollen belly. Looking at her, Tina said, "We're fine. You're the one that looks like you haven't gotten enough sleep."

"I'm fine, things have been crazy at the lab but all is well."

She grabbed her bag and keys. "I guess I should go. If you all need me again just call." Bending slightly, she kissed Tina's cheek and rubbed her belly once more. "Good night, Tina." She motioned for her not to get up and went out the living room. Making sure she locked the door, she headed for the car.

She enjoyed spending time with Taylor. Leaving the subdivision, she turned onto Clifton Street taking a different route home. She'd learned that in one of her self-defense classes to never travel the same route. This was the first time since moving to Seattle that she actually put it to practice, but after all of the voiceless phone calls and dreams she decided tonight was a good time to start.

Shortly after turning onto the street, she noticed a dark sedan in her rearview mirror. If there had been any traffic to speak of she might not have noticed. But there wasn't. The car had followed her every turn since leaving Tina's house.

There was a Mervin's department store a few miles away so, she decided to stop there. She made the right into the Mervin's parking lot. Going inside would provide the opportunity to prove that the car wasn't following her. The idea that it was, she knew, was a bit over the top. She might not have thought anything of it but the self-defense class had mentioned never stopping in dark areas and choosing well-lit areas with heavy pedestrian traffic.

There was never a reason for her to use any of this, but there was no need to take the chance now. The car drove past slowly as she emerged from her car. She didn't recognize the make or model, but what was more important than that at the time was he or she had driven on. Destiny relaxed.

Inside the store, she strolled the aisles looking for nothing, giving herself time to relax her nerves before going home. Maybe it was nothing. She was making too much out of this.

By the time she pulled into the driveway, she was feeling better. There was a small shadow of something sitting on the front porch. She squinted into the moonlight and stopped the car. Looking around she saw no one so she got out. Someone left a package outside of the house.

Getting a closer look, she saw it was a small chest. A little timid about opening it, Destiny peaked under the lid. There was a Philip Stein watch with a note attached that read, "One-day at a time."

Wow, Adam Wheeler was special. Although she loved the watch the note had the most meaning.

CHAPTER 16

When he awoke, Adam did what he always spent time with God. He prayed, read from his book of meditations and his Bible, and then he went into the bathroom to start his day.

After he showered, he went into the kitchen to eliminate the hunger pains he was feeling. While eating his bagel and drinking a weak cup of coffee, he couldn't help but think about the fact that if he had a wife, leaving home without breakfast would be a thing of the past. He had learned to be cautious in relationships. It was best to start off slow. Taking another sip of his weak coffee, he wasn't really sure of what he was feeling at the moment. But there it was again. As he bit into his bagel the feeling occurred again, only this time his mind instantly thought of Destiny.

What would she think about him if she knew all of his truths? Would she be kind and understanding? Or would she high tail it out of his life, avoiding him at all cost? The shame of his past mistakes still hurt but it was no longer an opened wound as it had been before. The past couldn't be changed but it was forgiven, and he knew God had thrown it into the lake of forgetfulness. He was free from that demon now choosing to make the right choices was a weapon he'd come to rely on in his everyday life.

Getting up from his seat, he put his dirty dishes in the sink. After grabbing his briefcase, he headed to his car. When the garage opened he was greeted with a friendly reminder that he lived in Seattle. Rain was pouring from the dark clouds hovering over him. It wasn't the greatest weather for the Internet Café, he thought as he navigated through the wet streets. That was all the more reason for him to make it to his meeting at the church. Today would be another day of washing away someone's past. Sexual addiction was as serious and dangerous as any drug addiction. The Internet Café was saving lives of countless men, women, and families in his community. He didn't like the fact that he was once bound to it himself, but now seeing how God used his struggle to free others made it all worth going through. Every time someone was delivered, it socked the devil in the face. So the rain didn't damper his excitement about his monthly meeting. No, he didn't mind challenges; as a matter of fact he welcomed them.

After picking up his needed materials he exited his office on the way to his meeting. Turning the corner he caught sight of Alexander, the church secretary, talking to a young woman. After a closer look, he saw it was Destiny. She was hugging Alexander before she turned to enter the door across the hall. He knew that Elder Ford held her Healing Virtue meetings in that room on today. Had Destiny been in an abusive relationship? He didn't have time to ponder that thought long; he had people waiting on him in the Internet Café.

CHAPTER 17

Destiny didn't have time to focus on the fact that she'd just seen Adam because she needed to get to her meeting. The tables were all pulled together and she quickly found a seat. After checking her watch she realized that she was about fifteen minutes early. As she sat waiting for the meeting to start, several friendly people stopped to introduce themselves and shake her hand. Some even held short conversations and asked a few questions but nothing invasive. She continued to watch as the group of women followed what she assumed was their normal routine, opening with prayer followed by praise reports of those in attendance.

"As most of you know, my name is Elder Michelle Ford, and I am one of the pastor's assistants here at Greater Community. I'm over the Healing Virtue ministry for Domestic Violence. We started this ministry three years ago for the survivors and those dealing with domestic violence. I myself am a survivor."

After a slight paused and glance around the room, she continued. "It was my goal to help others who were trying to find their way out of the cycle of abuse be it verbal, physical, or emotional. It may seem like a dark tunnel, but it is one that can be conquered with the help of God. Currently, we have twenty-three women active in our recovery group, and a few of the women have husbands who are involved in our partner recovery group."

"Now let's take this time to go around the room and introduce ourselves." Destiny noticed how relaxed everyone appeared to be. Turning toward her, Elder Ford said, "Today we want to welcome our newest member."

Destiny trembled nervously at the obvious attention she garnered from all those in the room, but when it came to her turn, everyone had such kind eyes and there seemed to be nothing judgmental held in them, only a silent understanding. She introduced herself and turned to Elder Ford who gave her a nod, letting her know she could begin.

Destiny began speaking with caution at first, tightly holding the information packet she was given. "I have never been through any therapy, so this meeting is a blessing. When I was twenty-two, my life was in the pits because I was raped my senior year in college. Things went from bad to worse when I moved in with a man for all of the wrong reasons, thinking he was going to be my savior. My aunt knew something was wrong, but she didn't know how to help at the time."

She signed before continuing, "I didn't think I needed all of this." Using her hands she gestured around the room. "But I was terribly wrong. I always felt I could handle all of these emotions myself." Her voice quivered, "Even this is uncomfortable and I know I'm really putting myself out here but it doesn't matter now. I should have gone to the police back then after the rape. I feel really bad because if I had gone to the police, maybe I could have saved some girl from possibly going through what happened to me. Maybe now I can impact someone's life with my story of survival."

"Everything that went wrong after that rape seemed to be my problem, I was the troubled one, I caused the rape. I started blaming myself, falling into what I now know was depression. My roommate was a blessing when she decided to adopt my child. My life changed, all I wanted to do was move on with my life— so I graduated and got a job. I just wanted to escape. Move on, you know?"

She looked at the faces of the women in the room. "So I latched on to the first person that showed me interest. It was a downward spiral from there." The woman sitting next to her handed her a tissue.

"I found myself depending on him to make me happy, learning too late that in order to stay happy, something had to be happening. But on the day he first hit me, I knew this wasn't the life

I was suppose to be living." She wiped her face with the tissue. "Why is it that we have to be slapped and beaten to realize that?" As she glanced around, she heard other women saying, "Amen, sister," "I know that's right."

Continuing she said, "In actuality, he slapped some sense into me, and I thank God for that. It took three years before I realized I was going to die if I didn't leave. I started spending most of my time in my room. I had no friends, because he wanted it that way. It got so bad that I was using pills to sleep and pills to get up in the morning. I foolishly thought I would be able to change him, but it didn't work. So, I lost many of the friends I could have had because I refused to listen to their words of advise, and on top of all of that, my relationship with my aunt was going down the drain fast."

Not saying anything for a few seconds, she watched as the eyes in the room searched her face, understanding her plight. There were some nods from the group members, which seem to relax her a little as she continued speaking.

"Sure some of my friends told me I needed to leave Stanley and focus on saving my life. But I was focused on making our relationship work, and it was destroying me."

She could see everyone was listening intently to what she was saying; the expressions on the faces of the group changed from frowns to tears, letting her know they understood. Everyone in that room had been where she once was. But what pleased her most was when the group walked over to embrace her, letting her know that she was not alone and that they were there to help each other.

After she finished they went around the room and had a chance to reflect on what each of them had heard from other group members and anything else they wanted to share. At the very end of the meeting they all joined hands and repeated the Lord's Prayer. This was a powerful moment for her because it was the first time since her rape and the abuse that she felt a common bond with others who'd had similar experiences. She no longer felt alone, like it was just her fighting her demons without any help.

Elder Ford wrapped up the meeting, letting everyone know that they were expected back in two weeks with their journals in hand. Everyone exited the room with a sense of joy and pride in what had transpired. Elder Ford stopped Destiny on her way out of the meeting.

"I want to let you know how proud I am of you for sharing what you went through. I think it would be a good idea if we met one-on-one for a few sessions, how do you feel about that?" Elder Ford asked as they walked down the hall.

Destiny looked at Elder Ford before responding, "One of my close friends suggested the same thing. When would you be available to meet?"

Elder Ford smiled. "Well, how about Thursday at two o'clock? We can meet in my office?"

"I'll be here. Thanks, Elder Ford. I feel better than I have in a long time after today. I want to get my life back and move forward," Destiny said with enthusiasm.

Reaching around her back, Elder Ford gave her a squeeze, "With God, Destiny, all things are possible."

"Thank you, so much." And with that, Destiny headed out of the building.

CHAPTER 18

Destiny walked into Bible study on Wednesday evening with a new zeal for her life. She saw Adam's eyes as he looked out in the audience and saw her. Her insides did cartwheels as their eyes met. Then he looked down at his podium, she assumed getting ready for the lesson he would be teaching.

He opened the Bible study after a short prayer by saying, "Forgiveness is not a gift to another. It is a gift to you. In Matthew 6:12-15, Jesus says, 'And forgive us our debts, as we also have forgiven our debtors... For if you forgive others for their transgressions, your heavenly Father will also forgive you. But if you do not forgive others, then your Father will not forgive your transgressions.'"

Adam went on to say, "I once hurt myself so deeply by judging myself that I hated the man I had become, I began to say every day, 'I forgive myself for judging myself.' That part of me that was hurt sneered and said, 'Yeah, sure,' and turned its back on me."

It wasn't just Destiny who was being inspired by what was being said, but everyone in the sanctuary had his or her eyes riveted on Adam. He continued by saying, "It took three months for your pastor to really mean what he said. There was a small spark of joy inside my soul at that point. However, it took another three months to completely win over the judging-myself spirit so that it would support me again."

There was a chorus of amens coming from the congregation including hers, because it was just this week that she'd attended her first group meeting for her past abuse and already she had a sense of knowing that everything felt better even if it wasn't better yet.

She watched as Adam looked at his congregation. She could tell he was speaking from his heart because his eyes spoke volumes, even if he hadn't said a word from his mouth. She knew that the Lord inspired this lesson because she needed to forgive her father for not being in her life and all of those she blamed for what had happened to her in the past. As she looked around, she saw Kristen, the young lady who had been with Marvin at the restaurant. She had seen her on some Sunday mornings but never at a Wednesday-night Bible study. She seemed to be in deep thought as he taught.

"Think about your past," he said. "Was there ever a time when you did something, even unintentionally, that hurt someone? Often, we are unwilling to forgive others when their actions remind us of our own. Think of how you would have wanted others to forgive you."

Destiny knew that was it in a nutshell. How could she ever expect to give forgiveness if she hadn't forgiven herself? Thinking about it now, Destiny had been seven years old when she began to ask her aunt about her father.

"Auntie Sara, why don't I have a daddy like the other kids in my class?"

Sara looked at her with an odd expression. "Auntie, why are you looking at me like that?" She was scaring her.

Sara knelt in front of her, speaking softly. "Baby girl, all families are different. You know I told you about your mommy living with Jesus, right?"

Destiny had bounced those two braids in her hair, acknowledging her question. "Yes, ma'am."

"Your daddy loves you; he just had a lot of other responsibilities after you were born. So I kept you." Her auntie searched her face for some kind of understanding as she brushed one of Destiny's braids out of her face, wiping the lone tear that had fallen.

"But he's going to come for you one day real soon." She pulled her close in a hug.

Sara stood and kissed her on the forehead, giving her the doll that was lying on the floor beside her. As she walked out of the room, Destiny began to cry softly. So from that day until she turned fifteen, she asked her aunt about her father. But he never came. After a while she stopped hoping. And then she started hating.

She hated her mother for choosing to live with Jesus and not her and she hated her father for being so weak, not wanting to raise her.

Her aunt was good to her. She provided her with things other children didn't have at that time. She always got what she wanted. Sometimes she wondered how her aunt was able to provide for her after closing her club. But she always said her sister left plenty of money to take care of her only child.

Destiny shook herself out of her reverie. It had been years since she had thought of her father. She pushed the memories of her childhood back to her subconscious so that she could focus on Bible study.

But it was hard to do especially after going to her counseling with Elder Ford. She knew others saw her as a woman who was smart and confident, with a great career. But it was all a façade.

Inside she now understood she was still that little girl who wanted people to like her, always trying to please others in hopes that one day her father would return. She had always been the type of person people could depend on. It had worked until her senior year in college when she was raped and met Stanley. Before that people always told her how fun she was to be around.

Despite all that, she longed for reassurance. And now after her counseling she knew why she was having feelings of loneliness and of inadequacy. She knew that's why she felt like crying for no reason at all. She had tried to hide the reality from everyone, including herself, for all of these years. No matter what outer trapping of success she wore, inside, she was still the uncertain little girl whose daddy had left her with her aunt and had not come back.

Destiny watched as Adam took a sip from his water and placed it to the side. He looked out at the people who were in the room.

"I think this will help to put it all in perspective for some of you. It happened to me. I have made mistakes in my past that I'm not proud of."

Why was he looking at her? It was as if he saw right through her after that statement. Then he added, "Fortunately for me, growing up in a Christian household taught me the right way to ask for forgiveness. I have gone before God and my family, sincerely asking for forgiveness. I know that God has forgiven me, as well as most of my family. Isn't it sad that even now, some of my family members are not only unwilling to forgive but anxious to mention my past sins, my mistakes, over and over again? But it's funny how God works because sometimes he will show you that the person holding you in condemnation is guilty of the same mistake they choose to keep condemning you for. You have to decide to be at peace with them because you have done the right thing. Your prayer is that they will forgive you and no longer harbor any ill feelings so that they may move on. There is a saying: 'Acid is more destructive on the vessel in which it is stored than on the object in which it is poured.' I hope that they will learn to forgive and ultimately find their own inner peace."

Closing her eyes, Destiny began to pray like he had just told them in Mark 11:25, "Whenever you stand praying, forgive if you have anything against anyone, so that your Father, who is in heaven, will also forgive you for your transgressions." Destiny released tears as she prayed; they felt like a flushing out of all the things that were in her past.

From a pew in the back of the church, she watched Pastor Wheeler's eyes jolt between the congregation and Destiny Harper. She got the name from a very informative woman sitting next to her with nothing better to do than gossip. Fury coursed through her blood, making her hands shake and her pulse thud. How dare he pay that much attention to her with a church full of congregants? How dare he, especially with her in the audience? Although, he didn't know she was present. She'd been planning their reunion for over six months. Her body vibrated with anger as she remembered the way he'd looked at Destiny from the pulpit. His gaze had reflected such tenderness, making it glaringly obvious that he cared deeply about Destiny Harper. Her eyes flashed with heat. In her mind she hissed, *You Mr. Wheeler are, annoying the hell out of me.* She was jealous. She hated admitting it, but she was positively vibrating with it. She held herself, rocking backward and forward in her seat, her hands were clenching and unclenching wanting to hit something.

Destiny, she learned was running from her past, just the memory of her informant's sob story about her life made her want to roll her eyes. What kind of woman let a man walk all over her? She'd feigned sympathy when she listened to the woman give her the story, all the while wanting to laugh at the stupidity of the woman. If she had been in Destiny's shoes, Stanley Womack, corporate executive or not, would have hit her once and then she would have killed him. Shelton, her initial informant, had gotten her some details of her life, but what she really appreciated was getting Stanley's information.

She'd only struck up this friendship to find out more about Destiny. She must have had some issues because this young lady had met her in a domestic violence class. Within a few minutes, she'd pegged Destiny as dull and totally useless to Adam as a pastor—that was until she'd seen the way he had looked at her during service. After that, getting to know as much as she could about her had been less about curiosity and more about keeping her enemy close.

Soon she'd have Adam Wheeler where he should have been years ago—in her bed. But this attraction he had with this woman annoyed her as much as the realization that if she did not do something soon she'd lose him again. Adam needed a real woman, not a weak fool who ran from the first signs of trouble. He needed someone like her. It was time to take Miss Goodie-two-shoes out of the equation. A smile lifted the corner of her mouth.

Reaching into her purse, she pulled out her phone and quickly left the church. She found the contact number for Womack Corporation and hit "talk."

CHAPTER 19

The loud ringing of the telephone woke Cynthia up from her sleep. She'd left the maternity ward of the hospital hours ago because the twins and Taylor had started getting sleepy, and she knew they had to go to school the next day. She and Sara came home to put all three children to sleep. Taylor had a fit because she didn't want to leave without seeing her brother. But Sara promised that on the next day she would take her first thing.

Cynthia, finally shaking off her daze, picked up the receiver.

"He looks just like Richard."

Cynthia clenched her fist and raised it in the air, shouting, "Yes!"

Sara heard Cynthia talking loudly and sounding excited. She rushed from her room, asking, "So she had the baby?"

"A healthy baby boy, seven pounds and twenty-two inches long. She delivered at three thirty-six this morning. Baby and momma are resting fine."

She handed Sara the phone; they talked for a few minutes, and then she hung up.

Walking into the living room, Cynthia turned to Sara. "I'm so excited for Tina. There's nothing like being a mother." She placed her hands on her stomach.

"You want another baby, don't you? Can't say I blame you. Every woman wants a chance to experience motherhood. It's a gift from God."

Cynthia realized she expressed herself without knowing it. Sara had never given birth. "I'm sorry, Sara. I didn't mean to make you sad."

"Child, I'm not sad. The best thing that ever happened to me was Destiny. I loved her from the day she was born like she was my own. I promised my sister I'd watch over her little girl, and I did. Sometimes I wished she didn't have to go through so much pain. But I know it's all about to change. Pastor Wheeler loves my baby, and I believe in my heart she loves him. They just got to get through all of the mess in their past in order to see the blessing in their futures together. They'll be good for each other."

"I can say with confidence that you've been a blessing to me and the twins as well. They love you like you were their grandmother."

"But I'm not. Child, you got to do right by them babies. They need to know their father, and they need to know their grandparents," she said, looking sternly at Cynthia. Sara walked over to the sofa and joined her hands with Cynthia. "I know you love the Lord, and I know you know that nothing happens in the life of a believer that God doesn't know about. It wasn't an accident that you had those babies. It was God's providential will. God knew." Laughing and patting Cynthia's hand, she said, "He knows his children, doesn't he?"

"If that's the case, and I know that it is, I sure wish he'd let me know so that I could be prepared for what was going to happen next in my life," Cynthia said, shaking her head. "Sometimes I think God has an awesome sense of humor. He must laugh at us making a big to do about something he already has worked out." Wiping the tears, she reached for a tissue on the table.

Standing, Sara looked at Cynthia.

"I'm sleepy, and in the morning, there will be three little people looking for me to cook breakfast, so I'm going to sleep. Will you do me a favor? Put that letter on the table by the door in Destiny's bedroom; somewhere she will be able to see it. I thought she'd be here sooner, but since she isn't, she can get it when she gets in." And with that, Sara walked back to her room.

Cynthia continued to sit on the sofa for a few more minutes. She decided to pray before going back to bed. She got on her knees in front of the sofa. "Father God, I know everything that you do is perfect and good. I need your divine guidance to give me direction. I love you, Lord, and I trust you with every area of my life. Instruct me, God, on what you want me to do. I know you respond to our prayers in a variety of ways. You have used signs and your Word to teach me how to trust you more. God, let your will be done in my life and my sons' lives. In Jesus's name, amen."

With that, Cynthia began to feel a sense of peace. She got up to go to bed. Going to retrieve the letter for Destiny, she put it on her pillow, closed the door, went to her room, and fell asleep almost before her head hit the pillow.

CHAPTER 20

Destiny opened the door to her room at exactly five o'clock in the morning. She was tired, but she was happy for Tina and Richard. It felt amazing to have held her god-son. Throwing her handbag in the chair that sat by the bay window in her room, she caught glimpses of a new day peeking through the curtains. Turning around to prepare for bed, she saw an envelope lying on her pillow. Walking over to pick it up, she looked for a return address, curious because all she saw was her name written across the front. She sat down on the bed, tore open the envelope, and began to read.

> Dearest Destiny, my precious little girl,
>
> This is my last expression of love that I have for you. You see, I'm desperate for you to know me, your mother. If you are reading this letter, then it's safe for me to say that you're at least twenty-six. Happy birthday, my darling. I wish I were there to see you all grown up.

Destiny hadn't even thought about it with all of the excitement. Her birthday was today. She was twenty-six years old. She never thought about birthdays. Hers were always uneventful and had always come and gone quietly. But this year, her mother had remembered, and it brought sad, happy tears to her eyes.

> More than anything, I wish I could be there with you to celebrate your day, but our God had a plan for your life, just as he had one for mine. I loved you from the moment you were conceived. Your father and I were desperately in love with each other. We met, fell in love, and not long

after, we were married. It was a magical summer romance. So much had happened in such a short period of time, but for us, it was the most wonderful time of our lives. One day we were a couple of foolishly in-love young adults and the next, we were husband and wife.

I love you so much, darling. It was my decision to keep our relationship from Sara. You see, your father left me to go home shortly after we were married. It was his intention to come back for me. We were going to share our marriage with Sara. I planned a beautiful dinner, but he never returned.

Destiny couldn't believe what she was reading. It seemed that her mother's life had been as lonely and hurtful as hers. She fingered the pale yellow paper, softened by age. The envelope appeared to be aged as well with no date, just the signature of her mother. There was love that still radiated from the paper, despite the years that had obviously passed since it was written. She continued to read.

It wasn't until weeks later that he informed me of the death of, first, his mother, then his brother and sister-in-law, who were killed in a terrible accident. They had one beautiful boy, Shawn, and were expecting a daughter. Tina was the name they had chosen. She was kept alive even though her mom was in a coma.

The paper slipped from Destiny's hands. She couldn't believe the words she had just read. There was no way that this could be a coincidence. Could there really be another Tina and Shawn? Her senses were going haywire. Her hands began to tremble uncontrollably. She found herself rocking back and forth on the bed. The tears were flowing like a dam that had been breached.

Reaching down, she picked up the letter. The words were a blur because of the tears in her eyes.

> I know you're wondering why you were never told about them being your first cousins. Please forgive me. It was my choice. Your father wanted to tell Sara. You see, I loved Sara so much, and she had no one else but me. I couldn't let her lose you. I asked your father not to take you from her. So that's why you're with her and not him.

It was at this time that Destiny noticed the handwriting. The words seemed to be strung together, frantically, with barely a space between, as if the letter had been written in one furious burst of energy. Destiny wondered when her mother wrote this letter. Had it been right before her delivery, or had it been written while she was at the hospital? She had questions that only her mother knew the answer to, or maybe Sara could fill in the blanks of this mysterious letter that seemed to be filling in the gaps if her life. Looking back at the paper in her hand, she continued.

> Destiny, life is laughter and pain; it is hope and despair; it is truth, and it is lies, beautiful and ugly all at the same time. And through it all, I want you to choose your own path, be what you want to be, do what you want to do. Because whatever you choose, you'll still be my beautiful, precious child, and I will love you always. It is my promise to you this day, on your birthday that your life will change forever. Your father has a special birthday gift for you. He loves you, Destiny. He promised me that he would always be close to you and that he'd never be far away. He never broke a promise to me, so I know he will do as he promised. Remember, I'll always be there to cheer you on, whatever road you may choose to walk. When he comes to you, love him just as I did. Willie Brown is a good man,

and I'm sure he's been a great friend, but he'll also be a great father to you.

May life be kind to you, Destiny, and may the sun smile on you. May you always find love and care, and that you give it in double measure. You will always be my Destiny.

I love you,

Mom

Destiny hastily refolded the letter into thirds and tucked it back into the envelope. She noticed her hand shaking as she hurriedly smoothed the envelope over the paper. Destiny had grown up believing that her mother was unwed and that she was an accident. She had been wrong about her mother and father. They had been very much in love, and they both loved her. Someone in deep emotional pain had written this letter. Someone who had been literally sick with love for her baby and her husband had written it.

Sara would talk willingly enough about her mother's first dates or what life used to be like in Kingstree before the interstate highway arrived. Once in a while, Sara would reminisce about the early days of her life, and Destiny would get a brief, precious glimpse of her mother as a baby or young girl. But questions about Destiny's father were met with awkward silence. The past, she learned, meant pain. And the last thing Destiny wanted was to cause her auntie any more heartbreak.

The only safe memories, the only ones Destiny could ask about and get a smile from, were the stories of Sara and Margret's childhood in Kingstree. She'd told her of her parents' courtship but never the mention of a marriage. Her mother's story had made a powerful impact on Destiny, who grew up believing that love would eventually lead to a broken heart. She'd made her way unhappily through high school, where being smart disqualified her from popularity and her frizzy brown hair, acne-prone skin, and only reinforced her brainy image. Destiny was forced to believe that fairy tales she had read about rarely ever happened in real life.

It wasn't until college that she met her best friend, Tina Brown. She was someone not as socially awkward but just as grade obsessed as she was. Tina was the youngest child of two. Her Uncle Willie had raised her. Destiny now knew that was her father. It was odd because he had always been there for her. Every major event in her life during and after college, he had been around. He saw her transformation from an awkward bookworm into a polished woman, her unruly hair then smoothed from a perm.

As Destiny thought about Willie, she realized that Sara and he were one of the few constants in her life. Friends who didn't understand her nonstop work schedule had drifted away—all accept Tina. Her social life outside the office was nonexistent because Stanley had wanted it that way. But Willie had been around even then. Never did a month go by that she didn't see him. He was always in town for a conference or a meeting, but he always stopped in to check on her. They had even had lunch on several occasions. Uncle Willie, her father, was the only person who understood her ambition. Not only did he understand it, but he encouraged it. Willie never seemed to approve of Stanley; he always told her she could do better, and she now knew he was right. It was often that his hands carefully brushed the tears from her cheeks when she was sad or disappointed. She knew, even through the pain and grief, that she was loved and that she was safe. Yes, he had kept his promise to her mother.

Lying back down on her pillow, Destiny clutched the letter close to her heart. She had a family, a family that was close. She found herself drifting off to sleep with the sweetest thoughts she'd ever had in her twenty-six years of life.

CHAPTER 21

Lying in bed, Stanley couldn't keep the thoughts of Destiny at bay. He was getting anxious needing to get to Seattle. After receiving a phone call a week ago from some woman, he knew exactly where she was then with the help of his own private investigator it had been easy. She had to know he would find her. His private investigator had told him she was currently seeing someone. But he seemed to think that they were only friends for now. Seven months ago he was furious when he got home to find her gone. She belonged to him and he'd convince her to come back with him. He had been her rescuer and he'd make her think she owed him that much. After all when she needed a job he offered her one. It had been easy to persuade her to move in with him, giving her a maid. And he was the perfect playmate. He would have never hit her if she would have listened to him, but she always wanted to do things her way.

Marriage was something that was eventually going to happen. After his best friend Curtis married his old girlfriend, he had decided to go ahead and marry Destiny. But she was always going on and on about how he'd hit her and harassed her for no reason. So, she left. Now his like for her was replaced with all of the hate he had for Curtis. She would pay for walking out on him. Leaving him meant she never loved him. He would never forgive her for that. She would pay and suffer for the pain she had put him through. His need to find her grew stronger every day and he sometimes found it hard to concentrate on the things that were going on around him. Even his current girlfriend was driving him crazy, always talking about how much she loved him. Every night she wanted to go out and show everyone that she was his girl.

He got out of the bed, throwing the covers back over her. He hadn't wanted to hit her but she kept going on and on about why he hadn't professed his love to her. There was no way she was going to distract him from getting Destiny back. He told her to shut up but she hadn't listened. So he made her shut up the only way he knew how. But he wouldn't hurt Destiny this time if she did what he wanted. Then once he got her back to South Carolina he'd teach her a lesson that she wouldn't soon forget.

Moving into the bathroom he yelled and told his date to get up and get out. He heard her scurrying around his room like a scared little rat. The laughter bubbled up inside of him and he couldn't stop even after he heard her leave his house.

Destiny woke with a gasp, sitting straight up in bed. She felt a strange lurching in her stomach; it occurred often when she had a dream that involved Stanley. Her sheets were soaked in sweat, as was every inch of her skin. Shivering and fighting the urge to jump from the bed, Destiny curled up into a ball underneath her covers.

The dream had been so insanely real. It was always like that when she dreamed about Stanley. There was another kind of chill when she saw a copy of the letter on her bedside table she laid there looking at it with her emotions reeling. Spotting the clothes she had on yesterday, she must have just thrown them on the floor before getting into bed. She shook herself to forget the train of thought that she had been on because that train had a destination she didn't particularly want to arrive at.

She glanced out her window at the daylight. Then looking over at her phone, she felt a strange sense of déjà vu just before it began to ring.

Her heart began to pound in her chest. "Hello?" she whispered into the phone, her voice cracking.

"Good morning, Destiny. Happy birthday," said the voice she had heard often throughout the years. It was Uncle Willie. He'd been calling to wish her happy birthday since she met Tina in college.

"Thank you, Uncle Willie." Destiny wasn't sure if he knew about the letter. She assumed he was just calling like he did every year.

"I was wondering if it would be okay to come by later today. I have something for you."

Was this a coincidence? Destiny thought. "Yes, I look forward to seeing you," she responded quickly before letting fear of the unknown frighten her.

"Thank you, Destiny. I'll see you after lunch." With that, they hung up the phone.

Destiny knew she would have a busy day. Adam was coming to take her to dinner later, and she wanted to get her hair done. So she swung her legs out of the bed, getting ready for what would be an eventful day.

She was sitting on the couch in the living room, staring out the window, but her mind wasn't taking in the beauty of the summer day on the lawn or Auntie's roses. She was in deep turmoil from the phone call she'd received earlier. Her mind was tumbling like a dryer full of wet clothes.

"I've got your favorite—banana pudding," Sara said, sitting next to Destiny on the couch.

"I'm not hungry right now, Auntie."

"I wish I could do something," she responded quietly.

"I know you do, but you can't." Secretly she wished there was an easier answer. But there wasn't.

"You could…"

Destiny shook her head as her aunt was speaking. "I know I could just accept him and make everything better, but I'm afraid. He's always been Uncle Willie, and I don't know how we'll move past that."

"If you told him how you feel, surely he would—"

Destiny shot to her feet. "Like I told Tina and Richard when they called earlier, I'm not sure if I'm ready for this next chapter in my life."

"You can't walk around feeling this way, Destiny. You have to talk to him," Sara said sagely.

Destiny wrapped her arms around her midriff, walked over to the window, and then turned to face her aunt. "You don't understand. You should have told me."

The doorbell rang before Sara could respond, slicing through the quiet house. Destiny walked to the door, wiping tears away from her cheeks, and reached for the doorknob clumsily. Then she went still. She dropped her hands, fumbling with them at her side. "Hi Uncle Willie."

After twenty-six years, Willie stood, looking at his daughter meekly. Tears were forming in the corners of his eyes. His aging crow's feet stood proudly around his eyes.

"Destiny…" he whispered, his voice resonating deep sorrow. He realized no one knew the depth of the grief she felt.

Destiny stood calmly, her hands reaching to open the door wider for his entrance. In actuality, she wanted to wrap him in her arms. She had so many questions that needed to be answered. Desperation made her step back to watch as he hesitated slightly before taking an uncertain step through the door.

He turned, angling his eyes at her. "How are you?" He handed her a bouquet of flowers.

Taking the flowers, Destiny turned to walk into the living room with Willie following close behind. She turned, meeting his eyes.

"I'm fine, considering..." Destiny told him mechanically. She turned to face him, her hands nervously fumbling with the flowers in her hands. Looking down at the roses, she said, "You remembered my birthday as always."

"Yes, always." Willie turned look around the room. He settled himself into the nearest chair. She was sadly surprised to see the distress in his eyes. He looked defeated, almost helpless, at this moment. She had never seen him in this manner. On most occasions, he was a pillar of strength. This was a side of Uncle Willie she'd never seen.

"I know you're a little shocked by all of the revelations in the letter."

"You know about the letter?" Destiny asked.

"Yes, I know. Sara told me several years ago."

Destiny folded her arms across her chest. "I really don't know what I am. I guess shocked would be a start," she muttered. "You really can't know how I feel. You've always known me as your daughter, but to me you have always been Shawn and Tina's uncle Willie."

He looked away, ashamed of the decision he and her mother made all those years ago. He was noticeably upset as he stood and paced the room a couple of times before he came back to stand in front of her. He held her look for endless seconds. "Destiny, your mother and I...we made a decision so many years ago. We didn't plan it out well. Our only concern was what would be best for you and your aunt," he said on a long breath, his voice fading away as his eyes traveled the room. Obviously, seeing the pictures of his beloved Destiny and her mother around the room had to be difficult for him. Destiny stood looking at him in silence. His gruff admission of guilt stirred her deep inside. She could tell it was unfamiliar territory for him.

Her eyes dropped from his, a frown pulling at her forehead. "But what about me?" The words tumbled out of her mouth. "What about all of the things I had to endure because you were not in my life?" The anger she felt was evident in her voice. "Why couldn't you have told me when I got older? Why weren't you there for me? What about all of the pain, the hurts, the disappointments in my life? Why weren't you there?" The words were falling out of her mouth on their own accord.

He didn't respond, but sat back down. Destiny sat down beside him, crossing her arms in front of her as she tried to gain her composure. It was the pain of abandonment that she was dealing with at the moment. That pain went back as far as she could remember. Her parents had made the decision for her to be raised by her aunt. She was given to Sara to help ease the pain of her mother's abandonment. In reality, she had been a pawn to right the wrong that her mother and Uncle Willie felt was done to Sara. It simply came down to that.

They sat in silence for an enormous amount of time with the memories and pain between them. At this moment, Destiny didn't know what to say. She didn't know how to say anything.

Willie drew in a sharp breath he'd gotten enough courage to respond and turned to look at his daughter. "I know you're disappointed, Destiny, and I can't really blame you. But just so you know, I shared more of your special occasions than you know about, always sending a card for your birthday along with making deposits into an account that my lawyer established for you. I was there when you were six at your first ballet recital, sitting in the back of the room—in the very, very back. I was nervous when you won your first spelling bee. I believe the word was *harlequin*, if I still remember correctly. You paused for a few minutes at first, but I cried when you spelled it correctly." He chuckled to himself, looking out as if he were seeing a movie of the event.

"I was at your piano recital when you were sixteen, and you told everyone before playing you weren't the best, but this was your favorite song, Sonata No.13 in Eb-Major, Op.27, No.1 Ludwig Van Beethoven and after that, it became my favorite."

Willie watched her eyes dance with surprise at these revelations. "I was and have always been proud of you. But I have never been as proud as I was on the day of your graduation from high school. You were simply beautiful. On your first day of school, you dragged your book bag because you didn't want to put anything on your Barney shirt."

Destiny couldn't help but smile. The realization that her father had been there for every special event gave her cause to believe he hadn't abandoned her. Maybe they had made a bad decision about who would raise her, but she had a father now. She just had to decide how to handle it from here on out.

"Aunt Sara told me that my mother died giving birth. Were you there?" Destiny had to know if he could fill in the blanks to her life. She looked at him with a sense of hope in her eyes. "When was the last time you saw her?" She patiently waited on him to respond.

"The last time I saw her was on the day you were born," he answered, slowly coming out of his shock at the question. "I had gotten the news of my mother's death. Then I had to deal with my brother and his wife's death; it changed all of our lives. His wife was pregnant with Tina, who we were able to save. It was too much for me to bear at first. But your mother was my saving grace. We didn't know it at the time, but she was pregnant as well. It was a lot for a young doctor. She seemed fine. I had no idea that in nine months she'd be gone."

His eyes were glazed over in memories of the past. "I loved her with all of my heart. When the doctor called me to inform me she was in labor, I cancelled everything to get there. She saw me standing at the door. I heard her tell Sara to take care of you."

She saw the way he was destroying himself now, slowly and painfully, and she nearly cried at hearing it. He was her father, whether she wanted to accept it or not. He loved her mother, and he was here now, saying that he also loved her.

"Willie, I love you because you have been a part of my life as an uncle for a while," she whispered, her heart breaking as the words came from a place deep inside.

His eyes froze on her. She hoped he realized that what she had felt was the idea of not being abandoned by him. She wasn't ready to call him "Dad" just yet, but maybe one day she would. He had hurt her, although the counseling she was receiving had helped. But she was still in the healing process. Today was a good day. At least now they'd both started the healing process.

Destiny watched as he seemed to struggle with old demons from the past. Silently she prayed. *Father, I bind every devil that's trying to come against this unity that you are trying to establish with Willie and me. Loose us in the name of Jesus and let the blood of Jesus come against Satan and cast him back to the pits of hell where he belongs! In the name of Jesus, amen.* She had been to only one deliverance service since being at Greater Community, and she hoped that short prayer for her father would suffice.

"I was angry at you for so long because I thought you'd abandoned me and my mother," she admitted, trying to give him time to decipher the words she was saying. "And as we stand here, I can't say for sure that I'm totally free from all of it, but since I've been here in Seattle, things have begun to change. Since I've been born again, I'm learning that the blood, grace, and mercy of Jesus covers a multitude of sins; it heals and delivers.

"Yes, maybe you were there for me behind the scenes, but I didn't know it. I had no way of knowing that you were there. But Jesus is different. I know he's always there because he reminds me in his Word that he will never leave me nor forsake me. All I can say for today is thank you, for being my unseen helper."

Destiny swallowed, holding back the tears that were threatening as she spoke from her heart. "God has done some wonderful things in my life. I've got so much to be thankful for. Everything has changed for me. Now I know God always loved me, even when I thought I was unlovable because of all the negatives that were in my life. I now know that God's love is complete, and it makes me the whole woman he wants me to be," she said, her eyes shining with tears.

He pinned her with his gaze. "The person you described before sounds like the man I used to be before I met Jesus," Willie said as he shifted in his seat, leaning forward to look directly at her. "What I'm trying to say is that when three of the most important people in my life died in the span of a month, I didn't know why God didn't just let me die. I wanted to, but he had other plans. I was left with a newborn baby girl who needed to know that someone in this world loved her and a nephew who was grieving for his parents and grandmother. Then I had to deal with the loss of both of my girls, your mother and you. It was too much for one person to bear without the strength that only God can give us. It was after I came to know him that I fully understood what Paul was saying when he said, 'When I'm weak that is when I am strong.'"

His heart was so full of gratitude for the second chance he had been given with his only child. Standing to his feet, he reached to wipe the tears that had fallen down her face.

"You and your mother were the best things that have ever happened to me. I watched you graduate from high school, go to college, and graduate at the top of your class. You have a wonderful career as a chemist, and you are the most beautiful woman in the world to me. You're my daughter, and I am and shall always be proud of the woman you've become."

Destiny watched the emotions that played across his face. His expression was crestfallen. She didn't know how or when she began moving, but before she could reconsider anything, she had her arms around her father, holding him for dear life. She was home at last in the arms of her earthly father, and they were both wrapped in the comforting arms of their heavenly father.

Willie wrapped his arms around his daughter in a way that he had never done since she came into his life through Tina. He held on to her with dear life. *This is what home feels like*, he thought. *This is what having a daughter feels like.* He didn't want the embrace to end, but the ringing of the doorbell drew them apart.

Smiling, Destiny whispered, "I love you," before turning to answer the door.

CHAPTER 22

When she opened the door, she saw the worry in his eyes. Adam scanned her face for verification that she was okay. He reached out and brushed a strand of hair from her face, his eyes compassionate and concerned. Destiny fell into his arms, clinging to him with all of her strength.

"Destiny?" He pulled back to look in her eyes. "Are you all right? I've been praying all morning. The Lord wouldn't let me stop praying. When I felt a break in the spirit, I rushed here as quickly as the law would allow. Are you okay?"

"I think I am," she said slowly, leaning into the comfort Adam offered. His eyes left her face to look at the gentleman standing behind her. Destiny sensed that her father was watching by the way Adam's hold on her relaxed. He recognized Willie from the hospital. She swallowed before placing her hand in his, leading him toward her father.

"Adam Wheeler," she said slowly, watching the two most important men in her life. "I would like for you to meet my father, Willie Brown."

Both men appeared relaxed. Reaching out, Adam shook Willie's hand. "It's good to see you again, Dr. Brown. I didn't mean to interrupt anything." Adam turned to look at Destiny. "I just wanted to make sure Destiny was all right. She was weighing heavy in my spirit."

Reaching out, Adam pulled Destiny close to him. He captured her hand in his, and Destiny allowed him to pull her close. She loved that his touch felt so right.

"Thank you for caring about my daughter." Willie reached for her other hand, slowly lifting it to place a feather kiss on the back. He lifted his eyes, seeing the smile in hers. "She is precious to me." He let go of her hand, relaxing for the first time since arriving at the house. He returned to the chair he had been occupying.

"I feel the same way about you, Uncle Willie." She said it so softly that he barely heard her.

Reaching beside the chair, he lifted a bag, extending it toward Destiny. "This is a gift from your mother and me. I've saved this for your twenty-sixth birthday. I pray that you will be blessed by its contents."

Destiny reached for the bag with trembling hands.

Willie sighed, rubbing his hands down his wearied face. "I have so much to make up for, Destiny. This is only the beginning. God will continue to show me how to repair the damage that has been done. I hurt you for too long, and I had to come today."

"We all messed up, Willie," Destiny said, surprising herself.

Willie stood and reached for her. He held on, looking her in the eyes. "And the thing that is so awesome about our heavenly Father is that he doesn't make mistakes. He knew this day was coming."

She held on to him, making sure she had his attention. "I'm not saying that I'm perfect in all of this, but what I do know is that God forgives, and because he forgives, it cleanses us from all of our sins. We are redeemed, and he loves us. He didn't cancel us; we still have a lifetime of seasons to go through." She smiled with a small laugh of humbleness.

Unknown to Destiny, Adam watched her with excitement in his eyes. A smile touched his lips. He was falling for his dear friend—her sparkling eyes and warm, laughing spirit. Yes, she just might be the one. This was the real thing, and God just confirmed it as she ministered to her father. At that moment, the thing he wanted to do most in the world was to kiss her to seal the promise of their future, but he didn't know if the time was right, not wanting to ruin their growing relationship.

Father, give me patience for our time. I don't want to mess this up by rushing her. She's been hurt too much already, and I don't want to be added to the list of people who hurt her. He looked over at her while she talked to her father. *But you know I could love this woman.*

"Destiny."

The simple way Adam said her name caused her to turn around from the conversation with her father. Adam reached out and gently turned her to face him. "I'm going to get out of here and let you have this time with your dad. I'll be back later for our date."

"I'm sorry, Adam. It's just that there's been so much going on today." Sighing, she looked at him, making sure he was okay with leaving now.

"No, I understand. I'm looking forward to our date later this evening."

Whispering, Destiny replied, "I can't wait either."

All of the energy had evaporated out of Destiny, and she let him hold her, comforted by his embrace having no desire to pull away. Placing a soft kiss to her forehead, he looked in the direction of Willie.

"Dr. Brown, it was nice seeing you again. I hope to see you again real soon and often." After saying his good-byes, Adam turned toward the door.

"I'll see you this evening," she said before gently closing the door.

"Hey, listen," Willie said, "I've tied up most of our day, and it sounds like your young man has plans for the both of you tonight." Willie was getting up from his seat. "We have plenty of time. I promise I'm not going anywhere. Go get your hair done on me," Willie said, putting some money in her hands.

Running her hands through her hair, she responded, "Are you saying that this hair is not perfectly styled?" Patting her hair, Destiny laughed, putting a smile back on her face. "You're serious?"

"Of course I'm serious. I could tell this date means a great deal to you."

"That means I have to leave now," she teased.

"I want you to always be happy. It means more to me than anything in the world."

She felt her heart flutter, suddenly nervous. "Do you think he's really interested in having a serious relationship with me?" she asked, figuring a father would be the perfect person to answer this question.

"If he isn't, then he sure has fooled me, and I don't fool that easily. Now I'm going to go. Thank you, Destiny, for allowing us to have this time together."

CHAPTER 23

Walking with her bare feet across the floor, Destiny was happy for the first time in years. Her father had given her a picture of himself and her mother for her birthday. It was taken on their wedding day. They were both standing on the porch of a beautiful Victorian home; it was a wonderful gift. She made her way into the bathroom, reaching for her favorite bath gel, and filled the bath with silky liquid. Destiny turned on the faucets in the tub, adjusted the water temperature, and then poured an additional splash of the gel into the bath. The space was filled with the scent of jasmine. She stripped off her clothes, leaving them in a heap on the floor. Before stepping into the tub, she pressed a button on the radio on a nearby shelf then slid into the lukewarm water and sat down. Her lids came down as she closed her eyes, willing her mind blank.

It was five minutes before six, and Destiny stood back, eyeing herself critically in the mirror. The elegant yellow sundress with its spaghetti straps flowed around her legs. She relished the feel of the silk against her skin. She adorned her earlobes with pearl earrings that matched the tiny row of buttons down the back of her dress. Turning first one way and then the other in front of the mirror, she tried to decide what Adam would think about the dress.

A knock on the front door brought her out of her daydreaming. It was followed by Sara's voice. "Destiny, are you ready? Adam is here looking handsome."

"He is so punctual. Thank you, Sara." She smiled, running her hands down her dress. "I'm so nervous."

"Well, if it's any consolation, he looks just as nervous." She chuckled to herself.

"Tell him I'll be out in a minute. I have to put on my shoes." She slipped into the shoes she purchased to match her dress and grabbed her purse, giving her long curls a toss that sent them cascading down her back.

Adam was watching her as she entered the room. He was lounging comfortably on the sofa; mesmerized it seemed by her appearance. Standing, his gaze drifted downward to her long, bare legs. She smiled as he noted the pink color on her toes in a pair of gold sling-strapped, high-heel, silk-covered sandals. She also hoped he liked the sundress she wore because she loved the way the silk fabric skimmed her curvy body, ending at her knees.

Destiny suppressed a sigh when she gazed at Adam in his tailored gray suit with a two-button jacket. This Adam her friend and pastor with his gorgeous face, killer smile, and bedroom eyes and voice. Destiny felt as if the spirit of the Lord had reached into her chest and gently squeezed her heart, making her nervous, saying, "This is the one."

He opened his arms to her without comment for a few seconds before saying, "Hello again. And might I say you look extraordinary tonight." Leaning over, he pressed a kiss to her cheek, his warm moist breath sweeping over her earlobe as he whispered those words.

Destiny's hands settled around his waist involuntarily, resting against his sides. Closing her eyes, she breathed in the warmth and intoxicating scent that was exclusively Adam Wheeler. Releasing him, she picked up her small shoulder purse from the chair and her keys from the table. "I'm ready."

Adam took her hand, squeezing her fingers as they descended the porch steps. Opening the passenger-side door, he waited until Destiny was seated on the black leather seat. As he strode around the car to the driver's side with his usual grace, it struck her that Adam looked handsome in his suit. Even though she'd seen him in many suits, this one was different. She was sure it was tailor-made. Adam epitomized the grace of the Lord and always worked at presenting the proper image. To Destiny, it seemed to never come naturally, but having this new sense of self-awareness gave her the confidence she needed.

Adam seemed to sense her thoughts. Reaching out with his right hand, he took hers. His touch was comforting, nonsexual, and nonthreatening. She looked at him and smiled, noticing how his eyes crinkled attractively as he winked at her, making her insides do somersaults. He didn't remove his hand, and she didn't ask him to. It wasn't until he maneuvered into a large public parking lot adjacent to the Edgewater Hotel that he removed his hand. The Edgewater was one of Seattle's finest hotels, showcasing the Elliott Bay, Puget Sound, and the Olympic Mountains beyond. He retrieved his jacket and then came around the car to open the door for Destiny. She placed her hand in his outstretched one. Tightening his grip, he assisted her with getting out of the car.

Curving a free arm around her waist, he pulled her closer. "Thank you for spending your birthday with me."

Lowering her gaze, she stared up at him through her lashes. "Thank you for asking me to share it with you. This has been the perfect birthday so far."

"I hope you don't get seasick because my plans include that ship docked just on the other side of that pier," he said, breaking the spell she had on him.

"What time do we sail?" she asked, looking in the direction of the ship.

"Not until seven thirty, but we can board anytime between six thirty and seven fifteen for cocktail hour."

Adam glanced at the watch hidden beneath his French-cuffed shirt.

"We can board now because it's six forty-five." He escorted Destiny up the gangplank of the extraordinary ship *Pictorial*. The beautiful sounds of a saxophone greeted them as they were having their names checked off the reservation list. They were escorted into the main salon, Destiny took the opportunity to take in the elegance of the ship. There was soft lighting, cloth-covered tables, burning candles, and beautiful flower arrangements on each table. The mood had been set for a romantic evening of gourmet eating and long hours of dancing.

As soon as Adam made sure she was comfortable in her seat, he took his and picked up the menu. The dinner selections featured everything from Dungeness crab and shrimp cake with lobster lemongrass sauce. Adam knew all of it would be a delight to both his and Destiny's taste buds. One thing was for sure: it was more than both of them could eat in one sitting.

"I hope your appetite is in mint condition this evening because everything sounds delicious, and this is a five-course affair."

She picked up her menu, glancing at it for a few minutes. "If I eat all of this, you will be going with me to the gym for the next six months."

"No problem. After we eat, we'll go upstairs and exercise those beautiful legs of yours while burning off calories at the same time."

She blushed at the comment and gave her dinner partner a smile over the menu in her hand.

"You've got yourself a deal. I love to dance."

Adam and Destiny spent the next ninety minutes talking about everything from the visit by her father to the upcoming events at Greater Community. They shared a bottle of Flora Springs Trilogy while listening to the soft sound of a live saxophone player that enhanced the romantic atmosphere in the dinner area.

After her first glass of Trilogy, she couldn't remember the last time she'd felt so relaxed. When the waiter came to refill their glasses, they both declined, not wanting to overindulge. She forgot about all of the years that she spent her birthday alone. There was something so powerful and compelling about the man sharing the same space with her that caused her to lower the walls that she'd built up so many years before with Stanley.

Touching the corners of her mouth with a napkin, she placed it on her plate. "I can't eat another morsel."

"Are you sure? What about the crème brulé we talked about earlier?"

Shaking her head, she said, "If I ate another bite, you would be rolling me around on the dance floor."

He inclined his head to acknowledge her surrender before touching the sides of his mouth with his napkin. "Are you ready to dance off those calories?"

A sensual smiled softened her lush lips. "Yes."

He came around the table and pulled out her chair. They joined hands as they headed for the upper deck. There was a DJ who had a variety of music, replacing the sultry sounds of the saxophone.

Encircling her waist, Adam led her out on the dance floor to join the other dancers. Closing her eyes, Destiny was glad this song was slow enough for him to pull her close; she reveled in the feel of his body next to hers.

Destiny felt the strength of Adam's arms and felt the slow, rhythmic beat of his heart, and at the moment, all she wanted to do was let her body melt against his. This man was the most precious man she'd encountered in her life. His presence made her think about herself outside of all the mistakes she'd made or all the negative things that had happened to her.

Then without warning she pulled away from him. Closing her eyes, she stood there, embarrassing herself in the middle of the dance floor. Dumbfounded, Destiny stared wide-eyed at Adam. For no reason at all something about the way he moved on the dance floor brought back a memory of Stanley. Only thing this wasn't Stanley. This was Pastor Adam Wheeler, a quiet, laid back type, not a bossy, outspoken guy who made demands of her. She thought of returning to her seat, but when Adam pulled her back toward him she lost herself in the music.

"What was that all about?"

Her eyes flew open, causing her to miss the next step. She wondered how long he had been gazing at her. She fell back into the rhythm of the dance.

"I let a memory of something throw me off. But I'm good now. You are a really good dancer."

"I have many talents besides preaching and teaching God's Word, Destiny. You have only seen a few, but if you give me the chance I want to share all of them with you," he whispered against her ear.

"I'm not sure if all of this was a good idea." She sent him a frustrated look as he grasped her hand.

Suddenly they were both serious. They stared in each other's eyes for a long moment.

Adam spoke first, "Look, I'm not trying to pressure you into anything, and I'm by no means perfect. There are a few things you may not like about me after you find them out."

She turned away from him just for a second, "I'm sure they are no worse than some of mine."

She turned to walk away from him just as the tempo of the music changed, becoming more upbeat and allowing both of them to distance themselves from each other.

Grabbing her hand, he pulled her back toward him, "Can you step?" he asked as he dropped one hand and took the other.

"I've been stepping since I was four. Sara taught me." Then she pulled away, moving to the rhythm of the music as she made her way back to him.

Adam swung her out, releasing her, and everyone stared as she used her dress to sashay back to him. Tiny beads of sweat left a glistening sheen over her beautiful caramel skin, and everyone took notice as she moved around Adam like a professional dancer.

The night was going too good, Destiny thought as she leaned against Adam on the upper deck as the pier came into view. Resting her head on his shoulder, she looked up at him.

"Honestly Adam, do you think all of this is a good idea?"

"You're kidding, right? This is a great idea." Using his hand he pointed to her and himself. He wanted to answer for her and say every day for the next fifty years, before she replied.

She shrugged a shoulder. "Maybe for you but my life is just getting back on track."

"What are you trying to tell me?"

She looked directly at him. "That we may be moving too fast, and I'm just starting my counseling. Are you prepared for what I might become after I've come through all of it?"

"Yes, I am. Friends can ask friends out right?" He didn't hesitate. His eyes searched her face. He so wanted Destiny to feel comfortable with him.

"I guess." When she looked up at him he tried to hide his frown.

"Listen Destiny…" he shook his head lost for speech. "For a friendship to develop we have to spend time together."

The frown didn't leave his face. He turned around looking out over the pier. She turned to look out as well.

"Destiny, it's one thing to get counseling, but that shouldn't stop your life. I thought we were moving in the right direction. But now you act like I'm the bad guy."

She looked at him, "What are you trying to say?"

"By all means I think you should get counseling. Lord knows it's helped me."

"Adam I appreciate your opinion, but this is about me and although you've had your own challenges, I've got to get through this the best way I know how."

He watched her as she looked directly at him, her eyes watering. "But when I told you I had some serious issues in my past, I meant it. Even today you saw my father reenter my life. It's all a lot right now. So excuse me if I feel overwhelmed."

"Destiny…"

"Don't say another word, please, Adam, and I mean it. I don't want to get angry and make this night any worse than it is right now," she said. "I appreciate your help tonight, but I don't appreciate being patronized by someone who has no idea what they're talking about when it comes to me."

"I'm simply pointing out that sometimes we let our past keep us in bondage. We all have a past and yes yours may have been difficult, but life can go on, is all I'm saying."

There was a cold, hard edge to his voice. He wasn't pleased with his reaction to what she was saying.

Her voice was low and controlled as she said, "This was suppose to be the best day and night of my life but look at us now." Adam watched as she wiped a tear from her face before continuing. "I'm not going to stand here and listen to you tell me what I can't do and what I don't know."

She turned around headed back into the dining room of the ship.

"I'll be at our table if you want to finish our date."

"Destiny…"

She ignored him as she walked past other guest on her way to their table.

Adam admonished himself and went after her. He caught up with her just as she was going to open the door to the dining room.

"Adam…" She tried to pull the door open but he didn't budge.

"I'm sorry, okay? I was out of line."

She looked at him her eyes had a cool stare. She wanted something more from him. Maybe an explanation for his insistence about their relationship would help.

He dropped his arms and took a step backward. He had no idea what to tell her. So many things were running through his mind. He'd picked her up tonight feeling proud and happy and triumphant for her. It was her birthday and in actuality she had received a perfect gift in the return of her father. He wanted to add to her happiness, but had gone about it wrong. All he wanted was for her to be happy and not see the pitfalls and disappointments lying in wait for her. Destiny was smart and resourceful, her life as it was had proved it. At least what he knew of it, but she didn't want him to be apart of her life at this moment. She didn't understand that sometimes it didn't matter what you did or how much you tried, some things couldn't be fixed with counseling alone. You needed friends who cared about you as well.

"Listen Destiny, I was a cyber porn addict. I know about counseling. I've been through it," he said.

God, he hadn't meant for that to come out. And since when did he sound like a grade school boy being disciplined by his mother?

Destiny stared at him for a long while with a look of shock and disbelief.

"But..." She blinked. "How? Is this the struggle you make reference to sometimes when you're ministering?"

"It's been three years ago. But I attend and teach a counseling group."

She shook her head, her eyes wide. "I didn't know. I knew something had occurred, but I had no idea."

He smiled grimly. "As much as I would have loved to tell you about this another way, it happened I'm not proud of it, but even in my darkest hour I needed family, friends, and counseling. It took me two years to get out of that dark pit in my life. But with the help of God and all of the resources around me, I was able to do it."

She mouthed something he couldn't interpret in the dimness of the corridor.

"I had a tremendous amount of support and a whole church of loving congregants praying for me," he said.

"But you're a pastor. How did you get involved in cyber porn? Guys like you are suppose to be good. You have such a powerful word from God in your mouth."

He didn't even know how to begin explaining his failure, the distance that had grown between him and the Lord, the anger as a result of it. He couldn't even explain his constant dissatisfaction with himself, the humiliation, and embarrassment of it all. He didn't fully understand it himself. He'd known it was wrong, a sin, but he hadn't comprehended the lengths it would drive him down a road that he had to fight to turn around on.

"Adam, I'm so sorry."

Suddenly her arms were wrapped around him, her cheek pressed to his chest, and her arms around his back, holding him close to her.

"I'm so sorry you had to go through that, but I'm also proud of you."

For a moment he stood very still. It felt good—her holding him like this.

He'd had female friends in the year since his deliverance, but no one had held him like they cared. Like she was holding him now. He wrapped his arms around Destiny wanting her to care about him like he cared about her. They were at a crossroad and he didn't know how it all was going to work between them, but he had to try. He wanted her. He hadn't realized how much until this minute. She could be his sounding board, his cheering squad, his devil's advocate and faithful sidekick. No wonder he'd been thinking about her so much lately. No wonder she'd been in his dreams.

Before he changed his mind he blurted out, "Go with me next week to a one-night conference in Tacoma, Washington."

She swallowed a nervous laugh. "You're kidding, right?"

He sobered just as quickly as she asked the question. "No, I'm not. I want you to accompany me if you don't have any plans."

Destiny was shaking her head, but she was really cautious as to why Adam was asking her to go with him.

"I don't know, Adam. What would people think?" She looked at him with concern in her eyes.

"Destiny, this is not about us sneaking off to do something that we could do right here in Seattle. I have to preach in Tacoma and I want you there with me. It will also give you the chance to be with me in a setting other than at Greater Community. We could make a day of it, returning late Wednesday evening."

Rising on her tiptoe, she kissed his chin. "I don't know, Adam. It's so soon. Can I think about it and let you know?"

Gathering her closer, he buried his face in her long, fragrant hair. "Of course you can, but you don't have to worry. We'll have separate rooms. It would be a blessing to me if you were there, and it would give us a chance to get to know each other away from here."

She smiled. There was no doubt he wanted her to feel comfortable traveling with him. "I'll let you know as soon as possible."

Curving a hand under her chin, he raised her face to his. Pulling back, Adam looked her in the eyes.

Destiny studied his expression, wondering if he thought she was too forward. Her heart was beating so fast.

"Happy birthday, Destiny."

"Thank you, Adam." And she had enjoyed herself up until this moment. She had grown to understand more about Adam than she anticipated for one night.

"How about us having breakfast at my place tomorrow?" He looked at her with a soft expression. "I want to spend as much time as I can with you this weekend."

She looked at him puzzled. "Can you make an omelet?"

"Yes."

"What else do you eat for breakfast?" She couldn't resist asking him the question.

"Muffins," he said while brushing a strand of hair that had fallen out of place.

"What time is breakfast?"

"Let's make it brunch. Is eleven too late?"

"No."

With brunch being at eleven, it would give her enough time to go over to visit with Tina and baby Richard before joining Adam. Maybe she would even have enough time to go to the gym to workout, especially after eating like a pig tonight.

The return trip home was rather quiet. Both of them were caught up in their own thoughts. Destiny was relaxing while listening to Smokie Norful through the sound system in his car. She told him Smokie was one of her favorite gospel artist. Closing her eyes, she smelled the scent of Adam's cologne. She knew he was staring at her whenever they stopped at a light, but that was fine with her. Never in her life had she contemplated a relationship with a pastor, but this was the sweetest man she'd ever met other than Willie, Shawn, and Richard.

Adam had planned a perfect evening. Which had almost ended in disaster. She opened her eyes and caught Adam looking at her in that moment. With the glow of the lights from the dashboard she couldn't see the expression on his face. Was he feeling like she was feeling? Destiny looked away first. He was pulling the car into the driveway to park. Waiting until he came around the car and open the door for her, she placed her hand in his, giving him her keys. They mounted the steps together.

"I'm glad they left the light on for you, but you need to get that one that's out fixed and the other one has flashed a couple of times."

She laughed. "I've been meaning to do it for a couple of days. I will take care of it tomorrow. We always leave the lights on because there are three females in the house. The Lord supplies us daily with his mercy, and we have our ministering angels keeping watch over us."

Adam unlocked the door and was met by yet another soft glow of light from a lamp by the door. He looked around and placed the keys back into her hands. Turning, Destiny laid them on the table by the lamp, dropped her purse in the chair, and kicked off her shoes.

"I'll see you tomorrow at eleven, but I need your address."

Reaching into his breast pocket of his jacket, he withdrew a pen. Destiny handed him a piece of paper she found at the bottom of her purse. He wrote down his address and number, handing her the paper.

Destiny stood motionless, staring at Adam. Drawing her close, his fingers tightened on her arm as he pulled her closer to face him. One hand slid down her arm to her hand, and the other claimed her waist, drawing her close. He held her for a moment as if in a motionless dance. The glow from the lamp outlined his head, but reading any facial expression was impossible in the dim light.

She waited. Her pulse quickened. Finally, he lowered his head as his lips brushed her cheek in a soft caress.

She took a deep breath to clear her head because she assumed he was going to kiss her. His fingers slid down her arms in a tingling caress as he relinquished the embrace. When he finally spoke, his voice was soft and husky.

"You are dear to me, Destiny. I don't want to mess this up, do you understand?"

"Yes, I do understand."

She couldn't see his expression, but she felt the tension mount between them. When he answered, his tone was serious.

"Outside of my mother, you're the only woman who has ever heard me say those words in the last three years."

Destiny smiled. Clearing her throat, she said, "Thank you for the wonderful evening, Adam."

With one last kiss to the cheek, Adam said, "I'll see you at eleven. Make sure you lock the door."

Turning, he opened the door, walked out, and then closed it quietly behind him. She watched the tail lights of his car disappear down the driveway. She let out a long breath and turned toward the bedroom, pausing in the doorway as a thought occurred to her.

She had a father and a good man in her life she was developing feelings for. Tears rolled down her cheeks. *Lord, who am I to judge anyone who has hurt me?* She clasped her hands together. *I know I'm not perfect. I too am saved by your grace, Lord. I'm thankful for having you as my heavenly Father. You cared enough about me to bring my earthly father into my life. You forgave me for all of my sins, and you have shown me unconditional love. For that, I want to say thank you. I know it's your will for me to love and trust again. I repent for any negative thoughts I've had about my past, and I close that door in my life. In Jesus's name, amen.*

Just as she got up off her knees the phone rang. Adam had just left and she couldn't believe he was calling her so soon. Maybe he changed his mind about their brunch. Picking up the receiver she said, "Hi, Adam you didn't forget anything did you?" She waited for a response.

Terror filled her as she heard the breathing. She slammed the phone down. She paced the room, nervous tension building up in her spirit. It rang again. Letting it ring a couple of times, she picked it up again.

"What do you want?" There was silence again and she hung up, stepping slowly away from the receiver.

When it rang a third time, she turned the phone off. Leaving her room, she went to check the doors in the house to just make her feel safe. Everyone was asleep but her. Amid the fear and tears, Destiny felt a little better. She had made up her mind—no longer would she be held in the bondage of her past. It was time to move on, to get back in the game. It was time for her to live, and in order for that to happen, she had to trust God completely. With that last thought she climbed in bed.

On the other side of town, thoughts came in what seemed like a dream. Too many thoughts were confusing. It was that Destiny woman who was quickly becoming the center of Pastor Wheeler's attention. For months after she arrived on the scene, the thoughts were always the same. Who was she, and where did she come from? But now she knew. She'd made that phone call to Womack Industries and found out that the CEO was Stanley Womack. After all of the planning, now everything was coming together. She was tired of going home to an empty apartment. This was a city full of eligible single men. The previous city was filled with singles, but none of them wanted to be in a committed relationship. She would be the First Lady of Greater Community. A slow smile formed and quickly changed into an outright laugh.

CHAPTER 24

Destiny heard the phone ringing and reached to pick it up before the ringing woke up a napping Sara. "Hello?" she spoke into the receiver. No one said anything so she hung up and picked her magazine focusing on the article she was reading.

She saw Sara's eyes open. "Another hang up?"

Destiny shrugged her shoulders, not wanting to make too much of the call and worry her aunt. It wasn't five minutes later that the phone rang again. Before she could pick it up, it stopped. Frustrated, Destiny was getting concerned about the calls that were being made to their home phone. It was almost as if the caller knew when she was at home.

She'd asked Cynthia if any hang-ups happened when she was home but she assured her that none had occurred. The calls were occasional when she first moved to Seattle but now they seemed to have become more frequent and at uncommon times. There were even times Destiny could hear breathing and knew there was someone there. She felt the caller knew her personally. It irritated her then but now for the first time, she was beginning to be concerned about it.

They had all agreed to change the house phone number and for a while the calls ceased, then they started again. Sometimes the sound of deep breathing, then a coarse whisper would burn her ear.

"He's coming." The caller in a singsong voice would say.

It was hard to understand the muffled words at first. But then panic set in when she asked the caller, "Who are you?" There was something demonic about the voice that caused a chill to run through her, she found herself trying to rub it away by running her hands up and down her arms.

"He's coming."

It was raining as Stanley exited the automatic doors of the airport. There were a lot of people waiting for car service, rushing to get out of the rain. After securing one for himself, he gave the driver the name of his hotel and for the first time since leaving South Carolina, began to relax a little. He knew he had changed since Destiny had seen him last. He had cut his hair off and was now bald. That wasn't the only change. He'd lost a tremendous amount of weight. But he was sure she'd be able to recognize him. Maybe these changes would give her pause, causing her to rethink her leaving him. He could even convince her that he was ill with all of his physical changes. All of it would help his cause.

Arriving at the hotel, he checked in and made a call to his private investigator. They were supposed to meet later to discuss the information gathered on Destiny's life in Seattle. His plans were to be here only for a couple of weeks. But he needed to see what he was up against. Deciding to take a nap, he picked up the television remote and lay on the bed. In two hours he would have all of the information he needed to put his plan into action.

CHAPTER 25

It had been raining all morning but Destiny wasn't going to let it ruin her day. Time flew by quickly for her. She had a little over two hours before she had to meet Adam. As she got dressed, she felt blissfully happy. It felt good knowing that her life was finally on track for the first time in several years. It was her ritual to do all her household chores on Saturday mornings, so she turned her radio to an old-school station. When she heard "Reasons" by Earth, Wind, and Fire, she couldn't help but sing along. After washing and folding the clothes for the entire house, she noticed the time. She now had less than half an hour until she had to meet Adam. Putting on a pair of white Capri pants, a pink tank top, and comfortable sandals, she was ready to go.

Her thoughts were on Adam as she walked down the hallway of the house. She kissed Sara on the cheek as she walked past her working in the garden. Today's brunch was a little unnerving because she would be at his home. They had many dates, but all of them had been in public places. What would it be like spending the day with him alone at his house? Even though she was nervous, she looked forward to spending time with him.

This would be the first time they would be able to see how they would react to each other totally alone without on lookers. Her first response to him was an instant attraction. But she wasn't the same woman who'd fallen so blindly in love with a man she knew little about. It took time, but now she understood what she'd been searching for in Stanley. It wasn't love, but it was security, a form of protection that she never received from her father. She learned that while attending Healing Virtue at Greater Community. Now she had purpose, a destiny, and a new life. It was changing her completely.

She turned onto the street to where Adam lived, peering at all of the beautiful condominiums in the charming neighborhood. As she entered the gated community and drove through, she was amazed at the beauty of the misty filled gardens that greeted her.

Looking for his home, she stared at the posted sign, which read Harvard and Highland. Looking at the address she'd written down, she knew this was where he lived. This area had a unique enclave of lovely condominium homes; they were all nestled among the tree-lined streets of Seattle's North Capitol Hill.

She strolled up the path, looking at the climbing vines and flowers that surrounded the wrought-iron gate out front. Taking her time to leisurely climb the steps, she approached the doorbell, ringing it once. The front door opened and she found herself breathless at the sight of him.

He had on a pair of faded well-washed jeans that hung around his waist, showing off his slim hips and molded thighs. His feet were shoeless, which made her smile because she walked around the house all day without shoes. Yes, Adam did a suit justice, but she thought he made an excellent casually dressed man. She knew she was staring because when she glanced at his eyes, he was smiling. Leaning down, he pulled her in a warm embrace.

He extended his hand, pulled her inside, and closed the door behind her. Then he wrapped an arm around her waist. Destiny closed her eyes as he hugged her close. She pressed her face to his shoulder, inhaling the scent of him mixed with the extraordinary smells of their meal.

"Good morning," she said. Her heart was racing. "You have a beautiful home."

He picked her up, swinging her around. After setting her down again, he looked into her beautiful eyes, which seemed to have turned deeper in color.

"Good morning," he whispered.

"You're in a good mood today," she countered. Adam bent slightly so that he could place a kiss on the tip of her nose.

She extended the bag she had been holding in her hand. "This is a little something for our brunch table." She reached into the bag to pull out a basket of flowers, perfect for a centerpiece.

His smile was dazzling. "They're perfect."

She arched her eyebrows. "I was hoping you didn't already have some."

"No, I didn't, and these are perfect. Thank you."

Their gazes met and fused for several seconds. "You're quite welcome."

He grabbed her hand, pulling her behind him. "I hope you haven't eaten anything this morning."

She grasped his hand, feeling the warmth of it. "I have to be honest with you. I was too excited about this brunch to eat."

"You must be starving. We'll eat first, then we'll talk about what to do for the rest of the day.

Destiny stood by the cooking island in his kitchen. After Adam poured her some orange juice, she sat, sipping and watching Adam move around the area like a skilled chef. He was dicing onions and peppers into tiny pieces on a cutting board for their omelets.

"You're really good with that knife. How'd you learn to cook?" she asked as he diced with abnormal speed.

"Mom taught Marvin and me how to cook when we were in middle school," he responded without lifting his head from his task.

"Can you cook a variety of meals?"

Wiping his hands, he picked up his own glass of orange juice. "I can cook just about anything. Maybe I'll have the chance to show you." Taking a sip from his glass, he sat it to the side and finished his chopping.

Taking the opportunity, she let her gaze sweep around the open spaces making up his kitchen. The entire floor of the house seemed to be constructed around openness; there were very few walls. It gave the place a feel of being outside. The oak floors and cabinets, along with the crown molding, were a perfect contrast to the wheat brown color of the walls used throughout.

Adam watched as she glanced around his functional kitchen. "I'll give you a full tour after we eat."

"Can I help you with anything? I don't like sitting around doing nothing."

"Something tells me you need to be treated like a queen. You deserve having someone wait on you." He took his chopping board and wiped its contents into a bowl. "So relax, you're my guest." His voice was soft as he said the words *my guest.*

She went still, her gaze fusing with his. "A girl could get use to being a guest?"

He put the bowl to the side, moving slowly as if he was in deep thought.

"That is just the way my mother raise us. Guests are catered to when they are in your home."

She squinted at him from her perch on the stool. "Smart mother."

He picked up his knife and began to dice an onion on the chopping board. "It's not often I get the chance to entertain in my home and I really want to impress you."

"Well you are. Just seeing you move with expertise around this kitchen has impressed me."

Putting his knife down, he scrubbed his hands under the cold water of the sink that was built into the island. After drying them, he reached out to take her hands and pulled her off the stool. Adam pulled her up close, flattening her against his chest.

"I'm not going to lie. This brunch was a way to get you to spend more time with me. I would love to rush what God is trying to do in his time. I want to be with you more each time I leave you. But I'm willing to wait on God. I want this relationship to be all the things he promised in his Word. I want to be satisfied with being with you everywhere but the bedroom."

Smiling, he brushed a loose strand of hair out of her face. "To be honest with you, my flesh screams every time I see you or touch you, but I have to conquer the flesh and let the Holy Spirit take control," he whispered against her cheek. "So yes, my flesh would love to take advantage of this situation, but I don't want to do anything that will cause us to damage God's blessing on this relationship."

"I've never met anyone like you. Why is that, Adam?" she whispered against his shoulder. Her voice was barely audible against the fabric of his shirt.

"I don't know, Destiny. All I can say is that from the moment we met, I knew there was something special about you and about this relationship."

"I want it to be that way, Adam. I just want to take baby steps for right now."

A soft laugh rumbled from deep inside Adam's chest. "I understand although I would like for it to be different."

"Good." It came out of her mouth like a sigh of relief.

"So now that we have that out of the way, we can enjoy our brunch."

Closing her eyes, she tried to still her heart. She knew he could feel it beating wildly in her chest. She wanted to tell him that she loved him and wanted to spend the rest of her life with him. But she decided this time she was going to get it right.

Releasing her, he turned, walking over to the refrigerator to take out the pitcher of fresh orange juice.

"Come on. I'll show you where we're going to eat."

Turning, Destiny followed him into the room across from the kitchen. She didn't know what to expect but certainly not the scene unfolding before her. The large space reminded her of an Italian villa. The room was filled with ceramic pots and beautiful flowers. There was a stone fireplace with a beautiful, carved table made of marble and wood. The walls had a beautiful painted mural of a villa's garden. After helping her into a seat, Adam slid her chair under the table.

Brunch lasted for two hours over several cups of tea; omelets filled with peppers, onions, smoked ham, a variety of cheeses; and sweet potato muffins. Destiny was happy. Never could she have imagined being at this place in her life and totally at peace.

She listened to Adam talk about his goals and future plans for the ministry. The afternoon progressed after they leisurely talked over coffee. Adam showed the rest of the house to Destiny. It was beautiful. He had excellent taste.

Cradling her hand, Adam led the way back downstairs. He pulled her close to his chest as they reached the landing. Turning to look her in the eyes, he asked, "Can I see you again tomorrow?"

He wouldn't take no for an answer, not that she'd exactly told him no yet.

Everything in her wanted to jump up and down like an excited child.

"You haven't told me whether you will go with me to Tacoma. It's not 'til next month, but I want to have all of the details worked out." Adam patiently waited for her to answer.

Without even knowing it, Destiny found herself drawn into the deep pools of his eyes. Yes, she would see him again. For the first time in a long time, she was eager for tomorrow to arrive. Images of their Saturday together stayed with Destiny as she pulled her car into the driveway.

In his kitchen later that evening, Adam stood, drinking a glass of water and reflecting on their day, only his thoughts were immediately interrupted by the ringing of his phone. After listening for a minute, he ended the call, grabbed his keys, and rushed out of the house. He could remember not wanting her to leave. Even after walking her to the car, he was sad when he went back inside the house, he should have convinced her to stay longer.

Destiny had forgotten to change the porch light again. She and Adam had just discussed it. She made a mental note to change the bulb tonight as she pulled into her driveway. This bulb was just a reminder that she needed to contact the police about all of the phone calls she'd been getting. It was one more necessary thing to add to her list. And she'd better not forget to do it or she'd hear about it on Sunday from Adam. Her aunt had also stressed it was time to contact the authorities.

She grabbed her purse from the passenger seat and opened the car door. The day had changed from the earlier rain and now it turned into a cool, dark night. Her day with Adam had been exciting. It could have been a whole lot better if she put on her big girl panties and told him everything about Stanley.

"You're going to have to tell him sooner or later," she muttered as she fished keys out of her purse and jogged up the porch steps.

A sound carried through the darkness. She could almost hear some kind of fabric rustling as someone drew near. Destiny stiffened, the hair on the back of her neck standing on end. She glanced over her shoulder, her heart leaping as she saw a shadow moving across the lawn. Medium height. Face hidden in darkness.

"Can I help you with something? Is anybody there?" She kept her gaze focused on the approaching figure as she shoved the key in the lock and tried to turn it. She wiggled the key, her palm sweaty and slipping on the metal door handle.

"Come on!" The key turned, and she shoved the door.

She screamed, her purse dropping as she turned to scream again and she froze not moving an inch.

"Whatever you want, you can have it." Another step and she'd be inside.

"Everything okay over here?" A masculine voice broke through the darkness as her attacker disappeared around the house.

This was her chance, so Destiny took it, jumping back and slamming the door, her fingers shook as she tried to turn the lock. She pressed her back against the door, her heart beating so hard she thought it might burst from her chest.

One hour later Destiny found herself in the police office with Sara.

The phone calls, trailing cars, and now this attack was just too much. She didn't know what all of this meant, but she wondered if it had anything to do with Stanley. She told the police about everything, even her leaving Stanley.

"Ms. Harper, why do think it may be your ex-boyfriend?" the detective asked almost as if he didn't believe anything she told him. "It really doesn't make sense why would he be that interested in finding you unless you took something from him when you left."

Destiny didn't like the way this conversation was going. Her aunt touched her hand in a matter that said, "I'll answer this one."

"Listen here, Detective, my niece didn't take nothing from Stanley but his pride when she left. That man beat my baby as if she was his piece of property. No man has a right to do that to any woman."

The detective turned to Destiny, "Is this true? Did he physically abuse you?"

Destiny looked at her aunt sighing. She told him, "Yes, that's why I came here to start a new life."

The detective seemed to ponder what she said for a few moments, tapping the pen he was using to take notes on his desk. "Well, it seems a little strange that you are only now coming forth to tell your story. Why didn't you go to the police in Charleston?"

Destiny looked at the detective, "Stanley Womack is a very powerful man in South Carolina, they would have never charged him with anything."

"So you are telling me that he has somehow found you here and is now threatening your life?" The detective seemed to roll his eyes at his assessment, which was pretty much what Destiny believed to be true.

"Yes."

He stood. "Well, ma'am," he looked at her aunt, "Ms. Harper, we'll see what we can do. We will be in touch. In the meantime, if you remember anything else, give me a call."

"Sure." They stood at the same time, thanked him, and left.

Despite the detective's obvious disdain, Destiny felt empowered. She was trying to take control of her life. For too long she felt like she was watching someone else's life. She felt so disconnected from her own. She now resolved not to watch it but to be an active participant in it. And that meant finding out who was trying to terrorize her, and why.

When they finally returned from the police department, Adam was sitting on the front porch. As he stood, Sara greeted him with a warm embraced then entered the house leaving them alone. The quiet stretched between the two of them until Destiny wanted to scream.

"Adam, What are you doing here?" She sounded as surprised as he looked, and her hand shook as she tucked a strand of hair behind her ear.

"I received a call tonight from one of the members of the church who works at the police department. I wanted to make sure you were okay. Especially since I was the last person you saw before coming home. Is everything all right? What happened?"

"Someone tried to attack me. They ran off after my neighbor rushed over after hearing me scream. I called the police to check things out around the house and then went to the station."

"Did you get a chance to see who it was?" he asked.

Her voice trembled as she scanned the area beyond the porch.

"No, I was so nervous trying to get in the house, and they had their face covered up."

"What about your neighbor? He questioned with concern. "Did he get a license plate number?"

"He told the police that if the intruder had one he didn't see it. But he did leave his number with them just in case they wanted to ask him more questions."

"Why don't you sit down, you look beat." He gestured to the empty rocker beside him.

Destiny's eyes widened. She wasn't expecting him to be here let alone stay with her for a while. "I think I am. Today started out great but now this." She crouched slowly, and reaching for her purse she'd dropped on the porch.

She watched Adam as he grabbed her hand, but he nearly released it again when she noticeably seemed to be agitated by his touch. All of the things that had been worrying her about Stanley simply shook her to the core.

She didn't want to hurt his feeling when she pulled her hand away from him, if he was he didn't show it. "You're right. I wasn't thinking." He seemed to be apologizing for his touching her.

"The sooner the police start looking, the more likely it is they'll catch the person." He said as they sat beside each other. Despite her seeming calm, her hand still shook and her eyes were filled with fear. She was terrified, and there was no way he planned to leave her alone. Not like this.

Destiny met his eyes, the wariness in her gaze unmistakable. She frowned again, turning her back on him.

"Are you okay, Destiny?" He finally blurted out. She knew he was concerned by the way his eyes were watching her facial expression. He turned sober eyes on her. "Not yet, but I will be soon enough."

She nodded, recalling the days and weeks she'd stayed in her room, too afraid to come out because she didn't want to face

Stanley. The prayers she'd whispered over and over again, asking God to help her get away from him and now that he did, she had to take control of her life. Her joy about being in Seattle and Adam was still firmly twined with her agony. She just couldn't hurt him; he'd been too sweet even coming here tonight. "Thank you," she said, in a voice a little too low.

"For what?" he asked.

"For coming here tonight. You didn't have to. I appreciate it." He shrugged. "Who's after you, Destiny?"

"I don't know." Which was the truth. She had an idea but wasn't sure about it.

He pulled out his phone. "I can call my friend at the department. He's a detective. Maybe he can help."

Destiny began to shake her head no. "I'll handle it myself, Adam."

She watched the muscles worked along his jaw. "Someone tries to attack you and you think you can handle it yourself? I guess that shouldn't be a surprise. But after everything we've talked about over the last two days, I feel like you still don't trust me."

She hated the sadness in his tone, but it ignited a flicker of anger inside her. All she could think about was the fact that she always depended on some man or woman to help her. But not this time! This time she was going to fight her own battle and win with the help of the Lord. For when she was weak, He was strong.

I've been co-dependent for so long. God, don't ever let me feel like that again, she'd prayed many times. *I won't depend on anyone. Especially since I want to depend on you.*

She wanted the life she longed for: an independent life, strong and in control.

"Adam this has nothing to do with you. All I'm trying to do is get my life back," she murmured more to herself than to Adam.

"The police will help me, I'll be fine." She looked at him with a renewed sense of determination.

"I understand, I guess… but if you need some assistance, let me know," Adam said, eyes blazing. "But tell me this, Destiny, why can't you tell me what's going on?"

She faced him, cheeks hot. "I'm not your responsibility, Adam. I don't belong to you." The glimmer of grief in his eyes made her breath catch.

"I know that and I don't want to own you," he said, voice suddenly soft. "I just thought we were friends or even more than friends."

Her cell rang. After looking at the caller ID she allowed it to go straight to voice mail she'd call Tina after she went inside.

"Thank you for being here when I needed you," she said. "You're a good friend, Adam, but this is something I have to do on my own," she whispered.

"I'm…I'm sorry. Maybe we have moved too quickly," he mumbled, getting up from the chair he was occupying. His eyes were questioning her.

She knew he was disappointed and she understood why, she caused him to believe she was ready for the next step in this relationship when in actuality she wasn't, she thought, because their date and the brunch told him a different story. Shaking away the conflicting thoughts, she smiled at Adam as he got up to leave. "Good night."

He smiled, but there was sadness in his eyes as he did so, sending her heart knocking against her ribs. She quickly turned to unlock the door and pushed it closed before she did something stupid. She double checked the lock and squeezed her eyes tight, praying for safety.

CHAPTER 26

Adam was restless when he returned home. He had a shower, turned on the television, tried to listen to some television ministers, and turned it off again. His body was tired, but his mind kept circling, thinking about the conversation he'd had with Destiny. His decision to go over to her house was last minute. He didn't even finish listening to the information he was being given on the phone. He just wanted to be there for her to help in any way he could. But she'd pushed him away.

Adam leaned back in bed. What was it that had Destiny so afraid? Didn't she know he was just trying to be a friend? Surely she wasn't going to keep him out of her personal life or end their friendship. He rejected that thought as soon as it occurred. He switched the light off around midnight. He had service in the morning. By two he was still staring at the ceiling. Sleep use to be a rare commodity in his life. But now he usually had no problems resting. When he was addicted to porn, he was used to being awake when most of the world wasn't, but he didn't like it.

He rolled onto his side. Back in the old days if he'd had trouble sleeping, he would have opened his laptop and find all he needed to keep him company. But this was a new day and he was a new man. A frown formed on his face as he thought about the conversation they'd had earlier. They needed to clear the air because this was beginning to be confusing to him. One minute she was eating brunch with him and the next she was pushing him away. She was important to him. Very. And he was determined to fix whatever had gone wrong between them if she gave him the chance.

Lying in her bed Destiny couldn't help but to think of how cruel it would be of her to continue to take advantage of Adam's generous and caring nature when she wasn't ready for their relationship to go any further. It didn't matter what her heart was saying or what the dates they had were like. Tonight proved that life could be random and unpredictable. Maybe it was God's way of telling her she wasn't ready for any relationship. Knowing that Stanley could possibly be the one harassing her didn't mean she should or would deliberately ignore the trouble it would cause for Adam or his church. And Stanley certainly qualified as trouble. All she wanted was a peaceful steady life. Not one with surprises or uncertainties. She'd had enough of that in her life. Adam had told her in a conversation that God would take care of those he loved. So with that she drifted to sleep.

A scream jolted Destiny awake from her restful sleep.

She bolted upright, scrambled to a sitting position against the headboard, and clutched the covers to her chest. Her heart thudded in her ears. Sweat covered her skin. Her gaze searched the bedroom room for any signs of danger. The scream echoed inside her head.

Sharp pounding at the door sent her stomach plunging with fear.

"Destiny!"

Then the banging got louder.

She knew that voice. It was Cynthia.

Jumping up from the bed she ran for the door, which she locked earlier. Her fingers scrabbled with the lock until it finally gave way. She yanked the door open.

Tears sprang to her eyes. "Cynthia."

"Are you okay?" Her gaze carefully swept the darkened room beyond her shoulder. "You screamed."

It had been her that had screamed. "I did?"

Feeling foolish for alarming everyone, she tried for a smile. Her lips quivered. "I'm sorry. I guess it's everything that has been happening lately. It was another dream about Stanley coming after me."

Cynthia smoothed a hand over her hair. "He can't hurt you now and if anything happens the police will be able to handle it. No one is going to hurt you."

She wanted to believe that. Needed to believe that. "You can't make that promise. That's not something you can control."

Her eyebrows drew together in a frown. "I understand that, but God can do everything; he will protect you."

"I know that, and I prayed before going to bed." She squeezed Cynthia's hand.

"God is in control." Dropping her gaze to the front of her pajamas she almost whispered.

"Lord, sometimes, it's so hard to…remember and trust. Help me do both."

Confessing that out loud lifted a weight off her shoulders. She hadn't realized how much she needed someone in her life she could talk to without feeling she'd be judged. Cynthia wouldn't judge her. She was sure of it. Adam had been right—counseling was good but she needed the help of friends as well.

Cynthia gave her a wry smile. "Believe me, I understand." Cynthia hurt for her, for the pain she carried because of her abuse. Cynthia looked her in the eyes and said,

"We're quite a pair." Turning she gave her sister friend a hug.

"You should try to get some sleep," she said.

This time Destiny didn't lock the door. If she trusted God then she had to have enough faith to believe he would keep her safe.

She had made Adam angry last night. Worse, she didn't know if he'd given up on her.

Destiny paced her bedroom, her mind racing with a million thoughts, none of them pleasant. If it weren't Sunday she would have stayed in bed wallowing in pity. Had she done the right thing with Adam? She wasn't sure, didn't dare to speculate it was over and she had been honest with him.

She wanted to blame stress on her lapse in judgment. But the truth was, Adam had a way of making her forget all the reasons why getting involved with him wasn't a good idea.

"God, can you help me out, tell me what to do? That's all I want. Some hint that will help me understand why You brought him into my life."

But she knew God didn't work that way.

Frustrated, she walked into her bathroom to get ready for church. She couldn't spend all morning thinking about him. But she did and now she had to rush to morning service.

As she opened the door to leave the house, she was thankful for the light of day. She was ready for a wonderful worship experience. As she drove she bobbed her head to the gospel song on the radio "Oh, Happy Day," which brought back a memory of her childhood with her aunt as they prepared to go to Sunday school. She'd been thirteen, old enough to be in the adult choir, and they sang that song on several occasions.

Reaching for and opening the sanctuary door, she let her gaze wander to the crowd inside. A typical Sunday morning at Greater Community with people passing by in the lobby, some hurrying to find places to sit and others meandering, talking about the weeks they'd had.

A young boy dawdling behind his mother stopped to stare at Destiny. She'd seen him on several occasions. She smiled and he lifted his hand in a shy wave. With a short laugh, Destiny turned her attention back to sanctuary. She walked in looking for a seat close to the front.

He'd been keeping an eye on her this morning, but she seemed to have recovered from his impromptu visit. Adam didn't think he'd ever forget the flash of relief he'd seen in her eyes when she'd walked through the door of the sanctuary and looked at him. *I can't lose her, not when I've just found her.* He wasn't sure where that thought had come from and there was no time to analyze his feelings. He'd played it cool for her sake, but he'd been hard pressed not to do something foolish like leaving the pulpit to acknowledge her presence, especially since he wasn't even sure she was going to come this morning.

The only thing that mattered at the moment was his sermon, but Destiny was there right now. He thought to himself, "Please, God, please, don't let her end what you're trying to do before we began." He didn't know what would happen, but as he walked to the podium he vowed he'd ask her to accompany him to his parents weekly Sunday dinner.

CHAPTER 27

It took some fancy footwork but he had convinced her to join him at his parent's house for dinner. He reflected on what she said immediately after he asked. "Before we leave, I wanted to say something about yesterday." He had groaned theatrically and clutched his stomach as they stood in his outer office.

Giving him a short chuckle, she said, "I'll be quick, I promise. I just wanted to let you know how much I appreciate everything you've done for me since I moved to Seattle and for last night. The way I was feeling could have been a disaster for us, a huge setback, but I can truly say God spoke to me through the sermon you preached this morning. "Finding Strength from God in the Dark' it really gave me the courage to walk in this season of my life. All I've ever wanted was to be independent. A new relationship never crossed my mind. This thing that's happening between you and I, wasn't my dream, but since I've been saved, I see that God orchestrates things for our good. Although I was comfortable in my past, it was comfortable discomfort. No longer will I be a slave to my past. I will always remember the kindness and generosity you showed me last night. From the bottom of my heart, I want to say, 'thank you.'"

She stood there looking at him. He was watching her with warm eyes.

"Destiny, all I want is what's best for you. I want to be in your life, but I'm willing to wait. I want you to trust me and trust us. The only way you will be able to do that is for me not be overbearing and let you move in this relationship at your own pace. I'm willing to do that."

So a half hour later here they were at his parents' house with him opening her car door. Destiny was happy that Adam decided they would arrive ahead of the other guests for the Sunday dinner with his family. She had seen them on several occasions and even exchanged hugs, but she still had not been officially introduced as Adam's friend. Destiny could do nothing but stare in disbelief at the beautiful home. It was a large two-story brown brick home. The windows were large with beautiful shutters, giving the house a warm curb appeal. There were columns that surrounded a wraparound porch. The hedges and trees were trimmed beautifully. She wasn't surprised by the beautiful home, but she was surprised to see his parents coming out to greet them.

Adam's mom, Mary, was wearing a floral sundress with a pair of gold slides. Her hair was styled with curls. Destiny admired the fact that her movements were so graceful, like she was royalty. It was intimidating knowing that this was the woman who had given birth to Adam. If she was nervous before, she was even more so now.

Bill seemed relaxed. He had strong, broad shoulders, looking very distinguished in his white shirt and loose, dark jeans. His alert eyes, the same as Adam's, were trained on her, and a smile was in place on his face. However, she felt as if he were watching everything about her to see if she was just as relaxed and comfortable as they were. His hair had a touch of silver around the edges. He was a very handsome man, and she knew where Adam and Marvin got their looks.

"We are so excited to have you here, Destiny," Adam's mother said, moving from under her husband's protective arm to embrace Destiny. She made Destiny feel as if she was already a part of their family. She couldn't help but notice utter happiness on his mother's face.

"Mom, she'll be here the rest of the day. So you can relax," Adam stated, surprising himself as he spoke those words.

"Oh, I'm just happy, Adam!" Mary replied as Adam's father made his way over.

"You both come on in the house. I was just about to take my roast out the oven. Adam, I want to chat with Destiny before you steal her away!"

Destiny smiled when she saw the small smile coming from Adam's father.

"Welcome to our home, Destiny. You have to excuse my wife. She's excited about your visit today." When Destiny's eyes made contact with Bill, he was watching her. Leaning in to whisper, he said, "She picked you out for her son some months ago before she met you."

Mary rolled her eyes while playfully hitting his arm. She started leading Destiny inside the house, talking fast about her meal and the day she had planned for all of them. Something about Mary made Destiny feel very welcome and very at peace, so she didn't feel too awkward or uncomfortable.

Destiny's eyes widened as she entered the foyer. "Mrs. Wheeler, you have a lovely home. Did you decorate it yourself?"

"Yes, the boys built this house for us a couple of years ago. To say we were surprised is an understatement. It was such a wonderful thing for them to do for us. We've never asked them for a thing. It was their way of saying they loved us, as if we didn't already know it." Mary watched her husband and son walk in behind them. "Adam told us that your friend Tina Wilson and her family will be joining us for dinner today. I'm glad. It's been a long time since we've had a gathering this large."

"Yes, Adam invited them after service. I hope it's not an inconvenience." She looked a little anxious as she watched Mary shake her head.

"No, I've cooked plenty. I asked Sara to come after Sunday school, but she told me she had plans with your father."

"They do have plans. My father is taking her downtown for dinner, and then they're going to a movie."

"Well, she's welcomed here any time, even your father. I would love to get to know Sara better. It's wonderful to have a husband

and sons, but sometimes, I'm positively sick of only male companions. Don't get me wrong. I love them, but they absolutely refuse to go shopping with me."

They both laughed as Destiny followed her farther into the house without saying much. She looked and listened as Mary showed off her home, stopping by the gourmet kitchen to take the roast out of the oven.

Adam, along with his father, went toward the back of the house. Mary sat on the sofa as Destiny followed suit. Relaxing on the sofa, Mary spoke. "Adam has done nothing on his visits but talk about you, Destiny. I must say, he really is smitten by you."

Destiny smiled, pulling a strand of hair from her face. "I have to admit, he's a special man. You and your husband raised a wonderful son, Mrs. Wheeler."

Mary looked curiously at Destiny. "It was easy because both of my sons had the support of a mother and father. I couldn't have done it alone."

"That's the way I want to raise my children when and if it happens." Sighing, Destiny looked everywhere but back at Mary.

Reaching out, Mary placed a hand gently on Destiny's arm. "Adam has always wanted children as well. I've watched you, Destiny, over the last several months, admiring what I've seen. Not every woman would have been as low key as you have been, getting the attention of the pastor of a ministry like Greater Community."

Laughing, Destiny replied, "The one thing I know, Mrs. Wheeler, is that Adam needs a strong, confident saved woman in his life. He's a good, sold-out man of God who only wants to glorify his Father in heaven. I believe I'm a good woman. I know for sure I'm saved, and yes, all I want to do is please God. There's still a lot we don't know about each other, but in time we will because I don't want us to have secrets that will cause hurt or pain later. I don't want us to have any skeletons in our closets. I could love your son if I don't already, but I want to make sure we have a good foundation."

Mary smiled with a look of relief. "I knew there was something special about you, Destiny." Getting up from the sofa, she looked at Destiny and asked, "So are you ready to help me in the kitchen?"

Destiny's eyes lit up as she stood. "Just lead the way. I'd be glad to assist you. I love to cook."

Mary took Destiny's hand, pulling her close in a warm hug. "And you like to cook. Adam always did have a good head on his shoulders."

CHAPTER 28

Did it always rain in this God-forsaken place? Stanley thought as he drove away from the hotel in his rental car. He'd been in Seattle for three days now and it was time to get out of this city. Finding the house was easy with the GPS in his rental car. He'd even been able to watch the comings and goings of the residents from down the street. The first time he saw Destiny caused his heart rate to increase.

She seemed happy each time he saw her. There wasn't that scowl on her face that he'd seen so often. He saw her leave home a couple of nights ago with the man he'd read about in his packet— the pastor. She was dressed like she was going on a date. It had been late when they returned.

Now he was on the road again, his report indicated that she attended the church of the pastor she was seeing. Since he had an address and a picture, finding it would be easy. His heart raced with anticipation. Maybe today he'd be able to speak to her.

There was no denying that Destiny was gorgeous. If she weren't, he'd never been bothered with her. She had moved on with her life as if he never existed but for the last seven months, he had been laughed at by all of his friends for being doped by a silly immature woman. If she hadn't fought with him that night, he would have never left her to go out with his friends. It was her fault he had to hit her with so much force. She was a woman after all. He wasn't trying to kill her, just teach her a lesson.

Stanley looked at the directions then at the street sign. One right turn and he'd be there.

Then he smiled as he looked at the church ahead of him. Once he had her with him alone, he would be able to convince her that he loved her and she'd come back home. He got out of his car at the church and stood looking at the building knowing she was inside. He breathed in the memory of her sweet smell and felt a flicker of something in his memory. He put a hand to his head, frowning as he tried to concentrate on Destiny instead of his pounding head. All of this thinking and planning was giving him uncontrollable migraines.

Stanley began heaving with each ragged pant he took through his nostril. He knew it would be just a matter of time. His fists were uncurling and his hands dangled at his sides. Destiny was always trying him. She had no right leaving him the way she did. He shook his head as if to make sense of it all. She should have known better. He was a big man, six-one, two hundred and twenty pounds. She couldn't wiggle out from his hold, let alone try to keep him from taking her back to South Carolina.

For three years he tried everything to drive her crazy, but she'd endured his subtle taunts, his jealousy and control issues, all his passive-aggressive forms of emotional abuse. She'd even made excuses to her friends for not being around them. There was no woman who could replace her in his mind and he wasn't going to try. He wanted her back. As far as he was concerned, she'd be with him when he left this god-forsaken state next week.

He didn't like being outmaneuvered. He'd run out of options until he'd gotten that mysterious call and hired a private investigator. The woman's name was Regina and they were going to meet later this week. Two days after she contacted him, he reached out to her. She'd told him everything she knew from the beginning to end with a timeline and, most importantly, names and descriptions. Stanley had contacted his own private investigator to see what he could find out about this Regina and Pastor Adam Wheeler. After a lengthy conversation Regina showed some interest in him and his money; it didn't matter she was just a means to an end. Maybe he'd been wrong to take such a drastic measure, but he'd been desperate to find Destiny. He was determined to bring her back and he could use all the help he could get.

So today was the beginning of his plan. He wouldn't stop or leave Seattle without Destiny. He had become obsessed with her movements around the city, even memorizing her work schedule. The opportunity would come, then he would have to move quickly. A smile lit his face. The same beaming smile he'd donned when he'd gotten the message about her being in Seattle. His thighs relaxed, he flexed his hands. Things were getting better by the second. Anticipation roared like a wild beast in his veins. Stanley hid his disgust when he thought about the information his private investigator had given him. Irritation etched into his aged features.

"I'll show Pastor Adam Wheeler who she belongs to, if he gets in my way." He was squeezing his fist so tightly, blood pooled in the center of his hands. "There's something between us and he'll see it when we are together again." His restraint snapped like an elastic band. He walked back to his car to wait. They'd be out soon. The only way he'd go into a church would be in a coffin, and that wasn't going to happen for a long time.

CHAPTER 29

Cynthia picked her son's up after school. She had breathed a sigh of relief when their last meeting ended, wanting to get to her parents home before it got too late. As she was about to leave the office, Marvin stopped by. He had gotten back from Atlanta the day before after finalizing his business deal. She reminded him she was going to her parents' house today. He was very caring knowing this was going to be a day of reconciliation for her and her parents. She had prayed about it this morning but some days she just felt tired, and today was one of those days. Yes, she loved God but she just felt burden, but God showed her he hadn't given up on her when Marvin suggested they pray for God to intervene on her behalf. Still dazed, she watched Marvin as he moved to escort her to the elevators. Picking up her purse, she quickly joined him.

Forty-five minutes later, Cynthia eased her car through the gate to the semi-circular drive of the Mason mansion. She remembered all of the times she'd driven through these gates. However, the last time was seven years ago when she left to go to college. It was a marvelous house—four-stories with an apartment on the upper level, bedrooms on the third level, entertainment on the first, and a huge cellar with a recreational area. Outside was all red brick and stucco in the front with a beautiful stone deck on the east side. The front lawn was decorated with an elaborate marble fountain on the left side of the cobble stone walk and a beautiful craved teak bench on the right, underneath the tall oak tree. This grand estate was once a place she never thought she'd leave. But things change and so do people.

Cynthia sat in the car nervously, twisting her fingers in her lap and gazing up at the house she had lived in most of her life. She had always loved everything about the house, especially her window seat, which looked out over the lake in the back. It was her place to read, think, or dream about her future. She couldn't believe she was actually back at home, vowing never to come here again once her parents began badgering her to break things off with Marvin and focus on a more suitable young man. She had gone through a lot in this place and with its residents, and now she was actually back.

Her legs were actually wobbling as she stepped out of the car to scan the surroundings she knew so well.

The tension she was feeling gave way to excitement as she watched Miss Betty swing the doors to the mansion open. She relaxed when she realized she didn't have to see her parents just yet. Betty always walked in heels; she still looked fit, no older than when Cynthia last saw her. Walking briskly down the steps to the car, her face was filled with excitement.

With arms outstretched, Miss Betty welcomed her back home. Cynthia went into them, closing her eyes and hugging her tightly.

"Cynthia! How have you been? Lord knows I missed my baby." Betty smiled, pulling back and exposing the sheen of tears glistening in her eyes.

"Miss Betty, I wanted to call, but I was afraid you'd tell Mom and Dad where I was. I didn't want to put you in that position." Tears were threatening to fall as she looked at the woman who cared for her like a mother most of her life.

Peering over Cynthia's shoulders, Betty spied the twins, who were looking just a little apprehensive about the scene that was unfolding.

"I see that congratulations are in order, although it seems to be…what, six years too late? Who do we have here?" Betty walked over to car, opening the door and peering in on the boys.

"You're right. They are six, Miss Betty," Cynthia interjected as she attempted to smooth over the awkwardness of the moment. She glanced at the boys who were smiling and shyly giving Betty a return hug.

"Jonathan, David, I'd like you both to meet Miss Betty. She was my nanny, sort of like what Miss Sara is to both of you."

They smiled. "It's nice to meet you, Miss Betty." Their eyes were curious as they looked at Betty.

"You both are cute as can be, I see you both look a little like your mom. So which of you is Jonathan?" She was gazing between the both of them after hearing their mother say their names.

Raising his hand reluctantly, Jonathan said, "I am, and I'm the oldest." He giggled, looking at Betty.

"So you must be David?" She looked behind Jonathan to gaze into the face of the second twin.

"Yes, ma'am. Do you live in that big ole house too?"

Betty smiled. "Yes, I do, but my house is out back. I'll show it to the both of you later."

"Can we go inside? Momma said our grandparents are in there," David said, pointing in the direction of the house.

It appeared to Cynthia that the twins had no issues about meeting their grandparents as they took Betty's hands and started for the house. Their eyes and smiles were identical as they walked toward the entrance. It pleased her that they felt a connection with Miss Betty. Cynthia sighed with relief. Could they really become a family again? She hoped so; she knew she'd like nothing better. She didn't know how her parents would react at seeing her again along with her sons.

A few minutes later, Miss Betty ushered Cynthia and the twins into the entrance hall. Edward and Gwendolyn Mason came out of the living room to greet their daughter and their grandsons. Cynthia saw tears shimmering in her mother's eyes when they settled on the twins.

The twins ventured forward curiously. "Are you really our grandmother?" Jonathan asked her.

"Are you really our grandfather?" David asked Edward.

Gwendolyn went to Jonathan while Edward walked over to David. The eyes of both Miss Betty and Cynthia were riveted on them. Neither of them spoke a word.

"Yes, I am." Gwendolyn spoke first, leaning down to look directly in Jonathan's eyes. "What's your name?"

"Jonathan William Wheeler." After saying his name, he proudly looked at both of his grandparents, smiling from ear to ear.

"And what's your name, young man?" Edward asked David.

"I'm David William Wheeler, sir." David looked at his grandfather with unrehearsed pride.

"How old are you, young men?"

"We turned six on our birthday," David answered.

"It was March the twenty-sixth," Jonathan interrupted to say.

Gwendolyn held out her arms to her only grandchildren. They both went into them without hesitation. Tears stung Cynthia's eyes when she realized how much having a family meant to her children.

Standing to his full height, Cynthia watched her father turn to her. With questioning eyes as if asking if it would be okay to speak, he went to his only child. For all the wrong he had done to his family by his treacherous ways, they could now only be righted by asking his only daughter, his only child, to forgive him. Now, as he watched her eyes grow huge, the silence of awareness fell over her. If he had his way, he would never have allowed the past to disrupt the future, but in order to get their family back, he had to admit he had been wrong all of those years ago.

His wife had cried herself to sleep many nights worrying about their child. That's why he arranged for her to have that home in Charleston without paying rent. What good was it being Edward Mason if you couldn't pull strings or call in favors every now and then? He made sure she never had to pay tuition. He'd arranged for her to receive special scholarships from the university. Yes, she was away from home, but they knew everything about her and the boys.

"Cynthia, how have you been?" her father asked. His voice was crisp, but there was no animosity. He wasn't being unkind.

"Fine, Father, and you?" she asked after clearing her voice, looking between her mother and father.

"Fine. A lot has changed since you left home. I've had a lot of time to deal with all of the demons that have tormented me since your departure. The hurt and pain I caused in all of our lives has eaten this old man up," he said, using his hand to pat his chest and emphasizing his point before continuing. "My selfishness and foolish pride almost cost me my entire family. I had to learn that forgiveness is a powerful weapon. It can be used for good or bad. I'm just blessed that I now understand what it truly means to walk in forgiveness."

Edward Mason looked at his only daughter. She was beautiful, and God had kept her in spite of all the anguish she had to endure because of his pride. How she even had the courage to come here today was a testimony of the woman she had become. She was a better person than him. But she had always been special. He knew his daughter was a survivor. It was in her genes.

"Let's have a seat." Edward directed his daughter to the seats arranged near the spiral staircase. They all sat, except for the boys, who were following Betty to the kitchen for cookies that she said were made especially for them. Before allowing Cynthia to take her seat, Edward stepped closer to her, reaching out to touch his daughter's cheek.

"I'm sorry, Cynthia. You didn't deserve what I did to you."

Edward pulled back, almost flinching as if he felt a shock ripple through his body. His eyes dropped in disapproval of his actions.

"I should have never assumed that I was God in your life. Justifying my actions because I was the man who once held your hand as you took your first steps, watched you as you walked into womanhood and then straight into the arms of a young man you constantly talked about loving. I had plans for your life—big plans—and it was hard to see you give all of that up."

Her father's eyes were shimmering with tears that refused to fall. "In reality, I was just a father who acted in ignorance, thinking he was God by interfering in your life even where Marvin was concerned. Sometimes as fathers, we forget the special role we have in our children's lives. Our pastor taught us about being a blueprint for our daughters."

Cynthia was surprised that her father even mentioned Marvin. The questioning of what he meant when referring to a blueprint must have been expressed in her eyes because her father continued as if the mentioning of Marvin's name was an everyday occurrence.

"He said as fathers, we embody our daughters' first blueprint of what it is to be a man, to be a husband, and to be a father. We do this both consciously and unconsciously because our daughters, just like you, Cynthia, generally base some of their choices of men they have relationships with on their observations of their fathers."

Cynthia was looking at her father through new eyes. Who was this man and where was the Edward Mason she knew? She looked at her mother for some sort of indication of what was happening. Gwendolyn just smiled and whispered, "Listen," low enough for her ears only.

"As you got older, it was my responsibility to help you separate from this blueprint and initiate the process of becoming a young woman who could make wise decisions on her own. My main task was to help you let go of the daddy image that I kept wanting you to see and gain your own sense of what you wanted in a relationship."

Now looking at Cynthia and his wife, Edward shook his head slowly with regret.

"But sadly, looking back on that time, I thought a person's worth was based on where they lived or what they did for a living. I didn't understand God's favor then as much as I do now. Marvin was a good man. If he weren't, then you never would have been with him. I now know that, even though it may be too late."

Edward reached back and pulled Gwendolyn, who was standing slightly behind his chair, to his side.

"I loved you, Cynthia. From the day your mother said she was pregnant, I loved you. It didn't matter that we never had another child or that I didn't have a son. You were all we"—he pointed to himself and Gwendolyn—"ever needed." The love he felt for her in his heart showed through the look in his eyes.

"David and Jonathan!" He called their names loud enough for them to come scurrying back into the vestibule. He glanced at his wife and daughter. Then he inched forward, kneeling in front of his grandsons.

"I'm your grandfather. My name is Edward Mason. It's my pleasure to meet my two extraordinary grandsons." He looked at his daughter, smiling proudly while opening his arms for his grandsons.

Cynthia smiled. She could tell that her parents were hooked on their grandchildren already. Her sons had a way with people that could wrap them around their hearts at first sight. They were good boys. She watched as her parents along with the boys turned to go into the living room, and then she looked nervously at Betty, who was signaling for her to follow them.

"Go ahead, sweetheart. They love you, and they have missed you terribly." She turned in the direction of the kitchen before gently ushering her in their direction. The tears that had been threatening were finally falling.

As she entered the living room, she smiled when she saw the interaction between her mother and the twins.

"Your hair is beautiful, Cynthia," her mother said. The look on her face was sincere as she rose from her seat to approach her daughter. She looked from her head down to her feet. It caused Cynthia's heart to break, and the tears would not stop.

"I didn't mean to make you cry, but I missed you so much. Sweetheart, you look wonderful," she said, watching her through tears. "Can you find it in your heart to forgive your father and me?"

It felt strange to hear her mother ask that question. She had wanted to hear those words for years. Here they were and she didn't know what to say.

"I forgave you both a long time ago," she said. Her voice felt small in the room filled with the five of them. She was nervous. Secretly she had always wanted them to love her boys and to accept her. She couldn't remember ever having a test that seemed so hard and she didn't want to fail this one.

"Thank you." Her mother looked surprised when Cynthia wrapped her arms around her, wanting to remember nothing but the happy times of her childhood, blocking out all of the negative thoughts that the enemy had been trying to plant in her mind. It was easier now because she'd learned to cast down every evil imagination that tried to exalt itself against the knowledge of her God.

"Welcome home, Cynthia." Her father took her in his arms, holding her so delicately as if she would break if he squeezed too hard. He pulled back to look at her, trying to remember every detail of his daughter and mother of his grandchildren.

"I'm sorry, Cynthia. I let so many things get in the way of my love for you, and because of that, I had to watch you grow into a beautiful woman and mother from a distance." Her parents looked at each other.

"You were never really alone, Cynthia. You didn't know it, but your father and I have been your secret angels for all of these years." Her mother sat in the chair and trembled slightly from nervous energy. Reaching out, she pulled both of the twins down with her.

It was Cynthia's turn to be surprised. She turned her head to look at her father. There were times when she had her suspicions about some of the favor she received. How could she have forgotten that her parents had a wealth of resources around them? Cynthia's eyes danced at this, but when she looked at her mother's face, she had no misgivings. She knew all of the coincidences couldn't have been accidental; and they had been arranged by her parents.

Her mother spoke first after that revelation. "I'm proud of you, Cynthia. We regretted our decision the moment we hung up the phone. I wanted my daughter back home with me. But we foolishly thought it would ruin our reputation. The firm had just begun to gain national attention. We were winning more cases... but everything changed after that phone call. I cried myself to sleep every night until your father made the decision that, without you, our lives were empty." Gwendolyn looked at the twins.

"What your mother is trying to say is that she demanded I do something." They both nodded with appreciative smiles.

Cynthia smiled gratefully at her parents.

"Thank you for sharing all of this with me because I realize you didn't have to," Cynthia said with a welcoming lift to her voice. She realized how difficult it must have been for her mother to defend her at the cost of her father's success. The decision had been made, and now they all had to move forward, hopefully for the better. They would, as long as God ordered all of their steps. She looked at both them, her eyes taking in every detail. With the smiles she received from each of them, she no longer felt the tense air that had been in the room when she entered it. Now, it had slices cut in it that allowed a flowing breeze to pass through.

"Mother," Cynthia went to her mother, hugging her, "I do love you both."

"I know. We both know." Gwendolyn hugged Cynthia back.

Edward joined them, whispering, "But it's good to hear you say it."

"Now we want to know everything about you and the boys," her mother stated.

"Why don't we go in and eat first?" Her father was by her side, and she hadn't seen him move. Cynthia was so relieved. Without knowing she was doing it, she reached out to grab her father's hand. The twins were holding their grandmother's hands, both talking at once, telling her about their school.

They moved to the dining room where Cynthia was sure their interrogation would continue. She suspected her mother was holding back on asking about Marvin, but she was sure it would come up when dinner was over. The dinner was served family style. Miss Betty brought all of the bowls, platters, and servers to the table. Bowls were passed around the table, and each person served themselves. Miss Betty assisted the twins. The smells about the room caused her stomach to rumble.

Betty had cooked steaks that were thick, tender, and juicy. A variety of vegetables shared spaces in beautifully crafted antique china, creating a colorful palate against the beautiful embroidered tablecloth.

The twins were actively talking about their lives and telling stories from school. Laughter seemed to be the word of the day. Finally, the meal came to an end. Her parents got around to questioning her.

"So, Cynthia, what are your plans?" her father repeated the question asked by her mother earlier.

Cynthia had relaxed, but with the question, she knew she was center stage. "Dad, why don't you and Mom tell me what you know so I can fill in the parts you don't know," she responded, waiting for either of them to say something.

Her father shrugged. "Fair," he said, folding his hand on the table. "According to what we've gathered…"

She looked at her mother. Her face was unreadable, but she knew it was her father who had this information given to him. He'd had her investigated and had not told her.

"You came to back to Charleston and lived next door to a woman by the name of Sara, who you currently live with, as well as her niece, Destiny." Her father was laying out her life. It sounded strange to have it related so concisely, as if she were a prisoner about to be sentenced.

A hush fell over the room when his voice faded. Both sets of eyes were on her. Miss Betty excused the boys, mentioning taking them to see the grounds around the house. Cynthia knew this meant it was time to tell her story.

"I went to Clemson, found out I was pregnant, and my life entered what seemed like the twilight zone. Saltine crackers became my best friend. It didn't take long for me to be the topic of most discussions in the dorm. Dad had given me enough money so I was able to get an apartment off campus…"

Looking at her parents, Cynthia began to ring her hands. "After the first six months of pregnancy, I met a girl named Crystal in my econ class. She was a great friend. Her family kind of adopted me. After I had the babies, it was her parents who allowed me to live in their vacation home in Charleston. They also hired a nanny to help me with the babies. Without their help, I'm sure I would never have made it. Eventually, things got easier. I got some scholarship money to attend college and keep the bills paid. I went to school at night, and the boys were in daycare until I met my neighbor Miss Sara."

She watched both of the faces around her. Her mother smiled, giving her courage. Her father winked at her over his cup of coffee.

"I got so many scholarships…" She related the story of how she discovered monies she never knew about. "The twins and I lived meager lives, but that was because I didn't want to waste the money given to me by the college."

"They never told you where the money came from because we asked them not to tell you. I thought that if you knew, you would refuse it," her mother stated. Cynthia shook her head. Her mother was as beautiful as the fashion model Shelia Johnson. But the look on her face was one of regret and sorrow. "Why didn't you come to us, Cynthia?" her father asked.

"After you both said how I was no longer your daughter because I wouldn't have the abortion, I just shut that door. After losing Marvin and losing both of you, my baby was all I had. It was not until…"

"You were five months when you knew you were carrying twins…" her mother finished.

Shock registered in Cynthia's face as she looked at both of her parents. She couldn't believe what she was hearing. Excusing herself, her mother left the room, returning with two large baby blue photo albums. She handed both of them to Cynthia. Taking the photo albums, Cynthia rubbed her hands over the silk covers. One had Jonathan's name and the other had David's name. Their pictures were on the front. She began to quickly flip through the photo albums. The pictures seemed to have been put in with so much care and love. She went back to the front of the first book, opening up the first page. She chuckled when she saw her two smiling little babies. Each picture meant something to her. There were pictures of them in the hospital, their first birthday, and each of their first steps. She couldn't believe her eyes. Her sons' lives were chronicled in these photo albums. Their investigator had gotten all of her negatives; these albums were the proof of it.

Cynthia blinked away the sudden mist of tears that threatened to overtake her eyes. She smiled at her parents. They had wanted her in their lives all of the time. She began to tell them about each of the pictures as she turned the pages to their individual books. Her sons had her parents love all of their lives, even if they were not aware of it. They were able to attend a preschool at the Charleston Academy, and now she knew it was courtesy of her parents. Her parents had orchestrated the scholarships that she had received. The money was enough to take care of all of the twins' needs. They were gifts Cynthia couldn't refuse, as much as it had irked her pride and independence. But she had learned the hard way that as a mom, she had to make decisions based on Jonathan's and David's well-being.

When she left home for college, she was on top of the world. When she discovered that the reason for her weight gain was not the freshmen ten but a set of twins, she'd been shocked and totally unprepared. Now she couldn't imagine life without them. Just like she could no longer imagine a life away from her parents, Marvin, or Seattle.

Cynthia told her parents the story of her lost years—a clean, sanitized retelling of her life that left out the ugly parts, the depression, and the tears in the midnight, the insults thrown at her by people she didn't even know, and the sleepless nights.

"Life was tough," she said as calmly as she could. "Some days I thought I'd have to resort to making negative decisions that could have destroyed my life and the twins' lives. But God had another plan. All of my decisions were based on the twins' safety and well-being."

"You were a better person than your mother and I," her father said, reaching out to take her hand as she continued to talk.

"I worked and went to school around the twins' schedule. I never wanted them to go to a day care center. Children are vulnerable. People think—"

"I know what people think," Gwendolyn interjected. "I also know that sometimes people don't think. For you to struggle because your father and I accused you of ruining your life was not fair to you or the twins, and we were awful to Marvin."

Cynthia felt her cold heart begin to thaw even more at those words. Her mother's tone was indignantly protective. It reminded her of all the times her parents took up for her when she was being mistreated as a child.

"What about your relationship with Marvin? Who broke it off? You?"

Cynthia nodded.

"Why?" Her mother narrowed her eyes. The light from the window cast strong shadows, so her face was not easily read. "Because he wouldn't listen to reason, and he was so stubborn back then?"

Cynthia laughed in spite of herself.

"It was a terrible time," Cynthia explained. "Both of our emotions ran very high on all issues. I wanted to try, and for a while I even considered telling him I was pregnant to see if we could get past it. But I guess that, deep inside, I couldn't forgive him for believing that he couldn't trust me. I knew what that meant."

"What did it mean?" her father asked.

"It meant he thought we were…" She wasn't sure how not to make it sound like a stereotypical case of class envy. "He thought we were rich and powerful, not just in income, but he saw our value system differently from his parents."

Her comment was followed by a small silence, but somehow she didn't feel she'd offended her parents. Her father tapped his fingers lightly on the dining room table. After a few seconds, she turned her head to gaze through the window.

As the sunset deepened, the landscape lights had blazed on. They could clearly see David and Jonathan, who had run ahead of Betty to the edge of the lawn and were throwing rocks into the lake. If they were concerned about their mother, it didn't show. They were enjoying themselves.

Finally, with a sigh, Edward turned back to Cynthia.

"Men can be very stupid," he said. "But they do sometimes learn from their mistakes. I did. What I did to both of you all those years ago was wrong. Have you considered the possibility that Marvin has learned from his as well?"

"I know he has. We've seen each other often since I've been back. But before I make any major decisions, it was important that I talked to both of you."

Gwendolyn nodded. I…probably shouldn't say this, but it's fairly clear you still love him, even to me."

Cynthia flushed. She opened her mouth to deny it but closed it again. What was the use? She'd already learned that her mother was almost preternaturally astute when it came to reading people. It was one of her many assets as a lawyer.

"Yes, Mother, you're right," she said. "I want us to be a family."

"I wonder." Gwendolyn folded her hands in her lap. "Years ago, my husband did a very stupid thing. It was even worse than what Marvin did in not trusting you. The woman he loved left him because of it, and she didn't merely break his heart she took it with her. He couldn't breathe or laugh. It was not until he made a promise to take care of his only daughter and her children in Charleston, South Carolina, that his wife returned home to him."

The subdued anguish in her mother's voice shocked Cynthia. She had naively assumed that her parents must always have basked in the glow of their love for each other. The fact that such sorrow could lurk behind Edward Mason's sparkling smile or Gwendolyn's gracious poise was almost inconceivable.

She didn't have a comeback.

Her mother lifted a hand and beckoned for Cynthia to come around the table to her side. She continued to extend her beautifully manicured fingers until Cynthia took them.

"Maybe you should consider telling him everything. He may be willing to forget the past, which is exactly what we all need to do."

"But..." Cynthia wondered if her mother or father could understand. She'd already endured years of withdrawal pains. She did want to start over. "If he...if we..."

Gwendolyn smiled. "I know. That's the risk, of course. But if I've learned anything in my years, it's this. No matter how much you'd like to be rid of it, love is difficult to kill."

They talked, really talked for what seemed like hours. It wasn't until Betty brought the boys into the room with them saying they were tired that they realized the lateness of the hour.

Her mother was on her feet, looking at Cynthia and then casting a look at her husband as if to say, "help me out here."

Her father eagerly jumped into the conversation. "Cynthia, please don't leave. As a matter of fact, we have something to show you. We never knew if this opportunity would present itself, but we were always prepared just in case you and the twins came home."

"We designed a whole suite just for the twins. We want you to stay the night. Come on. We'd love to show it to you." Smiling, her father grabbed the twins' hands, heading for the stairs.

Giving God the glory, Cynthia followed her family up the stairs.

CHAPTER 30

Destiny jumped at the sound of the doorbell. Laughing at herself, she couldn't believe how nervous she was. It was Adam, always on time. Not wanting to wake anyone, she rushed to the door. "You have perfect timing. I'm ready," she said, unlocking both the screen door and front door.

"I can't believe how warm it is already, and it's not even eleven o'clock in the morning yet," she said, running her hands up and down her arms. "Come on in. Would you care for coffee?"

Adam grinned. "Yeah, coffee would be great. That always helps to get my day started, other than prayer. Everyone's still asleep?" Adam asked, looking around.

"Yes, everyone's still asleep. It was a long but wonderful day yesterday." She looked around at him while walking toward the kitchen.

"Your parents are a joy."

Destiny was rambling, but she was also conscious of the fact that Adam watched her as she led the way into the kitchen. She wore a beautiful dress with a pretty lavender floral print, accented by a patent leather black belt and a pair of strappy-heeled sandals that showed off her long legs. After filling a mug for Adam, she paused to ask how he liked his coffee.

"A little cream and sugar," he requested. After doing as he asked, she handed it to him. "Like I said, nothing beats a good cup of coffee to start the morning. Mmmm," he murmured, taking a sip. "That's good."

"I made some biscuits this morning. Help yourself because if the twins were up, there wouldn't be any left for you."

By the time she came back into the living area, she was carrying her garment bag from her room.

He was dressed simply in a pair of blue jeans and a red polo shirt. He looked good for their journey to Tacoma. To divert her thoughts, she said, "I'll get my handbag."

Destiny's heart had stopped racing. She really had no reason to be concerned about their trip. Adam had promised her that the rooms would be adjoining.

"Ready?"

"Yes." Destiny was happy when Adam took the suitcase. Looking around, she was satisfied that she had left nothing to do before they went out the door. She set the alarm. Adam walked with her down the stairs.

After placing her bags in the back, he turned to her, helping her into the SUV without comment. Once she was settled, he crossed to the driver's side and climbed inside. Seatbelt in place, Adam took Destiny's hand, saying a prayer before they left. They were traveling along the interstate, which was crowded with the early morning traffic. Neither of them said anything. They were focusing on the passing scenery. The driving distance between Seattle and Tacoma was approximately thirty-four miles, but he'd planned for them to stop for lunch.

Destiny was doing her best to hide her nervousness, Adam seemed to see right through it. "Destiny, are you okay?" he asked, snapping her out of her thoughts. She smiled and relaxed her hands by rubbing them down her sundress.

"Of course, I'm fine. Just trying to relax a little." Destiny knew he had a wonderful trip planned for them. She had made up her mind to trust Adam so that they could enjoy themselves.

"Well, I am excited about these two days that we'll be spending together." Smiling, he looked over at Destiny. Taking her hand, he kissed it.

"So what are we going to do first?" she asked.

"We're going to check in, and then I thought we'd enjoy the sights around the hotel."

"Sounds perfect." She smiled.

They arrived at the Hotel Murano in the heart of downtown Tacoma. After settling in, they met in the lobby. He smiled automatically when he saw her. "So where are we going?" she asked.

"I thought we'd go over to the Proctor shopping district. There's a festival in town, so there are a lot of visitors in the city. I thought you'd enjoy it," he answered, taking her hand.

Sweet peace filled the air, lifting their spirits as they strolled out of their hotel. They were both silent, reflecting on their own thoughts. There was a feeling in the air that gave each of them a sense of peace. They were able to relax and enjoy each other without the feeling of being watched by people who may have known them.

Destiny thought Adam had planned a perfect trip. It gave them the time they needed to relax and enjoy each other.

Every now and then they'd exchange a look, smiling as they held hands. They finally made it to the Proctor district, a quaint three-block shopping district. The scent of warm bodies and cinnamon roasted almonds mingled in the gentle breeze.

Strolling hand in hand, Destiny and Adam laughed and talked continuously, enjoying themselves. There was a small jazz band playing, and Adam stopped, pulling Destiny toward him as they joined the other couples dancing on the lawn. Gently squeezing her fingers, he asked, "Are you having a good time, sweetheart?"

She smiled, loving the sound of him calling her sweetheart. "I'm feeling like we are the only two people on the earth."

He took her hand. "It's only you and me for right now. Let's enjoy our time together."

They were having so much fun. Destiny enjoyed all of the goods from the local vendors. She brought a pair of earrings to wear with her suit tomorrow night. She also saw a pair of cufflinks that she purchased for Adam.

After returning to the hotel, they went into the Bite restaurant, which overlooked four floors, giving each guest a view of the art below. There were several couples enjoying this local festival. Many of them were staying at the hotel. They were content watching the couples in the lobby mingling with each other below. Then they decided that they would have something light to eat, and afterward they'd return to their individual rooms for a nap before their evening activities. Sitting down at their table, Destiny looked at Adam.

"What?" he asked, noticing her stare.

"Oh nothing," she replied, smiling. "I've had a wonderful time, and we've only been here a few hours. I love spending time with you."

"That's wonderful to know because I love spending time with you as well," he said, giving her a quick wink.

Destiny finished her salad and rested her chin on one hand, still observing him. "I'm so honored that you asked me to accompany you on this trip. I hope that it doesn't cause problems tomorrow night at church," she said casually.

"Wha...what?" he asked, his forked paused halfway to his mouth.

"Since we've been seeing each other more, I have noticed some changes in some of the women at our church," she continued cautiously, not wanting to offend or cause him unnecessary stress.

"I'm not concerned about what anyone thinks. That goes for anyone at Greater Community or the church tomorrow night. This relationship is between you, God, and me. Everyone else doesn't even matter, we've been through this now on several occasions," he insisted hotly.

"Okay, just checking," she said soothingly. Adam stabbed his sandwich and avoided making eye contact.

"It's okay, but this is between us"—he pointed at the both of them—"and I want to enjoy what's happening between us without outside influences. Tomorrow will take care of itself, all right?" He took the final piece of his sandwich, popping it into his mouth as if to say that this subject was finished. Destiny looked at Adam, smiling. She loved him. He made her laugh. Each time he laughed, it caused her heart to swell all the more.

Taking out the small package from her bag, she handed it to Adam. "I saw these and thought they were perfect for you." Destiny watched as Adam removed the wrapping.

He couldn't hide his surprise. He admired the cufflinks that were a black-and-white checkerboard pattern. She had pictured how wonderful they would look with any of the suits he had in his wardrobe.

He smiled. "I love them, thank you. I'm going to wear them tomorrow," he said, putting them back in their case.

"I'm glad you like them." Destiny was elated. She'd never bought a gift for a pastor before. Adam kissed Destiny softly on the cheek. "I love them, and I love that you brought them for me. It means a lot." He then placed a bag in front of Destiny. She watched as he pulled out a box. Handing it to her, he requested that she open it. When she did, she was shocked to see a pair of expensive stilettos that were in the window of the hotel's lobby. "The moment I saw you look at these in the hotel boutique, I knew they would look extraordinary on you."

"Oh my, they're beautiful, Adam. When did you get them?"

"I asked the concierge to have them waiting for me here in the café." Adam winked his eye at her.

"The look on your face when you saw them was priceless. Is that look only for shoes? Or can a brother get a special look like that as well?" Leaning toward him, Destiny kissed him on the cheek.

"I promise to never put a pair of shoes before you." She laughed heartily as they continued to enjoy their afternoon.

"When do you think you can be ready to leave for our concert tonight?" He was content, ready to enjoy the rest of their evening he'd planned.

"Well, since it's a surprise and I'm not sure of what to wear, it will take some time. How about seven? That will give us a couple of hours to sleep." She exhaled, hoping he would break down and give her a clue.

"You didn't think I'd give away all my plans, did you? I've been looking forward to this since I first told you about the revival." He was laughing, and she loved the sound of it coming from deep inside his belly.

"Me too, so I won't ask any more questions. The rest of the night is in your hands."

"Well, I promise you won't be disappointed." Getting up, Adam grabbed their bags, and they headed for the elevators.

For the evening, Destiny chose to wear a lobster-red-and-cream silk halter dress. A pair of orange drop earrings, two trendy bangles, and a pair of cream stilettos set off the outfit. She felt good about her choice after looking at herself in the mirror one last time before joining Adam in the lobby to leave. Adam looked handsome tonight in his casual attire.

Her eyes were fixed on Smokie Norful. She couldn't believe he had planned all of this. It was a wonderful surprise that made the day perfect. She had told him on one occasion how much she liked his music. At that moment, Adam turned. His lips were curved in a smile, messing with her senses. Then he shared a light kiss with her. She was trying to keep it holy, but he was making it hard! She couldn't believe he'd remembered her telling him that she loved Smokie Norful.

Everybody in the audience clapped as Smokie sang his last song and her favorite "I Need You Now." The audience began to get up and mill around, strolling through the building. Destiny couldn't help but notice that some of the staff were beginning to move some of the tables and chairs, making the dance floor available for couples to dance.

"He was really good, wasn't he?" She looked over at Adam, finding him watching her.

"Oh yes, he was. I hear that he's up for another Grammy award. Are you having a good time?" Adam's whispered breath fanned her cheek. She looked over at him and smiled. "I loved it. Thank you for planning this evening. It was wonderful." The music changed, and they both decided to move upstairs to the balcony for some privacy.

"I just wanted you to be happy, but I must admit the performance was great and the event was well planned.

Adam's smile was affectionate as he moved closer to her. The way he looked at her made her heart thump with expectation. Her stomach was churning and she'd started to sweat. Suddenly her heart was beating fast because she wanted to kiss him without him being the initiator. She smoothed the creases out of her dress. Their eyes met, and he was smiling at her bashfulness. They both burst into laughter. It was almost comical.

Adam filled two glasses, giving one to her and lifting his in a toast. "To the lady in my life, I care for you deeply."

"To the most wonderful man in my life, I care about you as well." *If only he knew*, she thought, lowering her eyes to drink from her glass. She could feel him watching her. She shifted on her seat.

"Let's get out of here while I'm still thinking straight," Adam muttered. As if on cue, footsteps sounded on the stairs, then in the next minute, people were joining them in the room. Adam kept his arms around her and continued to send heated glances her way. They both finished their drinks and went back to the hotel.

They entered the hotel, walking toward the bank of elevators. He glanced over at Destiny once they were inside the elevator, thinking that he wished they were married already. She was quiet. He figured they were both caught up in memories of their day spent together.

Once they made it back to their rooms, Adam gave her a tender kiss good night and watched her close the door. Tonight had been tough, but they had made it. He didn't know how much longer he would have to deal with his flesh, but when he remembered Smokie's song, he smiled and sang, "Lord, I need you now."

The following evening, Destiny looked stunning in her pink, two-piece crepe suit with a ruffled skirt. He knew he should not have been looking, but her legs were stunning in the gray stilettos he'd bought for her. She sat in the front row next to the pastor's wife, smiling as she watched him. He had on the cuff links she'd bought him. She had told him earlier that he'd looked good in his tailor-made black suit. Even though they had not talked much since arriving this evening, he had enjoyed his day with her. Her thoughtfulness toward him was never-ending on this trip.

She listened as they introduced Adam to the congregation. As he walked toward the podium, she noticed he was watching her. He had winked at her as he got up out of his seat. She couldn't help but blush. She knew that the pastor's wife saw it because she squeezed her hand.

Listening to Adam as he was preaching was an awesome experience. Everyone was responding heartily to what he was saying. The spirit of the Lord came in that sanctuary and turned it upside down. Not a person was sitting as he began to close his message. Hallelujahs and amens were shouted out and followed by some calling out, "Preach, preacher, preach!" Destiny was proud of Adam, so proud of the way he allowed God to use him on every opportunity he was given. Even though most of the congregation had worked all day before coming to church, no one showed any signs of weariness.

After falling into bed, Destiny adjusted the pillows. Adam had kissed her before saying good night. She was so comfortable with him. Adam was the man for her. He had proven to be a perfect gentleman. Sinking further into the bed, she closed her eyes and slept.

CHAPTER 31

So this was Regina, and he couldn't believe how attractive she was as she stood there holding the hotel door opened for him. Stanley could imagine being with her if the circumstances were different. His chest tightened with that thought. As much as his contempt for Destiny tied his gut into knots, he was prepared to do whatever was necessary to have her again.

"May I sit down?" He couldn't believe she acted so surprised to see him standing at her door. After all, they'd discussed him coming over earlier this week. He couldn't afford her getting angry, so he made an effort to keep her calm and he had to stay calm himself.

He was grateful she had notified him with information that led him to Seattle. Since they had both been making anonymous phone calls to Destiny he thought they had some sort of camaraderie between them. He'd just returned from Destiny's house where he saw her and the pastor preparing to go on a trip because he saw him put a suitcase in the car. She was sleeping with the pastor. He shook his head in unbelief; it had taken him months to get her in his bed. That fact alone sobered him and gave him more reason for hating her.

"You're not going to change your mind about helping me, are you, Regina?"

The hungry animal look in her eyes gave him the answer he needed. It also let him know that this woman was in deep emotional trouble. But then again he had some deeply rooted problems of his own. Maybe that's why they could work together.

"I swear I'm not here to make you do anything you don't want to do, Regina." He held up his hands in surrender, prayed she would believe him. It was a lie. He needed her help. Somehow he had to persuade her to confront Pastor Wheeler. Maybe they'd have a happy reunion and an even brighter future together. She needed to face him so she could start living her life as the First Lady she wanted to be.

"My investigator said you were right. She hasn't told him anything about the rape or her past with me. I think it's time you pay him a visit." He lowered his hands back to his sides. "I can't get her out of your hair without you doing your part."

When she didn't immediately balk, he gestured to the sofa. "I'll just sit right here and listen." He eased down onto the sofa. He knew she needed money or she wouldn't be in this hotel. He was willing to give her a house and a generous amount of money if she just helped him with his plan. All she had to do was help him.

The suspicion hadn't totally cleared from her eyes. She didn't sit and she kept her arms folded over her chest in a classic protective manner.

"I'll help you but it's going to cost you," she said from where she was standing.

He relaxed at those words because he had plenty of money.

"Can you be a little more specific? How much?" This was definitely different. Usually he was the one negotiating.

Regina's gaze narrowed with uncertainty. "I don't want much, just enough to pay for my wedding. Being the wife of a pastor, I want a grand wedding; a hundred and fifty thousand should do the trick." She smiled but he noticed sweat forming on her forehead.

"When can you meet with him?" The idea that she'd be meeting him soon gave him immense joy. She'd done everything right so far and if she didn't come through on this, she would pay the ultimate price.

"First I need half the money to be sent to this hotel by tomorrow morning, postmarked from Atlanta. That way it will appear as if my parents sent me the money and no connection to you. Then I will call you by phone on my way to Adam's office. The rest of my money should be delivered by then."

Unable to keep the bitterness from his expression, he stood to make his point. How dare she tell him when to deliver the rest of the money?

"I know what you're thinking," she said, waving her hands for him to remain seated. "But I'll have him eating out of my hand by the time I leave his office. Adam loved me and still does, he just needs a reminder."

Struggling to maintain some semblance of composure, he met her scrutinizing gaze once more. "All right. But this better work. I'll have the money delivered here in the morning. You said he still loves you? What proof do you have?"

She turned and move to the sofa he vacated and picked up her purse from the table, removing whatever was inside. She walked back to where he waited and thrust it at him.

A newspaper article. "Pastor Adam Wheeler Admits to Cyber-porn Addiction." His heart raced with excitement. He looked at her. "Is this our Pastor Wheeler?" The surprise in his tone gave away the emotions twisting inside him.

"The one in the same. Don't you recognize him from the picture? He was so distraught after our break up, the poor man turned into a cyber-porn addict. I know every trick in the book. I'll get him back; you just get my money."

Yes. This woman was a freak. He couldn't help but get his hopes up with evidence like this. He handed the article back to her. "What else do you have?" He'd had his heart ripped out for the last time being gullible.

She snatched the article from him.

Regina stood looking at him in silence for a moment. He really didn't doubt her ability; he just wanted to see some of her talents. She reached behind her and unzipped her dress letting it pool at her feet. Revealing her body. She stood there, looking at him for a moment that seemed to last forever.

"Even you can't resist this," she waved her hands down her body. "If you can then walk out that door." She gestured to the door. "Just know that I am a woman with experience and not a little goodie two shoes like Destiny. I can teach you more than you have ever taught her. I don't need a teacher, just a man."

He wanted to be angry. But instead he lowered himself back onto the sofa and watched as she walked toward him.

CHAPTER 32

The time they spent together had been wonderful. Adam was an anointed speaker but she was glad to be home. It was just after nine in the morning. Sara had called earlier to say she had spent the night at Tina's helping them spoil the baby. Cynthia had been spending more time with her parents since she'd reunited with them a month ago, but today she'd gone to work and the boys were at school. All of their lives seemed to be coming together.

As they drove into her neighborhood, Destiny noticed a lone car parked across the street. She frowned. The man was looking down but something about his profile seemed familiar. Terror built inside her chest as she recognized Stanley. The fine hairs at the base of her neck quivered with apprehension. Tears welled in her eyes. Her temples throbbed and an alarm twisted in her chest. The need to jump out of the car came over her so suddenly. As if she felt his attention on her, she turned and looked toward the car once again. Their gazes locked across the distance as if it were mere inches rather than several yards. Tension exploded inside her. His head was shaven and his face seemed slimmer, but she knew it was Stanley. Then he rolled down his window, confirming her fear.

"Impossible." The muttered word startled her despite its having crossed her lips. How did he find me?" Now she could put a face to the calls she'd been receiving. Her hands began to shake and her stomach fell when she saw him get out of the car. "How did who find you?" Adam asked. Watching as he turned off the car she saw him glance in his rear view mirror.

"Stanley." She opened her door but Adam reached over to close it. Looking at her with concern, he asked again, "Who is Stanley? And what is he doing here?"

Her hands were fidgeting in her lap. Dropping her head she said, "I never thought he would find me." She reached for the door again. This time she slowly climbed out. Adam got out on his side rushing around the car to assist her.

Stanley's focus for the moment seemed to be on Adam; he hadn't looked in her direction. Adam squared his shoulders and protectively wrapped his arms around her.

"Is he the guy you left in South Carolina?" he asked.

"Yes," was all she could muster.

"I can get rid of him for you." Dropping his arm from around her shoulders, he approached Stanley. She panicked, not wanting anyone to get hurt. Her mind immediately thought about her dream. Not here and not now. They didn't need yelling, screaming, and loud, angry words. She didn't want Adam to be any part of her ugly past.

Rushing, she grabbed his arm before he met Stanley on the street. "N-no. Adam I don't want any trouble lets just go inside."

"I'm not worried about trouble Destiny. If this guy is here to harm you in any way, I'll protect you. Do you understand?" He looked into her eyes making sure she understood. "He can get back in his car and go back to wherever he came from."

She couldn't believe her eyes as Stanley powered toward the both of them with anger written all of his face causing her heart to race even the more. Stanley was mean and he would fight even if he weren't pushed.

"No, let me talk to him first." There was urgency in her voice.

"Are you crazy? I don't think so." He pulled away from her just as Stanley was walking up the drive. She took a shaky breath and gathered her courage; she couldn't let Adam get hurt because of her. She watched as Stanley looked from Adam to her. His eyes were black as coal and piercing. "Who is this, Destiny? I see it didn't take you long to find someone new, but sluts always do, don't they?" His hands were balled into fist.

It happened so quickly all she could see was Adam's fist connect with Stanley's chin. It surprised him because he tripped and ended up on the ground. He was cussing as he scrambled to his feet.

Her stomach was in a big knot as she held on to Adam slightly standing behind him. "Please, stop this!" He meant well, she knew he did, but Stanley was crazy.

"Go in the house and call the police, Destiny." Adam looked at her to reinforce what he had just said. "Now! Destiny." She came out of her trance, running toward the house and fumbled in her purse for the keys. Once inside she pulled out her cell phone to call the police. But then she became distracted when she heard yelling.

Opening the door and moving onto the porch, she heard Stanley yelling, "If you want to help, then go home." He walked right up on Adam so close she was sure he could see his tonsils. He came to a stop, his shoulders braced. "I'm dying, I need her to be with me."

From the porch Destiny saw Adam glance at her with the comment that was made by Stanley. Getting nervous she ran down the steps to hear him repeat himself. "Yeah, I said I'm dying!" He had his finger in Adam's face. Destiny saw his nose flaring from heavy breathing.

"Dying? Stanley, please! You're such a liar!" She couldn't believe what he was saying.

Then she saw him breathing rapidly and holding his chest, "Come on Destiny, why else would I come all this way? You know me; we lived together or didn't you tell the pastor about us?"

Time seemed to be moving slowly. All she could do was stare. Adam looked angry. His mouth was poised to say something but his lips didn't move. His eyes conveyed hurt. It was tough seeing his hurt. He only meant to help her and in the process he was hearing things about her that she hadn't had enough courage to share with him.

Turning to leave Stanley made one last quip, "I'm not feeling so good especially after being hit by your pastor, and I'm a sick." He held his side. "I needed his prayers not his anger." His hand went into his pocket pulling out a piece of paper. He handed it to Destiny. "This is where I'm staying and the number. I really need to discuss my illness with you."

He seemed almost defeated as he walked slowly back to his car. When he reached the driver's side, he leaned against the door in a resting position before finally opening it to get in. Destiny wasn't sure but it looked as if Stanley had smirked and winked at her before finally closing the car door.

Touching his arm, she looked at Adam as Stanley's car pulled off. "Thank you, Adam." He shifted causing her hand to drop to her side. He nodded once, saying nothing more and walked stiffly away from her, his gait tense as he opened his trunk to take out her suit case. He walked up the steps, placing her suitcase just inside the door of the house. She hadn't meant to wait this long. She'd made up her mind to tell him everything after their trip but now everything was messed up. She steeled her spine and gathered up all the courage she had. She wasn't good with uncomfortable situations. But right now she had to be. "Please, let me handle this situation with Stanley." She was almost begging him to understand. "We can meet later and I'll tell you everything."

Destiny looked sadly at Adam. He didn't even respond. He turned and silently walked out of the house. When she heard his car's engine, she knew he was gone. Stanley had done it again—without even throwing a punch he had beaten her once again.

CHAPTER 33

Adam knew his brother was watching him. So he wasn't surprised when he asked, "What's got you pacing around my living room this afternoon? Didn't you just get home from your trip with Destiny?"

He hadn't been ready to go home so he found himself driving to Marvin's house. To say that he was rattled by the events of earlier was an under statement. There hadn't been much conversation between the two of them since he had gotten there.

Adam winced at his brother's question. He knew Marvin was trying to get a conversation started. He just couldn't understand all that had transpired at Destiny's earlier. It was just like the enemy to show up after their wonderful trip. He moved over to sit in an armchair across from his brother.

"I met an old friend of Destiny's when I dropped her off. Guess who it was? The man she lived with before coming to Seattle."

"I gather neither of you were expecting him, and by the expression on your face it must not have gone well. You didn't know about him did you?"

Adam laid his head back on the chair, closing his eyes before saying, "No I didn't and to make matters worst, he says he's dying." He watched as his brother digested this information.

"That must have been a surprise."

"I can't believe she didn't tell me about him. I hit the guy for God's sake! I looked like a jerk in this whole situation." He rubbed his forehead, a small headache forming.

"You hit him? Why on earth did you do that?" Adam watched Marvin stand up to give him a concerned look.

"He called her a slut, and I punched him before I could think. I'm not proud of that, but I couldn't let him talk about her like that in my presence." He shook his head in disgust.

"That must have felt good. He must be a real jerk. She seems too nice to be with someone like that."

"My thoughts exactly." Adam got up out of the chair again, walking over to look out the window.

"I was just doing what any man who cares about a woman would do. I didn't know anything about the guy but I didn't like the way he looked and the way he spoke to her." Turning around, he looked back at his brother.

"Can you believe she wants to talk to the guy? She said she wanted to handle it alone." He shook his head. "I just wanted to protect her is all, was I wrong for that? Maybe he was telling the truth. Maybe his is dying."

Marvin joined him at the window. "Destiny has to be a smart and special lady. If she wasn't, you wouldn't have fallen for her."

"Marvin you should have seen her. She was standing straight and tall, her feet braced, her arms crossed in front of her like a shield. Almost like she was afraid. She didn't seem happy. As a matter of fact she called him a liar."

"Well, that seems like she knows a little about his character." Marvin's voice sounded as if he was relieved as he walked back to his chair and began to flip through the on-screen channel guide.

"It's going to be fine, man, she'll call you and you both will talk. Everything will be fine. Trust me, on this."

The one thing that stayed with Adam was that Destiny hadn't wanted him to help her. Everything in him wanted her to need him, wanted to stay there and make sure she was all right. He was torn between doing what he wanted and what she asked him to do.

He dropped back down in his seat, propping his feet on the ottoman in front of him, and stared at the program Marvin was watching without seeing a thing.

The last thing Destiny wanted was to have a confrontation with Stanley in front of Adam. Her hands were trembling as she tried to unpack from their trip. It had been more than she could have ever imagined. Their friendship had grown into more. But now that Stanley was in town, she had no idea what would happen. Needing to relax, she went into the kitchen to make a pot of tea. Still nervous about the encounter, her hands were shaking uncontrollably. She couldn't even hold the teacup steady. She hadn't been as frightened as she thought she'd be to be in his presence again. He was there to get her back even if it meant lying to do it. His behavior had always been erratic even more so during the last six months of their relationship. His mood swings were always up and down.

If it was one thing she knew from her counseling sessions at Greater Community, it was time to stop turning to others to save her from her own demons. After her rape in college and not knowing her father, she'd relied on Tina and Sara far too much. Then she'd allowed Stanley to become her rock—her savior— and it almost cost her life. His total domination of her life had destroyed something deep inside of her. She had no strength of her own. It was time she broke the cycle and it started today when she asked Adam to let her handle Stanley.

A smile tugged on her mouth, because she knew that from now on if there was a battle to be fought, she, along with the help of the Lord, would be fighting them. She felt free in her spirit—pure liberation flooded her soul. Yes, she would meet with Stanley because it was time to slay her Goliath.

The sound of a car engine caught her attention, but she resisted the urge to walk over to the window. It was probably Sara or Cynthia and the twins coming home. Stanley had left almost an hour ago with Adam leaving shortly after him. He hadn't come over to say goodbye. She really didn't blame him for that, either. His face held a look of being shocked by the whole situation so she wasn't surprised when he got in the car and just left. She'd lied to him from the moment they'd met, because she never really told him the truth about herself.

Destiny wasn't happy with herself at the moment, but it was hard to be sad about the relationship she'd developed with Adam, even if he hated her for what she'd done. He was an incredible man and he believed in her. It was easy for her to laugh when she was around him. Why couldn't she have met him three years ago? She poured her cup of tea and walked into the living room. Hearing the doorbell, she put her cup down and opened the front door without checking the peephole. Stanley was standing in the doorway. Shock registered on her face at the same time he offered an ugly smirk.

"Baby, guess who's coming to dinner?"

CHAPTER 34

Adam stopped reading his Bible. After closing it, he stood. Stretching his arms above his head, he yawned. He had been working nonstop since he left his brother's house. It had been a tremendously blessed couple of days in Tacoma. But everything changed with the arrival of Stanley. He hadn't talked to her since they got back earlier but she wanted to handle things with him her way. He hoped to complete this week's sermon, or at least most of it, but his thoughts were all over the place.

Adam returned to his desk and shut down his laptop. Glancing around the room, he found himself daydreaming about Destiny rather than getting his sermon finished.

At the sound of a knock at the door, he forgot those thoughts. Running his hands down his face, he moved to the door and opened it.

"Pastor, there is someone here to see you." His secretary seemed nervous. "She insisted on following me in here."

Alexandra, always the efficient secretary, was upset. But when Adam saw Regina, he understood why. As she walked into his office, her eyes danced around the room.

Turning around, her expression showed her annoyance. Her eyes darkened as she smiled. "That will be all, Alexandra. I promise not to bite him."

Adam knew his secretary and he could tell by the lines of tension forming around her eyes that Regina was getting on her nerves. It was only after he gave her a nod indicating everything was fine that she turned to leave. He knew she didn't like the way Regina presented herself.

Regina dismissed Alexandra, stating, "She doesn't seem very obedient." Her eyes were not warm as she watched her leave. "Did she come with the church?"

"Regina, that was not a very nice thing to say about Alexandra. She has been my personal assistant since coming to Greater Community." He watched her now, remembering why he'd called off their engagement. She was a selfish and spoiled woman, nothing like Destiny.

One of the first things he noticed was that she had changed her hair color to a rich auburn. Her thick curls went to her shoulders. She hadn't gained any weight, still a slender woman. His gaze automatically moved over her figure. A blue silk blouse was tucked into a short gray skirt at her tiny waist, which accented her long legs. He shoved his hands in his pockets, trying to figure out how to get rid of her.

She moved gracefully as she took the time to look at all of his pictures and plaques on the walls around the room. After watching her for a few moments, Adam asked the obvious question. "Regina, what are you doing here?"

"It's been a while." She walked toward him, stopping to grab his hands. "I've missed you."

He snatched his hands from hers. "How in the world did you find me here?"

"Come on, Adam. You've got the fastest-growing church in the Northwest. You are known all over the country for your seminars on the dangers of the Internet for pastors. It wasn't hard. You used to talk about Seattle all the time when we were engaged." She bent toward him, but he dodged her kiss. Smiling, she moved to sit in one of his chairs, crossing her legs at the knee and swinging them slightly. Regina's eyes twinkled with amusement as she slowly uncrossed her legs, the source of Adam's distraction.

"Daddy is in town for a revival, and since I was here, naturally I thought this would be a perfect opportunity to come see you. Don't tell me you haven't thought about me in all of these years." She smiled sweetly while twirling a curl around her finger.

"Everyone in this city speaks highly of you and the things you've done in this community. From the gossip I've been hearing, you're still very much a single pastor. I assume there must be a reason for that since we broke up years ago."

Adam couldn't believe she was even discussing this with him. They were finished.

"Adam, don't you think it's time our little break was over? I've forgiven you for leaving me, so now we can resume our relationship again. I presume you've realized the mistake you made when you left Atlanta...without me."

"Regina, what are you talking about?" He was staring at her as if she had suddenly grown two heads. "You are a piece of work."

"Adam, darling, let's go have an early dinner, then we can talk after I have eaten. My throat is parched, and I haven't eaten since earlier this morning." She began to prance toward the door, not giving him time to answer.

Adam trailed after her, searching for a way to get her to leave as soon as possible.

Alexandra was at her desk when they walked out. She smiled at Regina, but it didn't quite reach her eyes. "Is there something I can do for you, Pastor Wheeler?"

"Thank you, Alexandra. Is there still a tray of sandwiches in the kitchen from the Sunday school teachers' meeting earlier?" he asked her.

Standing, Alexandra turned, heading toward the kitchen. "Yes, there is. Would you like for me to fix you both something? I think there's even some lemon cake and tea left. I'll just be a minute."

When she returned with the sandwiches, Adam thanked her. "This looks wonderful, Alexandra." Adam pulled out two chairs as they sat down at the table.

"No cake for me, please." Regina smoothed down her blue silk blouse. "I'm trying to maintain my perfect size four." Her fingers were busy smoothing out invisible wrinkles that only she could see.

Alexandra discreetly rolled her eyes after she turned. Adam forced back a laugh.

Wanting to get this lunch over with, Adam asked, "So how are your parents?"

She sat opposite him, her nose crinkling at the sandwich and iced tea before her. Ignoring his question, she answered, "I came with Daddy, but it was you I really wanted to see. I'm here to convince you that we need to take up where we left off."

He watched as she pushed the tea glass away from her reach. "Why would I want to take up where we left off, Regina? You made it easy for me to understand that you wanted to stay in Atlanta when I wanted to come back home to pastor."

"And you've done a wonderful job. I'm not trying to take that away from you, but even my father, your mentor, feels it's time you find a wife. Your church needs a first lady. It would be ridiculous of me to ask you to leave all of this now. Besides, Seattle is your home." She turned in her chair when she heard Alexandra enter the dining room. "Please, come here."

Alexandra moved toward her. "Yes?"

"This tea is weak. I don't drink weak tea. Just get me some water." She waved her hand and sniffed her nose in the air.

"Here is your cake, Pastor Wheeler," she said through gritted teeth, not taking her eyes off Regina.

"Thank you." Adam reached out and squeezed Alexandra's hand.

"I'll get you that water." Alexandra snatched her unwanted tea glass. As she walked by her, she caused Regina's chair to rock just a bit.

"How rude," Regina commented, straightening in the chair. "If I were your wife, she would be fired. Why is she still here with that attitude?"

"You are not my wife, and as I stated earlier, she's been here since I became pastor. She's part of the Greater Community family. Please treat her with respect," Adam stated.

"Part of the family, huh? What about this Destiny woman I've heard so much about? Is she a part of the family as well?" She asked taking a sip of her water.

"She is and what does that matter to you?" He asked.

"I want us to be a family and she's keeping that from happening." Adam laughed. "Regina, are you joking?"

"No, I'm serious. I could move here," she responded while sipping her water.

Sitting in this dining room with Regina was the last place Adam wanted to be. But he guessed for her that desperation was an unwelcome persuasion. Because in all of the years he knew her, she prided herself on needing no one. So for her being here with him showed she had to be desperate. He didn't care if she did want him back. There was no going back down that road. Adam had heard rumors that things had not been going well at home for her.

Adam's heart was thudding against his chest. He rose abruptly because he couldn't believe what he had just heard. *The nerve of this woman! Couldn't she take a hint?* She was determined to drag him back into what he had walked away from years ago. And the worst part was that now Destiny seemed not to need him as well.

"Look, Regina, I have a lot to do today. It was great seeing you again, but what we had all those years ago is over. I've moved on. I'm sure you understand there's no going back for us. Now if you're finished, I'll ask Alexandra to show you out."

Stunned, Regina pushed back her chair abruptly and stared into the eyes of Adam Wheeler. He walked toward the door where she'd hoped to make her escape without being any more embarrassed than she already was. He'd pay for this. She'd make sure of it. He closed the door behind him.

"Walking away again. You do that well!" she yelled with a mocking smile on her face.

Regina kept her head held high and tried to appear calm while her insides quivered uncontrollably. She walked past Alexandra in the hallway; she didn't need anyone to show her out. She'd foolishly hoped that Adam had been pining after her since he hadn't married. But now she'd seen the foolishness in that.

She couldn't deny how handsome Adam still was. He'd looked good this morning, standing in a pair of black trousers and a crisp white shirt with the sleeves rolled up to his elbows. He looked older, more mature, and those eyes…she'd never forget the way they used to soften when he looked at her. Nor would she forget that day, all those years ago, when she'd allowed him to walk away from her. "I…this was a mistake. I shouldn't have come today, but soon I'll have the last word," she said on a breath.

CHAPTER 35

"Aren't you glad to see me?" Stanley brushed past Destiny to walk further into the house. "I thought I'd save you a trip to my hotel." He plopped down in one of the side chairs in the room.

Destiny left the door open on purpose and turned to look at Stanley. A jolt of unexpected adrenaline sizzled through her veins; she walked over to stand across from him as he tried to scare her with his sullen facial expression. He immediately put his legs on the coffee table, crossing them.

"Could you please take your legs off the table?" Destiny looked sternly at him. "Make me." He said getting up from the chair. He walked toward her, causing her to miss a step as she moved backward, stumbling and loosing her balance on a magazine stand on the floor. She tried to regain her balance.

Stanley took a glanced around the room without offering to assist her, wrinkling his nose. "So you gave up living in my mansion for this? Looks to me like a dump but I guess it's what you're comfortable with."

After steadying herself she blurted out, "What are you doing here? I thought you were sick earlier."

He smirked again. "Sick of being played for a fool. I was glad to get a tip that you were here."

She gaped at him. "But who?"

"Some woman, Regina something-or-other." Stanley went on; he was practically beaming at her. "Seems like you may have made some enemies."

Destiny had no idea who could hate her that much to contact Stanley. But more importantly, who knew him other than her family? They wouldn't have betrayed her.

Shoving those thoughts aside, Destiny met his eyes. "I don't want any problems with you. I just want to move on with my life.

You don't want me so why don't you go back to South Carolina and do whatever it was you were doing since I've been gone."

"So now you're giving me instructions?" He chuckled. "I don't think so, Destiny. We're going back together, to get married. And trust me, if you don't you'll be amply punished for the embarrassment you've caused me."

"Embarrassment?" A wave of anger slammed into her. For the first time, the sight of his face didn't frighten her. And his sheer nerve made her want to go toe to toe with him, but for now she just wanted him out of her home.

"It's over, Stanley. I was a fool for getting involved and moving in with you. But I'm not the same girl I was all of those years ago. I refuse to put up with you for even another second."

"Who do you think you are? You're absolutely nobody! Do you hear me? Nobody!" He laughed again, taking a step toward her.

She took a step back. Her gaze darted around, searching for something she could grab in order to use it as a weapon against him. But suddenly he had her against the wall, his large hands were going for her throat.

Destiny gasped and tried to pry his hands off, but he only squeezed harder. Then she thought about her dream and what Adam had said about praying. She heard Stanley yelling; "I've had enough of this you...you little—" he started dragging her body. "You're coming home with me whether you want to or not."

"The Lord is my helper," she choked out through tears.

"Who? I thought I was your helper," he said, with a malevolent glimmer in his brown eyes.

She said it again a little stronger. "The Lord is my helper. He has not given me the spirit of fear but power, love, and a sound mind!"

With a sudden blast of strength that shocked even her, she slid out of his iron grip and brought her knee up. Stanley squealed when she made contact with his groin.

As he doubled over in pain, Destiny unleashed her elbow against the crown of his neck, then flew across the room and tore out the door.

CHAPTER 36

Adam couldn't believe that Regina had the audacity to come to his church under the assumption that he'd take her back. His spirit was heavy as he drove out of the parking lot of the church. The realization that Destiny had not called made his throat tighten, but knowing that she was probably with Stanley hurt even more.

Although she insisted that he let her handle Stanley, he couldn't dispel the feeling that he'd made a huge mistake, despite the fact that his ever-practical brain was applauding him for the decision to walk away. He felt like he should have never driven away. But Destiny had lied to him. Why hadn't she told him about Stanley? It had made sense to leave yet since he'd left her house his inner man had been screaming at him—shrieking like the sirens on a fire engine—telling him that Destiny was in grave danger and that he had to help her.

Regina had distracted him, keeping him from leaving the church sooner. His foot shook so bad on the gas pedal that it was difficult to drive. He was on his way home but the nudging of the Holy Spirit refused to subside. There it was again that still small voice.

She needs you.

He'd heard those words for the last thirty minutes. He made the turn heading toward Destiny's house. *She needs you.*

He was halfway there. Maybe she hadn't gone to meet him. Maybe she changed her mind. Maybe she wanted him to go with her. At the thought, he pressed down on the gas pedal. The frantic tugging on his spirit got worse when he reached the street she lived on and spotted the rental car Stanley had been driving earlier.

"The Lord is our helper," was all he could say.

Adam almost jumped out before coming to a complete stop hurling himself out of the car; his panic rose to another level when he saw that she'd left the front door open. Destiny had a thing for locking doors and windows. This had to be a sign of trouble. After pushing the door open, he looked cautiously around, but there was no sign of either of them.

Maybe she hadn't left the door opened. Maybe she ran out of the door. Adam took his cell phone out of his pocket and dialed the police. He explained the situation to the dispatcher, asking for help to come quickly. Then he ran out of the house headed to the backyard. He should have come as soon as the Holy Spirit had whispered she needed help. With all of the distractions he'd had today it was a wonder he had heard at all. He knew nothing about Stanley but if Destiny had fled from him by coming to Seattle, then he had to have some serious issues.

Calming himself down once he was in the backyard he looked around for any signs of either of them. His eyes scanned the area. Then he heard a scream coming from a couple of houses over. With a burst of energy he jumped over the fence, running toward the direction of the scream. When he rounded the corner he saw Destiny in the back seat of Stanley's car. He was pulling out of the driveway.

Looking around for any signs of the police being somewhere in the vicinity, Adam was disappointed that they were nowhere in sight. Checking his watch, he counted five minutes had passed since he called. Without wasting time, he jumped in his car.

He knew it would take him a few minutes to catch up with Stanley; the expressway was about ten minutes away. He swore when it started to rain. Turning out of the sub-division he saw the back of Stanley's car in the distance. Maneuvering around a slow-moving car, he put his foot on the accelerator. Then he noticed Stanley weaving in and out of traffic. It was difficult to see and he lost them for a few seconds. Instead of getting nervous he focused on staying calm and kept his eyes trained on the road. Stanley had to be doing at least seventy miles an hour on these side streets. The rain was not letting up and the wind was making it even more difficult to drive as fast as he needed to. Despite the windshield wipers going at top speed, he still had a difficult time seeing.

"Lord, please protect Destiny." He signed, recalling the look of sheer horror on her face in the back seat of that car. Looking at the street and the standing water it would be easy for a car to hydroplane. He prayed Destiny was safe despite the maniac driving the car.

Before there was time to react, he watched as a Ford truck, moving too fast for the rain, barreled into the side of Stanley's car. The brakes on the truck screeched as it jack knifed into the side of the car. The impact sent their car hurling through the red light and into the intersection. It looked as if Stanley was trying to gain control before the car hit a light pole.

CHAPTER 37

"Something's wrong. Destiny would have never left the front door open," Sara said as she walked up the porch to the house.

"Call her on her cell," Willie said as he walked cautiously around Sara, making sure it was safe for them to enter.

"She's not answering," Sara walked through the living room into the kitchen where she saw a cup of tea.

"Sara, I think you're right. Destiny had to be here, that's her special teacup. Maybe she and Adam are together." Sara noticed he was sounding hopeful trying to keep panic out of his voice.

Sara disagreed by saying, "That's not likely, considering how she sounded earlier. She wasn't expecting him to come back today. But even if he showed up she wouldn't have left the door open."

"Well, we can't just sit around, doing nothing but worrying. Let's drive over to the lab; maybe she's there and left her phone off." Willie started walking toward the front door.

"Wait! I'm going with you," Sara called, grabbing her purse. She turned to lock the door.

Sara said nothing as they drove through the rain-filled streets headed to the Destiny's place of work. They were nearing the intersection when she shouted, "Slow down, Willie. There's been an accident and it looks like someone's been hurt, look at the car against that post!"

"I have a bad feeling about this, Sara." Willie's hands were shaking with fear. He slowed the car to a crawl and eased over to the side of the road. "That looks like Adam's car pulled over ahead of us. Come on, Sara. We've got to see if it's anyone we know."

A policeman was there directing traffic away, while the approaching EMS vehicle blared in the background, surrounded by sirens and a growing crowd, Sara was being pulled by Willie through the crowd. Tears of fear and disbelief were racing down her face as she neared the scene.

"Let us through; I'm a doctor," Willie said, showing his name badge from the hospital as he pushed over the onlookers. They pushed their way to the front of the crowd.

"Oh my God, that's Destiny and, Willie, she's not moving!" Sara sobbed, unaware that Adam had come to her and was holding her. Willie left her, rushing to Destiny.

"She's going to be all right. She has to be!" Adam insisted, as he wiped away her tears. They were clinging to each other for support.

"We have to get to her!" Sara tried to rush past the authorities blocking the way. "Why aren't they doing anything to help her?" She was trembling uncontrollably.

"Willie is with her. Let them do their job, Sara. They have to get them out the car." She knew her pastor was trying to comfort her but something he said confused her.

"Them? Who else was with her? Oh, my God not Cynthia and the twins?" Her tears were falling even faster.

"No. It was Stanley. He didn't make it. He died on impact."

"What was he doing here?" Sara was furious when she heard his name.

She watched them pull Stanley's body from the car, then cover his head with a sheet. The men were still working to free Destiny. They had to pry the car open to reach her. After getting her out, the paramedics along with Willie quickly checked her out and were soon wheeling her into the flashing lights of the waiting ambulance. Through it all, Sara noticed that Destiny never opened her eyes.

"Come on Sara. We've got to follow them to hospital." Adam stressed, bringing her out of her trance. As they rushed toward their cars, he prayed out loud for God to let his healing angels touch Destiny.

While Willie drove himself in his car, Sara and Adam followed him. It was still raining so the traffic was not moving fast. As they drove Sara called Cynthia and Tina. They agreed to meet them at the hospital. She told them what had happened and asked that they pray. When she hung up she saw Adam look at her, "Well?"

"They're all upset and they'll meet us at the hospital."

CHAPTER 38

After parking the car, Adam made sure Sara was comfortable waiting with Willie before sprinting toward the emergency room with a gut-wrenching fear unlike anything he'd ever experienced. He knew that as a pastor, his faith should have given him peace. But even as a pastor sometimes fear overshadows faith. This was an all-consuming fear that was dominating the faith he carried with him. The weight of it almost cut off his ability to breathe while he was at the accident scene. She had to pull through this.

He saw a nurse and asked about Destiny. "She's with the doctor. You have to wait until he's finished," the nurse answered.

Dejected, he scowled. He'd been hoping for some news. "You might as well have a seat, Adam. It's going to be awhile; Willie went back with a doctor he knew. He'll let us know something," Sara advised him.

He saw Cynthia and Tina come in together. They went straight to Sara. He watched as they took seats, giving each other silent comfort.

He was too restless. Getting up he began pacing the short hall outside the waiting area.

After he returned to the waiting area, Tina asked, "Pastor Wheeler, do you know what happened?"

Adam gave them a short version of what he knew. "Stanley showed up at her house, and I think he was trying to force her to leave with him. When I arrived and saw the house empty, I immediately called the police, but they didn't arrive on time. So, I decided to follow them. That's when I witnessed the accident. It's a miracle it didn't kill both of them instead of just Stanley. She's blessed to be alive."

Adam felt the tears running down his face. Wiping them away, he said, "She didn't deserve any of this."

"When did Stanley get here?" Tina questioned.

"He surprised us this morning when we got back. I had no idea who he was or when he arrived in Seattle." Adam tried not to show his frustration.

"She hasn't deserved a lot of things she's had to deal with in her life," Sara said pointedly.

It was then Adam noticed Willie dressed in his scrubs along with another doctor enter the waiting area. "Can we see all of you in the hall, please?"

They came forward. No one said a word as they waited for the news.

"How is she?" Adam asked.

Adam watched as Willie shook his head. "Destiny came in with head trauma, a broken left arm and leg, and a great deal of bruising to her shoulder and face. We've been able to set the leg and arm to make her comfortable. She hasn't gain consciousness, which we believe is from her head injury. Until she wakes up we can't do anything for the head trauma."

Adam listened as Tina asked the doctor, "How long 'til she wakes up? She will wake up won't she?"

He answered with slow caution, "We can't say how long she'll be unconscious. She may have a concussion, but we won't know until she wakes up. We're hoping it will be soon."

"When can we see her, Willie?" Adam asked anxiously.

"Soon, Adam," was all he said as he turn to walk away.

It was after midnight before she was given a room and the family was allowed to see her. She still hadn't regained consciousness.

Adam was the first to go in to see her. His emotions were all over the place. He stared at Destiny, filled with overwhelming relief that she was still alive. From the side of the bed he saw a woman who still captivated him despite the bruises, swelling, and the cast encasing her arm and leg.

He couldn't get past the constriction in his throat. He wanted to cradle her close to his heart and hold her until the fear of her dying finally went away. All he wanted was for her to open those eyes and then everything in his world would be righted.

As the others came in one by one, he settled in a chair in the corner of the room. He was out of the way but he wasn't going anywhere until she opened her eyes. He would silently pray until that happened.

The first day went by without any signs of Destiny's condition changing. Her eyes still had not opened. Watching the clock only reminded Adam that hours were turning into days. The ladies as well as Willie took turns sitting at her bedside, holding her hand. They prayed to God and pleaded with her to open her eyes.

Adam stayed in his same spot in the room. Everyone else took turns going home for a change of clothes, a meal, and rest but he stayed. He found himself constantly interceding with a host of fighting angels that she'd soon open her eyes. He refused to leave when Marvin stopped by and urged him to go home and get some rest. Although he was exhausted, he was determined to stay. After three stressful days, they all were showing signs of strain, even Adam.

He was rounding the corner, coming from the bathroom when he saw Tina and Cynthia rushing toward him in the hallway Adam could feel his heartbeat speeding up and the sweat forming on his brow as his gaze went from one to the other. He became even more nervous when he saw their tearful faces. Silently, he stood waiting for them to tell him the news about Destiny.

"What's wrong?" he asked looking at both of them.

"It looks like Destiny is going to be all right, she opened her eyes, Pastor." Tina gushed looking at him.

Adam closed his eyes giving God a silent "thanks" as he felt new tears run down his cheeks. "Are you sure, Tina, what if..." his voiced trembled as he looked at them.

"Nothing is wrong, the doctor just checked her out and all of her vital signs are good. As a matter of fact, she asked for you." Cynthia said, giving him a reassuring hug. "Oh, Pastor Wheeler," Tina cried, wrapping her arms around him and Cynthia.

"She's gonna be okay. Our prayers have been answered. We won't lose her."

The tears began to flow in earnest between the three of them. Then without warning, he bowed his head holding each of their hands to give a word of thanks to God. He acknowledged them, and then he turned and walked toward the exit.

CHAPTER 39

Even before Destiny opened her eyes, she knew she was in the hospital. At the blurred edges of her consciousness she vaguely registered the sound of shoes squeaking on polished linoleum and the swish of curtains and voices, both male and female, speaking in low hushed tones. She was sure she heard her family and friends. She blinked her eyes again trying to focus. It was then that she saw all of them as they surrounded her bed. From the moment she opened her eyes she was never alone. If it wasn't her family it was a doctor or nurse checking her vital signs. She'd been given every test known to man from x-rays, cat-scans, and blood test.

They told her she'd been in a car accident three days ago, which lead to her being in a coma. Upon first hearing about her ordeal it made her heart jerk like she'd been kicked in the chest. She frowned when she raised her head to see the cast on her leg and then wished she hadn't as it made her head ache unbearably. She put a hand up to her forehead, her fingers encountering a thickly wadded bandage positioned there. Upon further inspection she found that she had broken an arm as well. It frightened her when she couldn't remember the accident but the doctor assured her that it, as well as the headaches, were perfectly normal.

Tina told her about Stanley. "I am sorry to be the one to inform you of this, but Stanley did not survive the accident," she said without any trace of emotion in her voice.

Destiny blinked, shaken by the news. No one deserved to die like that. She vaguely remembered some of the events of that day. Shock had to register on her face when they informed her of Adam's vigil for her, staying by her bedside until she regained consciousness. She struggled to conceal her disappointment when she was told he'd left rather than staying to see her.

The accident was one thing not to remember but she knew distinctly what had transpired between Adam and her. In no uncertain terms she had indicated that she didn't need his help. But every time the door opened she couldn't help but to glance over, hoping it would be him. This time when it opened, it was Sara.

"You should be trying to get some rest." Sara gave her hand a gentle squeeze after walking over to the bed.

"I can't sleep, not with this headache, plus I've been sleeping for three days."

"We can ask them to give you something for it. What about the pain in your leg and arm?" she asked. "Because I could go talk to Willie. Maybe they will reconsider if he asks?"

"No, I don't want to be a bother. My nurse told me earlier that they were being careful about using strong medications with this concussion. It's not too bad. I'd rather suffer a little pain rather than risk going to sleep and never waking up."

Sara patted her hand. "You had us worried."

"I know, I'm sorry."

"Stop it. I'm just glad you're getting better. That's all I care about. I've been here a while so I guess I'll leave and see you in the morning." She leaned over to kiss her forehead. "Sleep well, I'll be praying for those headaches."

"Goodnight," Destiny said, yawning.

She was glad to be alone because it gave her some time to reflect on what happened that day. What must Adam think of her now? Restless, sleep seemed to be evading her. It was so difficult to relax with her bruises and sore body. Her mind kept asking questions. *Why had Adam stayed the entire time especially after everything that had happened with Stanley?* Every time she thought about it, her head would pound perfidiously, forcing her to push those questions aside.

With her eyes getting heavy, she shifted, moaning from the pain. Laying hands on her head she prayed for the pain to subside.

"Can I join you in prayer?"

That was the voice she wanted to hear since she opened her eyes.

Turning she saw him, "You came…"

Chapter 40

She watched Adam walk closer to her bed as he was taking off his jacket. "Is the pain terrible?"

"At times it has been," she admitted.

"Have they given you anything?"

"They're being careful with the meds because of the concussion."

Adam sat down in the chair by her bed. With his hand extended, he gently laid it on her head being careful not to cause her unnecessary pain. He silently prayed for her headache. Then looking at her he said, "I'm just happy your eyes are open."

"They've been opened since you left." Destiny stated flatly. She could see from his expression she had thrown him a jab.

"I had to leave at the time," he said in return. "You had all of us scared to death."

She felt, rather than saw, his eyes moving over her bruised and swollen face. She was grateful Tina had brushed her hair. Using her good hand she tried to make sure it was still in place.

"Don't worry about that, Destiny," Adam said. Destiny knew he was trying to make her feel better about being in such disarray. "It's nothing a few weeks of rest won't cure. The Lord blessed you. It could have been much worse."

She fiddled with the blanket covering her injured leg.

"Thank you for watching over me the entire time I was unconscious. They told me you never left, is that true?" When he remained silent, she finally looked at him. It wasn't until their eyes connected that she felt the power of the Holy Spirit overwhelming her with the fact that God had truly kept her alive.

"I couldn't leave you, Destiny. I had to stay."

"But why? We both know you weren't happy when you left my house. Why did you come? And why did you stay away today?"

She tried to ignore the way her heart hammered in her chest and the way her head pounded as she waited for his response.

"It was the God in me."

She didn't see a trace of humor on his countenance.

"Although I wanted to see you I was tired, almost dead on my feet. So, after hearing that you were awake, I praised God and went home to rest. I needed a shower and sleep arrested me after that." Shifting in his chair he continued, "I didn't know everything about Stanley but what you told me that day did not agnate the fact that you mean a lot to me."

He leaned forward, studying her. "Your head hurts, you're tired. Maybe this is not the place or time for this discussion. I don't want to cause you to become upset."

She absently rubbed her injured arm as she fought the urge to cry. "I'm so sorry Adam. I should have told you about my past before all of this happened. Being here has given me a reality check. Tomorrow is not promised. I could have died, never seeing you again."

Watching him from her bed she noticed him fidgeting with his hands. "Would it have mattered, Destiny?"

"Yes, it would have mattered!" She shouted although she immediately regretted it because of the strain she put on her head. "I need to tell you about me, Adam." She pointed her finger at her chest to emphasize her point.

Adam shrugged. "As I drove home all I thought about was us and what would have happened if you'd been the one to die instead of Stanley in that accident. I thought about where I wanted our relationship to go. But I feel like you've been holding some things back. I want you to be sure about this…" Using his hands, he pointed to her and himself. "Because I'm sure you know where we were headed before all of this."

When he stood, he towered over her bed. Then he seemed to brace his feet for what he was going to say next. "Your accident really got my attention. Thanks be to God we still have time to deal with our problems."

Destiny bit her lip. He was right. She knew from the moment that they met this relationship was more than just a casual friendship, even if she wasn't ready to admit it to herself. "Okay, you're right," she said, wiping a tear. All of the events of the day were catching up with her emotionally.

She took a deep breath before blurting out, "You see, when I was a senior in college, I was raped."

She watched as he dropped back down in his chair. The fine lines at the corners of his eyes showed signs of his concern. His gaze grew shuttered. "Oh, my God, Destiny. I'm so sorry," he muttered in a gravely voice. Adam moved closer to Destiny, but he did not touch her. He wanted her to know that he was there for her. "I had no idea you were dealing with something like this."

"No one but Tina, her husband, and Auntie know about it. It's been my secret for all of these years." She was leaning forward, trying with shaking fingers to reach the box of tissues on her bed tray to wipe away the tears that were flowing. "I can't keep all of this stuff inside anymore, Adam. I just wanted to be free. That experience caused me to hide behind everyone, even Stanley, because I thought I did something to deserve it."

"Your fault? No, Destiny, rape is never the victim's fault." There was deep concern in his voice as he touched her hand lightly with his own. Destiny was struggling to control her crying because she could feel her headache getting worst. "I went to a couple of counseling sessions in Charleston but never finished."

"But why? Didn't your aunt or Tina suggest it? Even the doctors could have assisted you with that, Destiny. My God, I cannot imagine what you had to deal with."

"I need you to take your time, Destiny, and tell me everything."

Dropping her gaze, she clasped the tissue with trembling hand. "I didn't think I needed it at the time. All I thought I needed was someone to adopt the baby. Tina agreed to do that, so I thought

I'd be fine. I was going to graduate and move on with my life." She glanced over at him with eyes filled with tears; she could tell he understood by the way he squeezed her hand.

"You know what I did, Adam? I pushed it so far back in my mind that I actually tried to pretend it never happened. I wanted to get on with my life." She paused. "I was so determined to move on that I absolutely refused to look back. I had the baby. Tina adopted her. I moved to Charleston and found myself in another mess."

Struggling to maintain some semblance of composure, he met her scrutinizing gaze once more. "All right. So you moved to Charleston. How? You said you'd let Tina adopt the child. Why did you feel this was a mistake?"

"It wasn't until I got saved, Adam, that I began to feel as if there was an extra weight in my life. Now I understand that God wants me to get rid of all the things that have caused my life so much pain. I got tired of hurting, tired of feeling like it was my fault, and tired of the dreams. That's why I started attending Healing Virtue counseling at the church." She looked at him now with a renewed determination in her eyes.

"I agree," Adam said, "that Elder Ford is the best because I believe the Lord had me put her in that position because of her compassion for hurting women. Plus, she has had firsthand experience. She was in an abusive relationship that ended in the unfortunate death of her husband."

Destiny was not surprised by this she knew Elder Ford's testimony.

"Destiny, I'm sure it has helped you work through some of your pain and hurt from that experience. You mentioned Charleston; what happen there?"

She knew if she was to be completely honest he had to know about everything. "Adam, do you have any idea how difficult it was for me to tell you this?" Trembling hands touch her forehead, praying to keep the headache at bay until she finished.

"The man who raped me was Stanley's best friend. Stanley and Curtis had been friends since their college days. Curtis was in love with a young lady named Denise. She was also in college with them. But something happened, and Stanley ended up with Denise. Curtis was mad because he really loved her.

"I was a pawn in a game they were playing with each other. Curtis raped me. But that wasn't the worst part. He threatened me and said I'd better not go the police or he'd make sure Richard wouldn't be able to walk or ever play football again. I loved Tina and Richard, so I made them promise not to go to the police. After having the baby, I moved to Charleston, took the job I was offered by Stanley, and eventually moved in with him because I thought I needed him to protect me.

She watched as Adam got out of his chair and sat on the side of the bed. Overcome by the wealth of her emotion, Destiny cried harder. She made a bit of a protest when he first cradled her against his chest.

He pulled back, placing a tender kiss on her bruised forehead, another on her nose. At the sight of tears pooling beneath her lashes, he tenderly gathered Destiny against him once again. Defeat sucked the wind out of his sails. "What kind of man treats a woman this way? God created a woman to be loved, cherished above measure but never man handle or used!" He hated the frustration that colored his tone.

"Please don't cry, it's okay, it's going to be okay. We can make it through all of this together. So, Taylor is really your child?" She lay there, looking at him for a moment that seemed to last forever.

Destiny heard the sincerity in his voice. Pulling back, Adam fluffed her pillow and helped her lay back down comfortably on the bed. "I admire you for not having an abortion. You gave that little girl at chance at a happy life. You did good Destiny."

"I'd done my research." She'd been a part of a single parent home since the day she was born and she wanted more for her daughter. The best research showed children with two parents in the home usually offered stability for a child. God knows she wasn't stable at the time. He had just said she had done the right thing. But now he was silent and that worried her. What was he thinking? If she were totally honest with herself, she would admit how good it felt to have him here. She'd always felt safe with Adam. She wanted to lean into those broad shoulders now just to have his strong arms around her once again.

"I want to help you work through all of this in any way I can. You are a strong woman in the Lord and God knows I celebrate the woman before me right now."

Those words took her breath away when her heart was already shuddering. Now she truly believed they could really make their relationship work.

"Why?" Her lips trembled. She bit them together. *Don't get your hopes up. This is Adam…he's too logical to really believe there's still a chance.*

His eyebrows shot upward. "Seriously?"

When she made no effort to amend her demand, he made a dry, pained sound that might have been an attempt at a laugh. "You're someone who means the world to me and from the beginning I've told you God brought you into my life at the right time. I want us to work, Destiny."

With all her heart Destiny knew he cared about her; that he would never stop. He was truly a believer. He had never given up on her. That gave her so much joy that even being in this hospital couldn't make her doubt that now.

CHAPTER 41

He'd gotten her to eat, which was a step in the right direction for her to get out of the hospital. She'd given him the story from the beginning. She was eating her ice chips, her dark eyes searching his, before asking, "You think I'm crazy, don't you?"

My God. How was he going to make her understand he cared more for her than any words would convey? He understood that awful place she was in and wanted to help her more than he wanted to draw in his next breath. He did not for one second believe she was crazy. "Destiny, I know you're not. Sometimes we all make mistakes but those mistakes can become miracles if we allow God to make them so."

A nurse came in to check her vital signs, so their conversation was put on hold for a few minutes. As she left the room he glanced around before he continued.

"Do you remember me telling you about a conference I attended when we met on the plane?" He asked in a voice that was toneless, showing no hint of emotion.

Destiny looked down at her hands for a moment. "Yes...yes I do..." she said, returning her gaze to his. "You said you conducted a seminar. On my birthday date you told me it was on Pastor's and Cyber-porn."

He lowered his gaze and sighed. "It's complicated...but I want you to know everything about me as well. I have always desired to have a relationship filled with the love of a God-fearing woman. I thought I'd found that in a young lady named Regina Webber who I met in college. Her father was a pastor, and I thought she was the one." Reclining back in his chair, Adam closed his eyes and rubbed his temples before continuing. Turning he noticed a surprised look in her eyes.

He watched as she searched his face. He wanted her to trust him. Her past relationship hadn't been based on trust.

"Did you just say her name was Regina?" She adjusted herself in the bed, her hands was shaking.

"Yes, I did." He watched her trying to see where this was leading.

"Oh my God, that's the same woman Stanley mentioned to me. He said she told him I was here in Seattle." She shook her head as if she was trying to figure out what was going on.

"I can't believe she did that. I knew she was having some problems because of the way she showed up at my office, but to do this to you is unbelievable." He got up from his chair.

"Adam, if you don't want to finish this conversation today it's all right, I understand. We both know you don't have to." He'd almost lost her a few weeks ago. He refused to let the enemy use any kept secret destroy what they were trying to build. He wanted Destiny to see that it was time for both of them to move forward. Sitting back down, he reached for her free hand.

"Because I asked her to marry me, but when I told her I was moving back to Seattle to minister, all bets were off and we broke up. After returning home I got involved with a young lady via the Internet on one of those social sites. One thing led to another and before I knew it I was addicted to cyber-porn." The silence thickened around them. Adam didn't have to tell her every detail, but she had to know some aspects of how serious it was. He moved his head from side to side, frustration setting his lips in a grim line.

"I hated the man I became during that time. All those years wasted because I was weak in my flesh. I couldn't see any good, only the bad or the potentially bad. I was a sick man sinking deeper everyday into the depths of sin." His gaze shifted to the row of windows beside her bed. "I am proud to say I'm delivered from cyber-porn. But just recently Regina showed up at my church. I haven't seen her in five years."

Adam wanted one thing to be crystal clear in all this. He was determined to go through with his plan to discuss all of this with her.

One of his broad shoulders rose and fell in a dismissive shrug that Destiny felt wasn't quite representative of how he felt. He waited a beat before continuing. "When I realized that she was interested in reconnecting, I told her I had no intention of getting back together with her, and I asked her to leave." He paused, his voice brimming with disgust. "Regina has always wanted the easy way out. She sees only the glitz and glamour. That's not true ministry."

She wiped an invisible piece of dust from her sheet before responding, "I know the pastor's wife role is different than any other and sometimes even undefined."

He took her hand. "God just wants any wife to be the best wife to her husband, everything else will fall into place."

"That's all I would know how to do." Destiny nodded adamantly.

In that moment, Adam realized his desire to protect and shelter Destiny had kept him from seeing how strong she was. She wasn't just beautiful and kind and generous. She was also smart and determined. He'd driven himself crazy with worry all of this time and what he should have done was trust her like she asked him to.

He lifted her hand and placed a kiss in the soft center. "Thank you for trusting what we have to share it with me today. You didn't have to do that."

Destiny felt tears burst from her eyes, hot scalding tears that ran unchecked down her cheeks. "No. I should be thanking you for staying," she insisted softly, lacing her fingers with his. "I didn't believe in myself or you. It wasn't until…" she didn't finish her statement.

He touched her then. His hand came down over hers on the bed, urging her to finish when she didn't he said, "until what? You started believing that I didn't trust you because of the past?"

"Yeah," she reluctantly admitted. "I was so angry that my past had caught up with me, I couldn't see how you could help at that time." She gave her head a little shake but it felt as if a jar of marbles had spilled inside. She groaned and put her free hand to her temple—confusion, despair and disbelief all jostling for position. Adam squeezed her hand with the gentlest of pressure. "I love you Destiny, and I know all this must be a terrible shock. There was no easy way of telling you."

Destiny rapidly blinked away tears, her throat was feeling so dry she could barely swallow. As if he had read her mind, he released her hand and pulled the bed table closer, before pouring her a glass of water and handing it to her.

"Here," he said, holding the glass for her as if she were a small child. "Drink this. It will make you feel better." She frowned as she pushed the glass away once she had taken a token sip.

"I don't understand…" She raised her eyes to Adam's gaze.

She swallowed. Was she dreaming? Was she hearing what she wanted to hear instead of what he was actually saying? That happened sometimes. She had done it herself, talked herself into thinking she had heard things, just because she hoped and hoped and hoped someone like Adam would say them.

"I have shut off my emotions since my break up with Regina," he said. "Saying 'I love you' is something I wanted to do. Please don't cry, Destiny. Talk to me," he urged softly.

She sniffed. "I'm crying because you said you loved me despite all that has happened. I love you so much," she confessed, using her good arm to pull him toward her. They shared a tender kiss. "I didn't know what to think when they said you had been here and then left when I woke up," she said.

Adam shrugged. "Believe me, you didn't want to see me then. After three days with no sleep, I was a wreck." He gave her a hard kiss. "I want you to get better and get out of here."

Destiny pressed closer against his chest, loving the feel of him. She softly said, "I will."

CHAPTER 42

Regina opened her eyes, slowly glancing around the bedroom. She was still in her hotel room. Everything had gone terribly wrong. She hadn't gotten the money from Stanley. That very thought gave her a reason to be upset. In her dream she was married and living in a mansion with Adam. The glow from the bedside lamp caused the light's reflection to accentuate her body's curves tangled up in the bed sheets. There was a look of jealousy on her face. Looking at the arm thrown across her breast, she moved to adjust her body, trying to get comfortable.

Next to her lay the pastor of the local church her father preached for a couple of months ago. He was married, but what the hell, she needed to eat and keep this hotel room. But she was tired of him. He was on his side, facing her with his eyes closed in peaceful rest. She had to admit, he was a wonderful lover, which made her sad that this affair had to end tonight. His wife really was a sweet woman and they had three adorable children. He should have been home with them rather than being there with her at one o'clock in the morning. She knew there was no excuse for her behavior, but what could she do—she may as well live up to the reputation she'd been given. Adam had made it clear he didn't want her, but she'd never give up on him, he was supposed to be with her.

He pulled her against his chest without opening his eyes. His nose was touching her hair. She didn't want to, but found herself snuggling closer. She felt safe while wrapped in his arms. What she really wanted was to be wrapped in the arms of Pastor Adam Wheeler, but he wanted someone else. If she had played her cards right, maybe she wouldn't be sleeping with every pastor in the city, instead she would be wrapped in his arms. She laughed, then she began to cry, causing him to stir, but he didn't open his eyes.

He just pulled her body closer, causing her to once again get lost in his capable hands without any effort on her part.

Closing her eyes, she imagined Adam being there. Whenever she thought about him like this, her jealousy caused her to hate Destiny even more. She was green with envy, and she knew she had no right to be. Her life was a disaster and it was all Destiny's fault. If it was the last thing she would ever do, Destiny's head would be on a platter and she'd make sure of it.

"I hope it's me that's putting a smile on your face. What are you thinking about, Regina?" He was kissing her on her neck. She was still staring at him. His eyes were still closed. He knew she was staring without having to look. Slowly, his eyes opened. The light caused his eyes to look even darker than they were. His arms drew her even closer protectively, and his grin broadened with pride at the play of emotions he was causing on her face. She was a beautiful young thing. He was fifty and never would have imagined being with a woman like her. She was a whore and a real freak in the bedroom- everything he didn't want his wife to be, but maybe a freak in their bedroom wouldn't hurt. He shook his head because she deserved better. But his grin widened again when he saw Regina's cheeks flare red.

"Say it, Regina."

"I love the way you love me." She hated it when he asked her to say that. Her brown eyes narrowed and she looked at him, daring him to continue.

"You love it, I know you do. I love it, too…" He suggestively accused before he collapsed on top of her.

"I know I'm only a means to an end for you. You need me to keep all of this." He flung his arms to emphasize his point. "I know our time together is over. I never expected it to last forever. Things change with time, and sometimes those changes aren't ones we foresee or expect and therefore, we cannot plan for them." He looked at her as if he was seeing her for the first time. Smiling, he slowly retracted his other arm from underneath her.

"There's never room for two in the heart, you know. The scripture says you will either love one or hate the other."

Regina couldn't believe he was quoting scripture when he was lying with someone other than his wife. She lifted her head from the pillow, looking at him in confusion. "Do you think it's cool to be quoting scripture when we've just had sex?"

He couldn't believe this woman. She lived her life on the edge, not caring about anybody but herself. She was going down, and he knew it would be soon. Her infatuation with Pastor Wheeler was going to be her Achilles heel. Smiling, he said, "So, now you want to get holy when you've been sleeping with another woman's husband? Come on, we both know you're a preacher's whore." She paused for a moment longer. Her hatred for him came back and she was forgetting everything she felt earlier being with him.

He knew she wouldn't put up too much of a fight about anything he said because she needed him. So she lay her head against his chest and felt his lips raining kisses on her cheeks like he had earlier.

"I'm sorry." His frown was replaced by a smile, if only for a moment. "I wouldn't make comments like that one anymore if I were you. Do we understand each other?" He reached out, stroking her hair before tugging it with force. She looked up at him, her heart thumping nervously when his strong arm settled around her shoulders. He drew her close and kissed her lips gently, and Regina surrendered herself to him completely. His hand quickly moved from her shoulders down her body as he gave her a squeeze.

"After tonight, it's over between us, but I must admit, I'm going to miss having this within arm's reach." He traced his fingers down her stomach slowly.

Regina reached up and wrapped her hand around his neck, drawing him near because she knew the funds they had discussed earlier were within arm's reach. "Then let's make it memorable." She purred in his ear.

He took her hand from around his neck. Turning slightly, he looked over at the money on the nightstand. Grabbing the money, he glanced back at her. Then, he took her hand. Opening it, he gave her the two thousand dollars enclosed in an envelope that he'd promised her.

Giving her a kiss, he almost sounded remorseful when he told her, "It's yours and what's really sad about this whole thing is that I gave you more money for sex than I gave your father for preaching the word." He laughed to himself. "He should take you with him to every revival."

After hearing his words and just to show him she was worth every dime of that money, she pushed him back on his pillow and slowly began to make a trail down his body. He moaned as if he was in pain. Looking at him, she smiled to herself. Match point. She'd just won again even if it was only for a night.

Much later, she cried herself to sleep in an empty bed with both hands holding her two thousand dollars. Her life was a miserable mess.

CHAPTER 43

The early morning sunrays came through the curtains of Destiny's bedroom. Trying to stretch in her tangled sheets, she managed to maneuver her recovering body out of bed with the help of her wheelchair, smiling because this was a new day the Lord had made, and she intended to rejoice and be glad in it on this Sunday morning. She felt a little tired, but she was happy it had been a month since her accident.

Lifting her good arm in the air, Destiny looked up, saying, "I am so happy, Father! There's never a dull moment with you. I lift my hands to you, Father, giving you praise for every tear I've ever cried because they weren't wasted."

Destiny was overwhelmed by the praise that was coming through her prayer. Wiping away the tears, she continued. "You took every one of my tears to your specialized laboratory, examined them, and saw my needs in each one. Father, I ask you to do for every woman, every man, and every child what you have done for me. Bless them, saturate their lives with your favor, protect them, and grow them up in your plans for their lives, plans for prosperity and not disaster. Let their pasts be just that, the past never to hinder their future. Give them plans for a future and a hope that only you can provide. In your Son Jesus's name, I pray. Amen." After praying, Destiny was ready for church. It was going to be a good day.

There was a buzz in the church parking lot as Sara and Willie helped Destiny get out of the car and into her wheelchair. Then they all headed for the sanctuary. Everybody was excited about the special guest psalmist for this morning. Last Sunday, Pastor

Wheeler had hinted that there would be a special guest, but no one knew who it was going to be. As always, the parking lot was full. They hurried into the vestibule and smiled at the greeters who welcomed them to the service. Not wanting to sit in the back of the church, Destiny looked around for Tina and her family. After spotting them, Sara rolled her chair down to sit on the outside of the pew they were sitting in. Usually everyone would still be milling around, but that was not the case on this Sunday morning. Everyone was already seated, waiting for the service to start.

Feeling a light tap on her shoulder, Destiny turned to look behind her, finding the smiling faces of the twins. She was a little surprised that Cynthia had allowed them to stay in the sanctuary this Sunday instead of attending the Children's Church. She never took the chance of Marvin seeing them, so having them out of the sanctuary was always safer. They were handsomely dressed as usual in their matching Polo outfits. Destiny smiled, giving them a pat on the cheek as she glanced at their grandparents seated with them. Smiling and mouthing a hello, she returned her attention to the boys.

"Miss Destiny, can we sign your cast again?" David said in her ear.

Destiny leaned back and whispered, "Yes, you may, but not right now. Now sit down because you don't want to disturb anyone's worship experience." Then she turned back around because Taylor had picked up her hand and was holding it.

"Auntie Destiny, are you going to marry Pastor Wheeler?" Taylor was playing with her finger as she asked the question.

Taken aback, Destiny adjusted the jacket of her suit, which needed no adjusting. She heard the giggles coming from everyone seated close by her. "Taylor, the praise team is getting ready to sing. Let's listen," Destiny responded.

The ministers had already taken their seats, but Pastor Wheeler had not come from his office yet. They waited for the musicians to start. Once the praise team was in place, the musicians began to play "Nearer My God to Thee." This gave latecomers time to take their seats. When they had finished, the praise team went into a melody of songs, causing most of the people in the audience to get up and praise the Lord. At the end of the last song, the spirit was high and the praise team leader signaled the audience to be seated.

Heads began to turn when there was a stir in the back of the church. The doors of the sanctuary swung open. There were audible gasps all around as the Shekinah Glory mass choir entered in synchronized movements through the doors of the church.

The Greater Community's band must have known they were waiting because they kicked into the beat of their first selection, "Yes." Shekinah Glory was dressed in blue-and-gold robes that moved and flowed with them as they came down the aisle. The church was saturated with the anointing coming through the hearts and flowing out of the mouths of these talented choir members. During their processional, they stopped and worshipped the Lord because the anointing was so heavy in the sanctuary. They finally managed to make it to the choir loft while waiting for the musicians to play the last chords of the song. Just as the congregation couldn't stop praising God, neither could the choir. The greeters had their hands full trying to help those caught up in the Spirit.

Destiny watched Pastor Wheeler as he came to the pulpit but didn't take his seat. It seemed the Spirit had pulled him out of his study. She knew it was going to be a high service in the Lord, because the manifestation of it was all over the worshippers in the church. God was doing it this morning. Looking across the audience, it was easy to get caught up in all of the praise as she sat there, the one person she didn't have to search for gave her a nod of recognition. The sparkle in Adam's eyes seemed to say she looked beautiful this morning.

She was biased of course but he seemed to always look handsome, but this morning he'd taken it to another level. The tan suit he had on fit like an athletic cut. To say he was fine was an understatement. He was a gorgeous specimen of a man. Seeing his nod, Destiny winked at him before turning her attention back to the choir.

Pastor Wheeler walked over to whisper something into the director's ear. The director then signaled for the choir to stand. After telling the musicians which song was going to be played, the band began to harmonize once again with the choir. Destiny's attention was diverted for a second when she heard Cynthia's voice whisper, "Good morning." Reaching her hand back, she squeezed the fingers of her sister before the choir took them on another anointed journey with, "How Deeply I Need You."

The leader took the microphone. "Here is my heart. I give it Lord to you. Here is my life. I lay it before you. Where else would I go? What else would I do, if I did not know you? How deeply I need you."

The sanctuary was enthroned with the presence of the Lord. The worshipers could feel the Lord's weighted glory. People were walking around in the sanctuary, weeping. Some even went to the altar, kneeling in worship. There were tears, clapping, and shouts of "Yes, Lord!" coming from everywhere.

Marvin sat quietly in the back of the sanctuary. Although he wanted to praise the Lord his eyes had been riveted on the two boys seated beside Cynthia. He'd been running behind this morning and took a seat in the back of the church. Who were they? There something about them that sent chills through his body; he didn't want to think beyond that because that would mean Cynthia had deceived him.

CHAPTER 44

Voices could be heard saying, "Hallelujah," coming from all over the sanctuary as Pastor Wheeler walked up to the mic. The choir was trying to close the selection, but every time they tried, the praise would continue.

Pastor Wheeler took the mic in his hand, and as if God himself was leading him, he walked out into the audience. Looking up, he began to sing, "I need you, Lord, like the desert needs the rain. I need you, like the ocean needs the streams. I need you, like the morning needs the sun. I need you, Lord. You are my only one." Tears were rolling down his cheeks as he gave God his all. His congregation knew he was caught up in the Spirit, and they began to praise God with him.

Pastor Wheeler returned to his seat while the congregation settled back down. Minister Samuel came to the podium, and after settling his spirit down a little, he asked the church, "Are ya'll feeling like I'm feeling? I'm happy in the Lord right now. Not later, not after a while, not after my bills are paid, but I'm happy in the Lord right now!" He pulled back his head and gave the Lord a loud shabach, followed by most of the folk in the audience.

After everyone had been settled down and the offering was collected, Pastor Wheeler came to the podium. Opening his Bible, he told the congregation, "Open your Bibles to Psalm 30:5, and after you have it, say amen." Once he heard "amens," he began to read. "For his anger endureth but a moment; in his favour is life: weeping may endure for a night, but joy cometh in the morning."

Looking out over his waiting audience, he asked them, "How many of you know today that in God there are no wasted tears?"

Many responded by saying, "Amen." Pastor Wheeler told them to look at their neighbors and say, "No wasted tears."

Folks turned toward one another and said, "No wasted tears."

"I'm here to tell you today that weeping may endure for a night, but joy comes in the morning. If you know it, then give God some praise."

People got up and started cheering, giving God praise, and then took their seats.

"Have you ever felt like crying? There are times in every life when each of us feels like crying. Crying is universal. Everyone cries. Babies cry and adults cry. No matter what sex, race, or nationality we happen to be, we cry. Usually our tears represent the condition of our spirits at the time. When our spirits are full, one way or the other, we cry."

Willie lifted his hand, saying, "Amen, preacher! We all cry sometime. Thank you, Jesus." Sara looked at Willie. Reaching over, she rubbed his back.

"Yes, Lord, we all have to cry sometime," she said as she looked back at Pastor Wheeler.

"Sometimes we cry when we are sad. Death, sickness, failure, and disappointment are powerful emotions that control our spirits and move us to cry." Walking away from his podium, he looked out in the congregation. "David wept over the sickness of his son. Jesus wept at the tomb of Lazarus. It is not unusual for us to weep in times of trouble or despair. It is a way of emptying our souls." Looking back at the guest choir, he said, "Can I get an 'amen'?"

"Amen, Pastor."

Swinging his arms around in the air, Pastor Wheeler did a two-step back to his podium. People were up shouting right along with him.

"Sometimes we cry when we are happy. We cry at weddings, reunions, graduations, and special ceremonies marking academic achievements. If we watch a movie that has a happy and sentimental ending, the tears flow like a river. They are tears of joy."

The church was rocking, and there was an anointing on Pastor Wheeler that had the church on fire.

Looking at the audience, he said, "A month ago God performed a miracle in the life of one of our members, and I cried tears of joy." He smiled at his family and said, "Can I get an 'amen'?" Then the church shouted it right back at him. It was as if they were playing baseball. He threw it out, and they hit it out the park every time.

Cynthia stood up, and before she knew it, the spirit of the Lord hit her in the top of the head and moved down to the soles of her feet. She began dancing in the Spirit right then and there. Smiling, Tina stood, watching her.

"Praise Cynthia, 'nobody knows like you know."

Cynthia wasn't the only one. There were others around the sanctuary that understood what their pastor was saying, and they gave God some praise for it.

"They're tears of joy. These are moments when we are so happy we cannot contain ourselves." Pastor Wheeler twirled around so fast in the pulpit and then gave God a Holy Ghost squall.

"But there is a day coming when God himself will be with us, and John said it like this." Looking at Destiny, Adam said, "And God will wipe away every tear from their eyes; there shall be no more death, nor sorrow, nor crying. There shall be no more pain, for the former things have passed away." He saw the look in Destiny's eyes and knew she understood. Even with the death of Stanley, she understood what he was saying.

Adam went on to preach that sermon like none he'd ever preached before. The congregation was blessed by the word that came out of their pastor's mouth through the aid of the Holy Ghost. Finally, as he closed his message, he walked down the steps from the pulpit and stood in front of the audience.

"Church, when David penned this psalm, he was looking back over his life and saw the merciful hand of God that helped him endure his own weaknesses and personal trials. He thanked God for being with him during his weeping and lamentations."

Walking to the right of the congregation, Adam looked at his members and saw their tears. He knew that as a church, they'd endured a lot. They had stood beside him even in his most difficult times, and he had stood by them during their trials.

Continuing to talk, Adam said, "David's reflection upon his life is the same as that of any believer. We too have shared the same three experiences that David shared in his lifetime. God's anger is a terrible thing. Generally, we bring down the wrath of God upon ourselves by some deviant act or another."

Throwing up his hand, he said, "I've been there. Have you?"

"Yes, sir, Pastor, we've been there," Edward Mason said as he gave God praise for delivering him.

Adam walked over to the other side of the church. "Then there's God's favor. It's the ultimate blessing for any believer to receive the favor of God. When a person is a favorite, he receives special treatment, access, and considerations that may not be required."

Turning to walk up the aisle, Adam stopped beside Destiny's wheel chair. Looking at her for only a few seconds, he said, "When we realize that we have been favored, that's when we can truly say, 'He didn't have to do it, but he did. He didn't have to bless me, but he did! He didn't have to heal me, but he did! He didn't have to save me, but he did!' While others revel in the fact that they have been blessed, those who have learned this truth are able to say, 'I'm more than blessed. I'm enjoying the favor of the Lord!'"

Everyone seated in that section and in the sanctuary began to rejoice at the awesomeness of God.

"Yes, Lord, you've been good!" was being shouted throughout the congregation. The members were on their feet.

Tina shouted, "Yes, sir, you've been good to me!" as she held her son in her arms. Cynthia reached for the baby as Tina began turning around, and with each spin, she said louder, "Yes, sir, you've been good to me." Richard stood to watch over his wife, but tears were in his eyes as he looked at their daughter, who was watching her mother, and their son in Cynthia's arm. God had been good to them. He was worth all of the praise she was giving him.

"Then there are times in our experience when we've had to weep. The very first thing we do when we get into this world is cry. But shedding a sentimental tear at a wedding or at the happy ending of a movie is not the same as weeping. The Hebrew word for *weeping* in this text means continuous like steady dripping." Using his hands, Adam illustrated a continuous motion, making sure that the congregation understood what he was saying.

"I want everyone in this sanctuary to know that in God, there are no wasted tears. Hallelujah!" He jumped up and down at the excitement of that statement.

He wasn't the only one. The organist began to back him up, and folks all over the sanctuary were on their feet, giving high fives and praising God.

"I've found out in my own life, just as many of you have, that the darkest nights are followed by the brightest days! A great and heavy burden is followed by a multitude of blessings!" Pastor Wheeler was really feeling the Spirit now. His voice had begun to rise and fall as the organ and drummer kept beat.

"The sorrow of today is followed by pleasant times of tomorrow! The weakness of the moment can be the blessing of the hour!" The organ roared in unison with his voice.

"The difficulty of the day can prove to be the blessing for the week! I've found that no matter what comes my way, the Lord is able to make a way out of no way! He's able to lift up a bowed-down head. He's able to dry a tear-stained eye!"

No one was in their seat. The whole congregation watched as he continued to preach his heart out.

"So Destiny, go ahead and cry right now because, in Jesus, there are no wasted tears."

Destiny heard those words with her heart, and before she knew it, she was rolling her wheel chair forward and backward in the aisle. She had seen people in wheelchairs praise God before but this was a first for her. She praised God like she'd lost her mind. Her eyes were closed, but the tears were flowing. It was over now. Everything from her past was not in vain because in God there were no wasted tears.

"Your tears are just temporary relief. Your tears are just a release of the pain, sorrow, and grief. Your tears are expressions that can't be controlled. A little crying is all right, but after a while, you won't have to cry any more. Don't you worry. God's going to wipe every tear away. Because, in him, there's never wasted tears, just a transportation to a new day. Weeping may endure for a night, but joy will come in the morning!" Pastor Wheeler was using his high and melodic falsetto voice.

People stood all over the sanctuary with their arms lifted in the air. Some were praising, and some were crying, but all of them knew that God was in this worship service.

"It's time to give it to Jesus. No wasted tears this morning. Let's give Jesus our all."

A couple stood in the back of the church, followed by several more people all over the church. Pastor Wheeler surveyed the audience; looking for one more if it was God's will. After getting peace, he asked all of those who stood to come to the altar. There were twenty-seven people at the altar, all wanting to give their lives to Christ. Pastor Wheeler asked for the assistance of the ministerial staff. Then he went to each one, hugging and speaking to them personally.

After walking back into the pulpit, Pastor Wheeler said, "I know you all thought that Shekinah Glory was our main guest today, but there is one other guest here to worship with us in song. I had the opportunity to take a wonderful woman to his concert recently while in Tacoma."

Adam looked at Destiny. Then he looked up in the balcony of the church. "I'd like for you all to welcome Mr. Smokie Norful to Greater Community."

Smokie moved through the sanctuary and walked into the pulpit. After giving Pastor Wheeler a hug, he looked out at the people in the congregation, who were standing on their feet, waiting for him to sing.

"Oh my God, I love Smokie." Destiny leaned over to tell Tina. "I can't believe he's here."

Tina turned to her, smiling.

Smokie waited, and as the musicians were getting ready, he said, "I got a call from Pastor Wheeler about two weeks ago. He asked me to come because he wanted to surprise a very special woman this morning." He laughed before continuing. "This was the first time I'd been asked to sing a specific song, but after talking to your pastor, I understand why." Looking out into the audience, he asked, "Destiny, will you please roll your chair down here?"

"Girl, you better roll up there," Destiny heard Tina say as both of her sisters stood. The congregation watched as Destiny moved down the aisle. "Stay right there," he stated as the band began to play. "This is from Pastor Wheeler to you. Many of you may not know this song, but it's by an old R & B legend, Willie Hutch."

People must have known it because Destiny could hear them whispering all around her. "Pastor is doing this thing right," was one comment she heard in the audience.

Sitting there, Destiny looked at Adam. She had no idea what this was about, but she was obedient and sat where she was as the choir began to sing, "I, oh, I choose you, baby. I choose you baby." Then Smokie joined in singing, "And I'll tell you why. You were there when no one else would be in my corner, Destiny, and it's you that I've learned to love and place no one above. Oh, how can I ever thank you, except take you home and make you my lovin' wife so we can always be together? Oh ain't that nice."

She watched Pastor Wheeler walked down from the pulpit and slowly walk toward her. With each step, she thought of all the things that made him special. People were cheering, and some were even crying as Smokie and Shekinah Glory continued to serenade them. "Oh, I choose you, baby. Destiny, no longer do I have to shop around anymore. No, no, no, no. I've found that once-in-a-lifetime girl who I've been searching for. My baby, you're all right. How can I convince you, girl, that you're truly out of sight."

Adam kneeled down, drawing a crying Destiny into his arms. He held her, telling her how much he loved her. Pulling back, he got up and took over the last part of the song. "Destiny, you're the kind of woman that any man would be proud to know, the kind of woman that'll have a man bragging anywhere he goes. Oh, I choose you, baby, 'cuz you're sugar. Oh, you're spice, woman, love, you're everything nice. Oh, my goodness, oh, I feel real bright. Oh, I choose you, baby." He continued to hold her hand. Adam pulled back, looking at Destiny as she cried. His eyes were filled with love as he reached out to touch her cheek, an offer of comfort and love.

"You better work that song, Pastor!" was yelled from somewhere in the sanctuary, followed by several, "Yes, Lord!" After the band played the last keys of the song, Pastor Wheeler dropped back down on one knee.

Someone yelled, "Lord, have mercy!"

He looked up at the woman who was the other half of him. She was surprised that his hands felt damp and a film of perspiration began to form on his upper lip.

The feelings that overtook Destiny were indescribable. Happiness was bubbling up on the inside of her. Through her tears, she smiled as he knelt down in front of her. Then he cleared his throat before looking around one time and setting his eyes back on his Destiny.

"I wanted to do this in a romantic, sweep-you-off-your-feet kind of way. I hope this"—Adam waved his hand around, indicating everything he'd done during the service—"was romantic enough, because if it isn't I could—"

Nodding her head, Destiny was trying to tell him it had been more than enough, but the words wouldn't come. Tears kept rolling from her eyes.

Laughing, he said, "I guess that's a yes."

Destiny placed a hand on his cheek, rubbing her thumb up and down his face.

"I've loved you since I met you on the plane. I love you more every day, more than I can ever tell you. My life was empty and incomplete before you came along. Only God could have found you for me because only he knew what I needed. Destiny, I don't know what I did to deserve you, but I thank God that you love me. You mean everything to me, and I want to spend the rest of my life causing you to love me more. I love you, Destiny."

The greeters had passed out so much tissue that they didn't have enough for all of the tears flowing in the sanctuary. One of the sisters on the front row yelled out, "Lord, he's messing us up this morning! I can't take it. God, send me one just like my pastor."

Adam continued, "When you're not around, I miss you. When I can't see your smile, it seems like the sun doesn't shine as bright. Because you're"—he took a deep breath—"you're the best thing that's ever happened to me. So, Destiny Harper, will you marry me?"

Destiny continued to look down at him, her hair falling around her face. Adam wiped a tear that fell from her eyes. She knew the answer to the question right away, but she couldn't believe that this was happening and Adam was asking what she'd hoped he would someday. That someday was today. She shook her head in disbelief that this day had been so glorious and now the man she loved was asking to marry her.

"Say yes, Destiny. Say yes." Everyone started chanting, "Say yes." Looking over at her family, Destiny saw everyone she loved chanting along with everyone else. She smiled from ear to ear as happy tears rolled down her face, she remembered the sermon from earlier in the service, "no wasted tears." Reaching for her hand, she watched him as he leaned down to kiss her hard on the mouth, pouring all their emotions into the kiss. As they broke apart, she was able to speak.

"Yes!" she said, resting her forehead against his. Adam pulled a black velvet box from his pocket.

Adam glanced over to his right. Following his eyes, she looked to see her sisters. Each of them was giving her the thumbs-up with a smile. Adam placed the three-carat, canary diamond on her finger and sealed it with a kiss. The organist began playing the first cords of "My Name Is Victory" as the choir joined in, giving God praise for this special moment. Folks all over the audience were praising God for blessing their pastor with a wife.

Adam broke into a smile as he hugged Destiny. "I love you."

Destiny laughed as she threw her arms around Adam's neck and hugged him, forgetting about everything but the two of them in this moment.

Praising God right along with the choir, Adam grabbed Destiny's hand, looked at her, and said, "You've just made me very happy, Destiny." Pulling back, he gazed at her with misty eyes and smiled.

Destiny pulled his face down to her and said, "You've just made me very happy, Adam. I loved you when we first met. I never thought I'd find someone who'd love me for me. No one knows me better, and no one makes me feel the way you do. You see past my past, and you make me feel so special. I know you're always going to be there for me, and when it all goes wrong, you'll be there to make it right. I want to wake up in your arms every morning, go to bed with you at night, and do everything in between with you every day for the rest of our lives."

Marvin sat in the driver's seat, knowing he needed to put the key in the ignition and drive away from the church. He didn't. Couldn't. His hands were trembling too much. He let out a slow breath, adrenalin, anticipation, and anger racing through him in equal measures. He'd just seen his sons. They had to be his; they looked just like him and they were with Cynthia.

Marvin forced himself to relax, forced the memories back, memories of their teenage romance, and that unforgettable night. Why hadn't she told him about them? Well things would be different now, Marvin promised himself. Nothing and no one would keep him from his sons…and certainly not Cynthia.

EPILOGUE

THREE YEARS LATER

"Destiny, push, baby, push!"

The sweat was pouring down from her forehead. The pain was almost unbearable. Her hands squeezed the railings of the bed so hard that they had lost some of their coloring.

"C'mon, Mrs. Wheeler, just a little bit more. Keep your eyes on your focal point."

The nurses were all excited that the world-renowned pastor, author, screenwriter and producer of the movie *No Wasted Tears* was in their hospital. The hospital administration had been put on alert earlier today that Mrs. Destiny Wheeler would be a patient. The movie had done better in theaters than any of the critics expected. The first week out, the movie grossed over forty million dollars. Now, nine months later, they were in California for the Golden Globe Awards. But their little bundle of joy was trying to make an early appearance.

"Mrs. Wheeler, you're nearly there!"

"It feels like I'm dying. Baby, please, I changed my mind. Let them give me something for pain. I can't do it again!" Destiny was crying as she looked at Sara, Willie, and Adam. They were doing everything they could to make her comfortable.

Adam moved closer to the bedside, taking her hand. "Come on, baby. Dad says all you need to do is push one more time. Little man is looking for his sister." Adam smiled at their son, who was born five minutes earlier.

Squeezing her eyes shut, Destiny mustered up all of the strength she had left to push.

It was almost immediately after that last push that the room was filled with the soft cries of their new baby. Leaning over to kiss her brow, Adam said, "Thank you, Destiny," as he watched the nurses clean up their babies.

"It's a girl," Dr. Fuller said as he walked their daughter over to the bed for both of them to see. Gently taking the baby in her arms, Destiny smiled at yet another miracle that had been created by their love for each other. Each of their babies were beautiful and the spitting image of the both of them.

Sara walked over to look at the bundle of joy in her arms. "She's precious, Destiny, almost identical to you as a child."

"I concur," Willie said from the other side of the bed. "They're both adorable babies, and I can't wait to spoil them."

Adam took the baby from his wife to place her beside her brother, staring down at their beautiful babies in their hospital carriers.

"She has your eyes," Adam said softly, smiling.

"And he has yours," she mumbled, feeling tears slipping from her eyes.

It seemed as if they had only been with them for a few minutes before the nurses came back in to take their babies to get baths. Neither one of them were ready for their babies to leave the room. Adam stood, looking at his beautiful wife. Even after twelve hours of labor, he couldn't help but praise God for the blessings that continued to pour into their lives. It seemed that God was on a continuous journey of rewarding them for every tear they'd shed in their lives.

"Are you sad about missing the Golden Globes?" Destiny asked him as she watched the nurse leave the room with the twins.

"Baby, I'm not worried about anything tonight. I just received the best picture award, and you gave them to me. You and those babies mean more to me than any Golden Globe." Adam leaned over, kissing his wife.

"You did it, Destiny. I'm so proud of you." Sara moved around Adam to look at her. "Willie and I are going to the after party, but only because Adam asked us to. You know we would love to stay here with you and our grandbabies."

"I for one voted against it, but since he is our pastor, we're going." Willie grabbed Sara's hand, pulling her to the door. Turning around to wave, they blew kisses and left the room.

"We did it, baby," Adam said as he took a seat by the bed. His smile was contagious because, before she knew it, she was laughing. "Oh, how I love our Jesus!" Destiny exclaimed, throwing her arms in the air. "I'm so happy, Adam."

"I know, baby, you have every right to be." He chuckled at the happiness of his wife. Placing a small kiss on her forehead, he said, "This has been our season of miracles." He wrapped his arms around his wife as she sat in her bed.

"I think you need sleep." He spoke softly, watching her eyelids get heavy. Trying to fight off a yawn, Destiny shook her head, not wanting to sleep yet. "The babies might be back, and I don't want to miss them, Adam." She fought off another yawn, as Adam adjusted her pillow.

"Your dad told the nurses to bring them back in an hour. That'll give you a little time to sleep before their first feeding from you."

"You promise?" she said groggily, already closing her eyes.

Pulling a chair closer to the bed, he made himself comfortable as he watched his wife close her eyes. "I promise." Adam was sure she hadn't heard what he said, but that was fine. He'd wake her when it was time.

"I love you, Destiny." Adam leaned back to close his eyes. Just as he was about to get in his real sleep zone, he felt the vibration of his phone. Looking at the screen, he saw Richard's number. "Hey, man, what's up?" Adam listened as Richard asked about Destiny and the babies. After telling him that the mom and the babies were fine, Richard asked if he had awakened him.

"Not yet, but I was just about to before the nurses bring the twins back. Why?"

Adam heard Tina in the background yelling something, but he couldn't understand her. There was a lot of noise.

"Pastor, I had to call because you just gave birth again."

"Again? What do you mean?"

"Your movie, *No Wasted Tears*, just won best short film! Congratulations!"

"Oh my God, what did you say?" Adam couldn't contain the excitement in his voice.

"What is it, baby?" he heard Destiny ask.

Turning to look at her he said, "Baby, our movie just won best short film!"

Destiny almost jumped out of the bed. She was screaming so loud that the nurses ran into the room. Seeing the both of them huddle together on the bed crying, they immediately became concerned about their patient.

"Is everything okay, Pastor Wheeler? Mrs. Wheeler, are you in pain? If you are, we can give you something so you won't have to cry," one nurse said as she was looking at the IV attached to her arm.

Smiling, Destiny looked at the nurse. "There's nothing wrong. We just found out that our movie won a Golden Globe for best short film. So you see these tears running down my face?" Destiny pointed to them. "They're not wasted. Praise the Lord! No wasted tears in God!"